THE REOCCURRENCE

DOUG MEIGS

THE REOCCURRENCE

DOUG MEIGS

WORKBOOK PRESS LLC
187 E Warm Springs Rd,
Suite B285, Las Vegas, NV 89119, USA

Website: https://workbookpress.com/
Hotline: 1-888-818-4856
Email: admin@workbookpress.com

Ordering Information:
Quantity sales. Special discounts are available on quantity purchases by corporations, associations, and others. For details, contact the publisher at the address above.

Library of Congress Control Number: 2015916635
ISBN-13:   978-1-953839-56-5 (Paperback Version)
                                  978-1-953839-57-2 (Digital Version)

REV. DATE: 26.09.2020

CONTENTS

CHAPTER 1

THE STAKEOUT

THE AIR IS dry, but the mornings are still tolerable, as the month of May is winding down; it's a good time of the year in West Texas, not too hot—yet. But even for a ranch that banks some twenty miles on the Concho River, the summers will get too hot, too dry, too dusty, and a little too everything except comfortable. This slightly desolate hill country seems to generate large boulders, mesquite trees, and a large variety of cacti, and has a knack for growing some of the best beef in the state of Texas. Our story begins on a large piece of this terrain called the Calahan Ranch. It covers some three hundred thousand acres and runs about twenty thousand head of cattle. Its primary income, however, is from natural gas and not the type derived from pinto beans, an old saying fondly used by the granddad of this modern-day empire.

Into the late hours on a Thursday night, the county sheriff, Ben Thompson, paced the floor in the library of the Calahan hacienda. Ben was a medium-sized man in his midfifties with a small pot belly, which was probably caused by an overdose of draft beer consumed on a regular basis between the office and home. He grew up in San Angelo, working in his dad's grocery store, but joined the local law enforcement right out of high school. Now some thirty-five years later and well grayed, he had held his elected post for fourteen years.

Ben's eyes wandered over the library, a room where he had spent many nights waiting during the last few weeks. The library was a man's room with plush leather furniture. A large stone fireplace stood at one end, with a first-class gun collection on both sides. A walnut desk was set at the opposite end and behind it a full wall of rich leather-bound books. Animal heads and a trophy-mounted mountain lion blanketed the room.

Ben moseyed over to a large map, which covered the top half of one wall. It was a detailed map of the Calahan Ranch, showing windmills, creeks, tree lines, and cross fencing. Twelve red flag pins stood out from the map, indicating the positions of the stakeout crews. Ben was studying the map when Walt, one of his deputies, wandered over. The old clock on the mantle struck as Walt spoke. "Hey, Ben, it's eleven o'clock. How late ya wanna keep this stakeout going?"

Ben, reaching up to rub the back of his neck, turned and looked at the owner of the ranch. "Levi," the sheriff stated in his slow Texas drawl, "I think we'd better keep at it for a couple of more hours, don't you agree?" Everyone turned toward the man at the far end of the study.

Levi, leaning back in his big leather chair with his boots propped on the desk, looked up from deep thought. "Yeah, if it's okay with you, Ben, I'd like to keep it up for a coupl'a more hours anyway." Levi came to his feet while he talked. His six-foot-four-inch lanky frame and rugged features made him look a little more mature than his thirty years. Although quiet-spoken and a little shy, his dark hair and green eyes would make any girl weak-kneed. However, girls were not his priority—right now.

The ranch is losing cattle, and no one can figure out how. Ben and everyone else are bumfuzzled.

Levi walked over to the window. Looking out at a clear sky and a full moon, his mind wandered for a second to his granddad who had passed away only a year ago. His sister, Dyanne, was away at college, and it seemed he had to cope with this cattle-rustling problem alone. He had hoped to have this mystery cleared up before the semester ended. Levi hadn't mentioned anything about it in his letters or his phone calls, knowing she would only worry, and it sure wouldn't help her survive until finals or graduation. Now school was over, and she would be coming home tomorrow. He was anxious to see her; Dyanne was the only family he had left since his granddad died. Their parents had been killed in a small plane crash when Levi was eleven and Dyanne only three. It was hard to imagine little Dyanne at twenty-two, half owner of one of the largest ranches left in the state.

The sheriff looked back at Walt. "Well, we've already missed supper. What else can we lose except a little sleep?" A little chuckle came from Ben. Then his face straightened up. "We've got twelve of Levi's ranch hands out there. We might as well take advantage of it for a while longer. Something's got to break soon."

Walt had been studying the map. "Hey, Ben, what's this Dorado Ciudad?" Walt wasn't the smartest guy in town. You might even say he's running with his choke pulled out. So his butchering of the Spanish pronunciation would come as no surprise.

"What?" Ben replied. Ben overlooked Walt's shortcomings because he was honest and a good officer and not to mention the son of Ben's only sister. One stipulation Ben insisted upon when he hired him was for Walt to stop calling him Uncle Ben. There was something about that "handle" Ben couldn't handle.

"What's this Dorado Ciudad?" repeated Walt.

"Where?" Ben asked as Walt raised his finger and pointed at the far west corner of the ranch.

"Oh, Dorado Ciudad. That last d sounds like th, ciudath. It was an old mining town," the sheriff replied with a little Spanish lesson thrown in.

"Really? What kind of mine?" Walt asked.

"Well, the name would tell ya if you'd studied your Spanish. Dorado Ciudad means 'Golden City'," the sheriff remarked loudly with a little pride in his voice for his knowledge of the Spanish language.

"I guess that means there must have been a lot of gold around there, huh, Ben?" Walt questioned.

"Yeah, that's right, but it was a long time ago," the sheriff added.

"I never even heard of the town. It must be a small place. There ain't too many people living there, huh?"

"Living there? You mean now?" Ben questioned as a large grin covered his face. "There's nobody living there. I guess nobody's lived there for a hundred years, wouldn't you think, Levi?"

Still staring out the window and only half listening, Levi remarked subconsciously, "Huh? Oh yeah, Ben's right. The town shut down about nineteen hundred."

"You mean the old town's still there?" Walt's eyes lit up as he found the subject intriguing.

Levi turned from the window, realizing he was engaged in a conversation with Walt. "Oh yeah, it's still there. You're right, it's not a very big town now, but it was a lot bigger back then when they were mining gold."

"What ya mean?" Walt asked.

"Well, one of those emperors out of Mexico ordered those mines to be opened. They were trying to raise money to send back to Europe. I think they transported all the Mexican prisoners up here to work the mines, and that's how it got its name … well, almost its name. My granddad told me it was called Ciudad de El Dorado at one time.

"Wow, what a name," Walt commented as everyone listened to Levi's story.

"Yeah, it was a mouthful." Levi smiled. "There were already a bunch of settlers around by the time the gold ran out. So after we won our independence from Mexico at San Jacinto in 1836, it went from Ciudad de El Dorado to Dorado Ciudad, but it's still there."

"That's neat. I don't know how ya remember all that stuff. How many people ya think lived there, Levi?" Walt asked.

Levi moved closer to the map and thought for a moment. "Well, I guess about a thousand, maybe twelve hundred. Wouldn't you think so, Ben?"

"Yeah, that's about right."

"You mean you've been up there, Unc … Sheriff?" Walt asked,

very enthused.

"Oh yeah, Levi's dad and I used to go up there a lot when we were in school," Ben commented as his chest expanded.

"Is that right, Ben?" Levi asked.

Ben turned from the map and faced Levi. "Sure is. Why, I remember the time Tom and I planned our first trip to the old ghost town," Ben started off.

"Ghost town!" Walt exclaimed.

"Oh, that was what we called it. It gave the old place some character. But anyway, I had spent the night out here with Tom. We got up real early, I mean, four-thirty, four-forty. We were saddled and on the trail by five o'clock. It was during summer vacation. Luckily, that scorching sun was to our backs." Levi looked at Ben and paid close attention to his story. He very seldom got to hear stories about his dad, and most of the ones he had heard were from his grandfather. This would be a totally different kind of story, coming from an old school friend of his dad's. "We'd filled our canteens and robbed everything we wanted from the refrigerator." Everyone smiled as Ben carried on with his tale. "We had those saddlebags loaded down. Well, anyway, we took off from here and crossed the Cagle fences, about here," Ben commented as his finger pointed to the spot. "Then we crossed back over, about here. We had a good road all the way to Dorado Ciudad. I think it was an old road that separated the two ranches, wasn't it, Levi?"

"Yeah, it was the road that all the ranchers around these parts used to go into town. I think my great-great-great-grandfather had donated the land for a public road, and when the town closed down, he just took it back, or his son did or his son's son. I don't remember which," Levi commented as he tried to recall some ol' hearsay. "But go ahead with your story."

"Well, anyway, Tom and I made it there about eleven o'clock that morning, the best we could tell. We ate our lunch by a huge oak tree in the middle of town. The wind picked up, the tumbleweeds were rolling, a few whirlwinds were in the street, and

7

we started hearing noises. You know how those old buildings will creak when the wind blows. Well, neither of us wanted the other to know we were a little scared, so we decided to go into the old saloon. It was right on the corner of the main street. We walked up to those swinging doors and busted right in, like we owned the place." Ben chuckled as he recalled the incident. "Then we started across the room toward the bar, and a loud thump came from upstairs. I guess the wind had knocked something over, but Tom and I got out of there in a hurry. We got to the horses and were five miles down the road before either of us said a word. Of course, we convinced each other we had really heard someone walking up there. We couldn't save face if we hadn't." Ben smiled as he reminisced. "We never told a soul about that trip." Levi smiled as the other men laughed.

"Ben, I know how spooky that old ghost town can be when you're a kid," Levi said chuckling as he patted Ben on the shoulder and walked over to where a table had been set up for a two-way radio. "Bob, why don't you let all the guys check in, and let's see if they've seen or heard anything?"

"Sure, Levi," the deputy said as he straightened up from a slouched listening position. He was also intrigued by the sheriff's tale and had gotten a little lackadaisical.

"Maybe you can also tell 'em to hang in there till one o'clock," Levi said, as the problem at hand came back to mind.

"Okay," Bob said as he started his checklist. "Checkpoint 1, this is home base. Come in."

"Yeah, this is checkpoint 1. Come in," someone with a heavy Mexican accent replied.

"Juan, is anything stirring out there?"

"The only thing I've seen exciting was a falling star. It's been real quiet out here," he answered as a little static broke up the conversation.

"Well, hang in there. We'll close it down around one. Over and out. Checkpoint 2," he continued, "this is home base. Come in."

There was a long hesitation, and Bob looked at Levi. Then, "Yeah, yeah, I'm here, I'm here. I was just taking a leak. Y'all must have a camera on me. It works the same way at home. When I'm sittin' on the toilet, the phone rings. Well, I ain't seen nothing, and I ain't heard nothing, but I sure could use some soft young thing to keep me company out here. How much longer we gonna keep this up?"

Bob smiled. "You can always count on Carlos to be out of socket," he jokingly commented to the group huddled in the study. "Give it till one, Carlos. Home base out. Checkpoint 3," Bob continued. The program had gotten too routine. Boredom had set in, like watching an oak tree grow. The only solution was to catch the bastards with their hands in the cookie jar. The problem with that scenario was to find a hand in a three-hundred-thousand-acre cookie jar. Levi walked over to the map, where Ben was standing over. "I don't understand it, Ben. I'm losing eighty to a hundred head a month. We've got all the roads covered, and we've flown over every fencerow a thousand times, but those rustlers are still getting in, and better yet, they're getting the cattle out."

An excited voice echoed through the two-way radio. "Hey, come in. Hey, base, come in."

"Yeah, this is base. Come in!" Bob yelled.

"Hey, I've spotted some lights, but they're a pretty good ways off, maybe half a mile or so."

Levi darted over to the table and prompted the dispatcher. "Who is it? What's their location?"

Bob responded, "Who is this?"

"This is Randy" came the reply. Randy was new at the ranch. He started cowpunching for Levi when his shop had a layoff a few months back. He was really a city fellow at heart, but Levi knew him very well. He thought of Randy as the best wide receiver he had when they played high school football as he listened to him come back again on the radio. "I'm number 7 Randy. Position 7," he repeated.

Levi and Ben both raced to the map to check Randy's location. They could almost feel the heartbeat in his voice as he came back on the radio. "I'm going to move in a little closer to the lights." Only moments before, Randy had started to pour him some coffee. The slow pace had just about to put him to sleep. Now nothing was needed; his adrenalin was flowing. He mounted his horse and headed straight for the lights, as they seemed to be traveling in a due west direction. He gained a little distance on the riders, close enough to hear the sound of the moving cattle. He stopped to radio back in. "I can see three or four riders herding forty to fifty head to the west, just south of the river."

"We're coming, Randy," he heard Ben reply. Ben had watched Randy grow up playing all the local sports and thought a lot of his athletic abilities, but he knew Randy would be no match for the rustlers.

Reaching over Ben, Levi grabbed the hand mic. "Stay put, Randy. We're on our way." Levi knew that Randy's patience sometimes operated on a short fuse.

"Let's go!" Levi yelled as he and Ben ran out the side door of the library into the yard. Bob stayed back to radio the other cowboys on stakeout. They all needed to merge on the west end of the ranch, just south of the Concho River.

"It's sure good you've got a helicopter, Levi," the sheriff said as the two men climbed aboard. "We'd never get to that end of the ranch before you turned white-headed and definitely not before those rustlers got away."

Always thinking about chasing girls and playing football, Randy figured the only chance to catch anything was to keep his eyes on it as he whispered to himself, Stay put, hell. He knew his only chance to keep them in sight was to get closer to the lights. Still monitoring the herd, he watched the rustlers move the cattle between two high canyon walls. Randy, knowing there was no way out for them, slowed down to report in. "Home base, come in," he whispered.

"Yeah, Randy, come in."

"Hey, Bob, they're headin' due west," he stated with a chuckle, "right up a box canyon. There's no way out."

"Home base to Randy."

"Yeah, come in, Bob." "You mean the one where the creek runs back to the pond?" "Yeah, that's it." He laughed. Randy, lagging behind, had lost the sound of the cattle. He decided to ease a little farther up the draw. He approached the pond with only the light of the moon; the men were gone, and so were the cattle. The herd had disappeared.

Completely dumbfounded, he ran his horse to the edge of the pond; he scanned the area and saw nothing. His mind raced as he noticed the water was still churning. The only sound was the roar of the waterfall. He stared at the waterfall for a second and then plunged his horse into the pond and headed for the deeper water. His horse gasped for air as Randy drove him through the pounding force of the waterfall. Coming up inside a cave, Randy's heart was beating like he had just run the length of the field for a touchdown. The cave was running about a foot of water, but he could now hear the sound of the cattle. Easing his skittish animal through the dark tunnel toward the light, he reached the mouth of the cave. He could now hear the voices of the rustlers, shouting orders. Once outside the cave, Randy could see the cattle being herded into a makeshift catch pen with a forty-foot trailer backed up to a ramp on the far side.

While the men were busy with the cattle, he managed to make his way behind some large boulders. Randy dismounted and continued to sneak in closer … when all of a sudden, "Position 7, come in," the radio blared. "Hey, Randy, come in. Stay put. Help's on the way."

"Oh shit, I left that damn walkie-talkie on," he muttered under his breath. Angrier with himself than worried about the consequences, Randy raced back to his horse. As he reached for the walkie-talkie, he heard the deafening sound of a gun firing at close range.

He felt the hot, sharp pain from the bullet in his back; his knees buckled, and he fell to the ground.

His semiconscious state seemed like a dream as he felt someone kneel down beside him, and the hot steel barrel raked across his cheek. "Hey, Mac, this prick has a walkie-talkie!" the man yelled out in a gravelly tone, "Let's get the hell out of here."

As the rustler turned to run, the remaining strength contained in Randy's body mustered one shot aimed at his assailant. A trembling finger squeezed tightly on the cold steel trigger. The sound of the shot reached the outlaw as fast as the hot lead entered his back. He twirled around, totally surprised that the cowboy was not dead. A mean, devilish-looking face stared at Randy as the man dropped to his knees. The victim's fiendish eyes fixed on him as a cold chill penetrated Randy's body. The evil face plowed into the dry, powdery dirt just ten feet from Randy's wilting body.

Another voice yelled out, "What about the cattle!"

"Hell with the cows!" a louder yell replied. "Get in that damn truck, and let's get the hell out of here."

The two men jumped from their horses; one shouted in a terrified tone, "I hear a plane coming over those trees!"

"No, it's a chopper!" the other one yelled. The shaken rustlers were now unconcerned that their cohort was lying shot only thirty yards away.

"Let's get the hell out of here!" The big rig spun away from the pen.

Ben spotted the truck as they came in over the trees. "There it is, Levi, dead ahead."

"Yeah," Levi acknowledged, "but I think I've spotted a body right back there. Let's set the chopper down, Ben." Levi paused. "It may be Randy."

"Sure, set 'er down, son!" the sheriff shouted over the roar of the engine as the eighteen-wheeler was fading out of sight. "Don't worry about those rustlers. We've got that road blocked about a mile ahead."

The chopper came down in a hurry as Levi leaped from the landing strut. He headed straight for the man lying in the dirt. As Levi reached the body, he grabbed the man by the arm. Not feeling any life, he dragged the body over on its back. The victim's eyes were open, with a penetrating blank stare right into Levi's eyes. "Oh my God," Levi moaned under his breath, as the dead body seemed to be looking straight at him. He checked the pulse. *God, what a face!* That's the meanest-looking bastard *I've ever seen*, he thought as he heard a moan. "Ahhhh, ahhhh." Levi stood as he sensed its direction and dashed over only three or four yards in the high grass. The twirling blades from the chopper had the dust flying thick, while the sheriff, not as agile as Levi, climbed down to the ground.

"Hey, Ben!" Levi yelled, "It's Randy, and he's still alive. He's been shot in the back, but I think he's better-off than that bastard who shot him."

The sheriff stopped to check out the rustler still gripping a pistol in his hand. He did a double take as their eyes met. "My God, that's the meanest-looking son of a bitch I've ever seen."

"He's dead, Ben. Let's not jack with 'im right now. We gotta get Randy to the hospital fast." As Ben and Levi placed Randy in the chopper, Levi told the pilot to radio the hospital to ready the emergency equipment. "This man's gotta make it," he said, "and if they don't have a cleared area for this chopper, they better get one cleared." The chopper's path was right over the road being used by the rustlers. The eighteen-wheeler plowed through the barricade and burst into flames, just as the helicopter passed overhead. Levi and Ben looked at each other with relief, but not a word was spoken.

The sheriff knew the wounded cowboy was an old friend and knew Levi was very concerned. The chopper dropped down in the parking lot of the small hospital, and the medics were standing by. Randy was placed on a rolling stretcher and wheeled straight into the emergency room.

While Levi paced the hall, Ben decided to check with his office. "I'll be right back," he stated as he headed toward the phone.

Levi nodded and walked over to a very enticing wood bench, which felt good as he leaned back for what he felt would be a long wait. But only a few minutes had passed when the doctor came through the emergency door.

"Levi, haven't seen you in a while," the doctor said as he walked up.

"Yeah, Doc, I guess it's been about a year," Levi said without any enthusiasm.

"Oh, I'm sorry, Levi, I wasn't thinking." The soft-spoken elderly gentleman had delivered Levi some thirty years prior, but their most recent encounter was the passing of Levi's grandfather. Doc had forgotten it momentarily.

"That's okay, Doc. How's Randy doing?"

"You got him here in time." The doctor smiled. "I think he's going to be just fine," he replied as he grasped Levi's arm.

"That's great, Doc."

"Yeah, from looking at the X-ray, the bullet entered his back about here." He turned slightly and pointed to a spot on his lower back. "About in line with the bottom of the lung, but it was deflected by a rib and came out his side, about here. It did chip that bone, but it's nothing too serious. He'll be sore for a few weeks, that's for sure."

"Boy, when we found him in that high grass, I was sure worried." Levi shook his head and smiled. "Oh, Doc, you think I could ask 'im a couple of questions?"

"We've got him out already, Levi," Doc said as he shook his head. "Can it wait till tomorrow?"

"Oh, sure. It's no big deal."

"I'm going to sew him up right now and put 'im to bed. He'll end up with a couple of small scars, but your friend is a lucky man.

A couple of hours out there, and he could have bled to death."

"Well, I really appreciate it, Doc. I guess I'll just wait here on the couch. Let me know if I can help with anything."

"Levi, you'll do no such thing," the doctor stated very seriously. "This boy will be asleep till tomorrow afternoon. There is nothing you can do here. My prescription for you"—he smiled—"is a good night's sleep in your own bed." Levi grinned. "Now you go home and get some sleep before I check you into one of these hospital beds."

"Thanks, Doc," Levi replied. He shook his hand and turned to see Ben walking back toward him.

"What'd the doc say?" Ben asked.

"He said Randy is gonna be fine." Levi's face looked a little wilted from the many nights of worrying and the long hours he had been keeping.

The sheriff was tired too, but he was also pumped up. "I knew Randy was too tough to let a little bullet stop 'im. Well, the boys caught one of the bastards, the one they left behind. The other two got a little crispy in that burning truck. Their cattle-stealing days are over," the sheriff said with a touch of pride in his accomplishment.

"What about the one we found by Randy at the corral?" Levi asked. "Did ya tell the boys about 'im?"

"Oh yeah, I called 'em from your chopper. They stopped to pick up that body when they spotted the live one. He was trying to get away on horseback"—the sheriff laughed—"but they got 'im."

"Hey, you don't think there are any more of those rustlers running around the ranch, do you?"

"Nah, I think the one we caught and the one Randy killed, the ugly one, were the last of 'em."

"Who was that guy, Ben?"

"I don't know. We don't have any information on any of 'em yet," the sheriff explained.

"Something about that guy's face gave me the creeps," Levi remarked.

"I know what you mean. That guy looked vicious," Ben added.

"Let's talk about something else." Levi's head and shoulders shook like a rabbit had run over his grave.

Ben could tell the man's face really did bother Levi, so he changed the conversation. "Levi, can you come by the office in the morning and sign the complaint against those rustlers?"

"Sure, I can. No, even better, can we go by there right now before I head home? I want to make reservations for Randy's parents to fly over from San Antonio anyway. I can do it from your office. Then I can call 'em in the morning with the flight numbers and time."

"Okay," Ben said. "That sounds good to me. Let's go."

"You mean *vámonos*. Ben, you've got to be bilingual around here," Levi said with a chuckle. You could tell a lot of pressure had been lifted. It was the first time he had joked around in months.

One of the patrol cars was waiting for them outside the hospital. "Well, Ben, you think of everything. I didn't even think about not having a car here," Levi said.

"Your chopper's still here. We'll run down to the station, and I'll drop you back off here on my way home, okay?" Ben suggested as he looked for approval from Levi.

"Sure, that's fine. Let me tell the pilot, and we can go."

In a few moments, Levi returned and was getting into the patrol car as Ben spoke. "You know, we still don't know how those rustlers got those cows around that mountain and up that canyon so fast or where they crossed the fence line."

"Yeah, you're right," Levi said with a long thinking pause. "I know Randy'll be able to shed some light on it. He got there just as fast as they did."

"Yeah, that's right. He did."

"Well, we'll be able to ask 'im about it tomorrow afternoon. Doc Bernard said he would be awake by then," Levi stated as they pulled up to the curb.

"I sure hope so. It's sure got me puzzled," said Ben as they got out of the car and walked up the steps. "Or as the old boys say, 'It's mind-boggling.'" Levi laughed as he opened the old wood-framed glass door with a waiter's bow.

The sheriff reached across an untidy desk and pulled out a standard form, trying not to disturb the deputy watching a late-hour western on a small black and white. He looked the form over and laid it in front of Levi for a signature. "Well, that's all you need to sign. I'll fill in all the blanks tomorrow and mail you a copy."

"That sounds fine. Why don't you let one of your deputies run me back down to the hospital? It's out of your way. You go on home and go to bed," Levi insisted.

"If you don't mind, I think I will. Hey, Gary, run Levi back down to the hospital, will you?"

"Sure, Ben," the deputy replied as his feet came off the desk.

Ben turned for the restroom. "I've got to drain my lizard. I'm about to pop. Hang on a minute."

Levi nodded and grinned and then reached for the phone and dialed the airport. The deputy grabbed his hat and buckled on his gun as he started toward the door. Levi finished his conversation and took a few steps toward Gary as the sheriff stepped from the restroom.

"Levi, did you make those reservations?" the sheriff shouted as he came across the room with a paper towel wiping off his face.

"Yeah, I sure did, while you were in the baño, taking a shower," Levi replied jokingly as the sheriff walked up.

"I didn't think I could drive home without that wash job. Boy, I'm wide awake now," he said vigorously as they started out the door.

Ben followed to the steps. "Where was I, what did ya say?" he questioned as Levi stepped into the patrol car.

"The *baño*, the restroom," explained Levi. "You have to start studying your Spanish, Ben." Levi laughed as the car sped away.

When the helicopter landed at the ranch, the ranch hands were anxiously waiting for some news about Randy. Levi stepped off the chopper as the engine noise ceased, and the rotor wound down.

"Randy's gonna be just fine," Levi stated. He looked over the crowd and noticed a few faces were missing. "I guess some of the boys on horseback stayed at the line shack again. I don't blame 'em. It's a long ride. Y'all might want to tell 'em about Randy tomorrow when they get back, or better yet, somebody could use the two-way radio tonight."

He knew everybody wanted to know because Randy was well liked among all the men on the ranch. "We'll be able to see 'im tomorrow afternoon. According to Doc Bernard, Randy can have visitors then, and I'm sure he'd appreciate the company."

Sounds of relief came from the group of worn-out cowboys as Levi spoke. "The sheriff said we got 'em all. Y'all did a good job of playing detective, and I appreciate it. Maybe we can get back to a normal routine next week." They all smiled and agreed as they started walking back to their own living quarters.

The pilot was tying down the chopper as Levi turned to leave. "You need some help with that?"

"Oh, no, that's okay. I'm just about through. Thanks anyway," he said.

"Well, I'll see ya tomorrow. Good night."

"Good night," the pilot replied.

Levi headed up the sidewalk to his own hacienda, where he had lived all of his life. As he reached the porch, he slowly turned, leaned over, and clutched the banister. Looking up at a full moon, he was more at peace than he had been in months. His mind wandered back to a time when he and his granddad sat on that porch when he was just a kid. He had a lot of good memories of that old porch rocker. He had a few bad ones too. The last few months his granddad was alive, Levi had set in that rocker many nights, worrying as the senior Calahan lay incoherent in the hospital. But now all the old memories were just good ones. A lonely feeling went through him, but he bounced right back. Dyanne was coming home tomorrow. "You've got to think of the good things," Levi said out loud to himself.

"Mis-ter Lee," came a light whisper with a heavy Mexican accent.

Levi was startled from his daydream by the familiar voice. "Yes, Manuel, what are you still doin' up?" The small-framed Mexican cowboy appeared from the shadows and walked into the moonlight. With the manners of a gentleman's gentleman, the aging caballero took his hat in hand as he reached the porch.

The old ranch foreman had been working on the ranch way before Levi was born. As a kid, Levi had sat and addressed many questions to Manuel about his parents. On just some simple little memorabilia, he could ask Manuel, but on a subject too emotional, he discussed with his granddad. "Oh, Mis-ter Lee, you say to me that as soon as this rustler problem was over, you was going to the line shack and go fishing."

"You're right, I sure did," Levi replied.

"When you leave, Mis-ter Lee? I can handle ever'thin', no problem."

"Are you trying to get rid of me?" he questioned with a grin.

"Oh no, Mis-ter Lee," Manuel defended.

"I'm just kidding. It's a good thought. Dyanne comes home tomorrow. I'll see if she'd like to spend a week or so on the lake." He looked up into the clear dark blue sky covered with stars. "That'd be good for both of us," he added with a smile of contentment.

"The line shack's got plenty of food?" he excitedly asked as he looked back at Manuel.

Manuel could tell that Levi was really enthused. "Oh, si, Señor Lee. She is stocked with plenty of food. Some vaqueros stay there through the stakeout. The place in good shape," Manuel said as Levi nodded his head and smiled.

"It's good to have Miss Dyanne home from school, no, Mis-ter Lee?"

"Yes, it sure will be. It sure will," Levi agreed as he turned to open the front door, and Manuel set his Texan sombrero back on his head.

"Manuel, hasta mañana."

Manuel tipped his cowboy hat once again and replied, "Hasta mañana, Señor Lee."

Levi shut the front door, and as he walked across the entry, a high-pitched voice in broken English spoke. "Mis-ter Lee, would you like Rosita to fix you something to eat?"

Levi looked down into the massive sunken den and scanned the room. He spotted Rosita standing by the huge rock fireplace, just coming out of her quarters. Very sleepy-eyed, the short heavyset Mexican woman, still in an old flowery flannel nightgown, was rubbing her eyes.

"No, Rosita. I'll just wait on a big breakfast. Right now, I only need sleep. *Gracias.*" "De nada," Rosita replied as she slowly turned for her room.

Levi drudgingly headed up an imperial circular staircase to the second-level balcony as Rosita slowly returned to her room.

All the bedroom suites were entered from this magnificent, picturesque balcony. Levi's suite was one of the most elegant. It was once shared by his parents but had remained empty for a number of years. Only one suite was more massive than his, and it had always been occupied by his grandfather.

Now it held no life. Levi felt that, with the passing of time, Dyanne would take the larger space for herself. But for now, he was only interested in his bed to end a very long day.

CHAPTER 2

THE REUNION

LEVI BOUNCED OUT of bed with only a few hours of sleep. He was back to his old self again. The smell of bacon frying and coffee brewing drew him downstairs to the kitchen. "That sure smells good, Rosita."

Rosita smiled as she took the biscuits out of the oven. "Ever'thin' is ready, Mis-ter Lee," Rosita replied.

"Oh, I'm ready," Levi stated as he sat down at the kitchen table. Rosita brought over a huge plate. "Ahh, huevos rancheros, my favorite. Rosita, you spoil me." Levi absently spoke with a Mexican accent as Rosita giggled and set his coffee beside him.

"Miss Dyanne is coming home today?" Rosita asked.

"She sure is, Rosita. I'll be glad to see her. I know you've missed her too," Levi said with a grin.

Rosita nodded. "Oh si, Mis-ter Lee. It'll be good to have her home."

"Yeah, I know, you just want another female in the house so y'all can team up on me," he said jokingly. The old woman knew how to take Levi; she had raised him from a pup. She too had been around the ranch since before Levi and Dyanne were born. Levi proceeded to eat.

A loud knock came at the back door, and Levi looked up from the table. "It's Manuel," he said as he stood. Levi took the last sip from his coffee cup and handed it to Rosita. Then he walked over and opened the door. "Buenos dias, Manuel," Levi stated cheerfully. He looked over Manuel's head to see his horse trailer all opened. A couple of the cowboys were loading some gear. "It looks like you've already loaded some stuff in the horse trailer, Manuel."

"*Si, Señor*, all of your fishing gear and some tools also," Manuel stated.

"Tools? Don't you plan too many things for me to do while I'm up there! This is a trip to rest, not work."

"Oh, Mis-ter Lee, you say me—" Levi stopped Manuel in the middle of his sentence.

"I know, I've told you to always send tools with me to the line shack," Levi confirmed as he patted Manuel on the back and stepped on to the back porch. "Something always needs fixin'," Levi added as he was laughing between the words. "I was only kidding, *mi* amigo." Levi looked around to the stable. "Manuel, maybe it would be good to take Crimson out of his stall and loosen him up a little," Levi suggested.

Manuel turned and shouted, "Juan, ensilla el caballo del Señor Lee y dale un poco de picadero!"

Juan jumped from a comfortable seat on the corral fence and speedily trotted for the stable as he yelled, "Si, señor, ya voy."

Levi walked over to his solid black horse trailer with the Calahan Ranch emblem on each side. He opened the storage door on the front. "It looks like you've packed everything but the kitchen sink," Levi remarked.

"*Que, Señor?* You want the kit-cinn sinnk?" Manuel questioned.

"No, nothing, I'm just kidding. I'm in a good mood," Levi stated with a grin.

Juan came riding out of the stable on a huge strutting sorrel. The long-legged Tennessee Walker started toward them.

"Magnifico," Manuel remarked, always amazed at the beautiful animal.

Levi stopped the animal as he came by. "Hey, big fellow," he said as he patted the stallion on the side of his face. Crimson was excited. Levi had spent very little time with him the past few weeks. "Would ya like to take a little trip? Huh, boy?" Levi added as he and Manuel watched Juan gallop off on Crimson.

"Well, Manuel, I guess I'd better drive to the airport and pick up our princess. I'll be back later." He climbed into his black Bronco. He drove down the long gravel road and then over a cattle guard and hit the main highway into San Angelo, Texas.

He had made this trip many times before. So accustomed to the beautiful scenic view of the rocky, mountainous terrain, his mind wandered off into the past with his sister and their granddad and the good memories they shared. Before he knew it, he was at the airport, pulling up to the front of the exit doors at baggage claim. He whipped over to the curb, hopped out, and went inside. As he entered, he spotted Dyanne retrieving her luggage from the conveyor. She was a beautiful girl with long legs and long black hair. Levi picked up speed as he headed for her.

Dyanne swung around and spotted Levi coming toward her. She dropped her bags just in time to catch Levi with a real bear hug. "Oh, Levi, it sure feels good to be home."

Levi stepped back, holding Dyanne by both arms. "You sure look grown." He was proud of his little sister, but she really wasn't little anymore. The dark hair and blue eyes made for a heavy family resemblance. The tall and slim but shapely body and beautiful face had matured quite well over the past couple of years.

"I am grown," Dyanne said as other voices interrupted.

"Hi, Levi."

"Hi, Mari, how've you been? I guess better since finals are over, huh?" Levi remarked jokingly.

"Yeah, I'm glad that pressure's over," Mari replied.

"I know what you mean," Levi said, while thinking to himself, *If she only knew pressure.*

Dyanne spoke up, "Levi, do you remember Anna?"

"Sure, I do, but I wouldn't have recognized her. Y'all look like college grads." Levi felt proud for all the girls.

"These are my parents, Levi," Anna said, introducing her parents.

"Sure, I know your dad. How are you, Bill?" Levi asked as he shook his hand. Levi had stopped at one of Bill Johnson's service stations many times over the years and, because of the girls being good friends, had often chatted about them. Then looking at Anna's mother, he added, "Nice meeting you, Mrs. Johnson."

"Nice meeting you too. We hear a lot about you from the girls."

"I hope it's not too bad," Levi replied.

"Oh, no, it's all good," she stated, laughing.

Mari, holding both her parents by the arm, spoke next. "Levi, do you remember my par—"

Levi interrupted Mari. "Of course. Ray, Susan, how've you been? Haven't seen y'all in a long time."

Ray answered, "It sure has been a long time. You doin' okay?" Ray was a PR man for Brackston Oil and a sharp dresser, with a personality that fit his position. They were both golfers and had run into each other on several occasions at the country club.

"Oh yeah, everything's fine," Levi responded, "I guess we're all glad to have the girls home, or maybe I should say young ladies." Everyone laughed.

Both mothers agreed. "It was just too quiet around the house. It'll be noisier, but that's okay."

Bill spoke up, "I guess if we're all going to the country club, we'd better get started, huh?"

"We're going," Ray and Susan chimed in.

"I've been staying pretty busy. What's going on out there?" Levi asked. "It's the annual barbecue," Bill replied.

"Oh, Levi, let's go, okay?" Dyanne pleaded.

"Well, sure, if you're not too tired," replied Levi as he winked at the parents.

"Too tired! I'm coming home from college, not the hospital," Dyanne remarked.

Levi smiled as he grabbed the luggage. "Well, okay, let's go," he replied, and everyone walked out, still talking. The women were talking, and the men were listening and carrying most of the bags.

The luggage was stacked in the rear of the Bronco. Dyanne waved to her friends, still loading their trunks, as Levi pulled out of the parking lot.

"This isn't the way to the country club," Dyanne remarked as Levi headed on down the road. "I thought we were going—"

Levi interrupted, "We are. I just need to make a stop at the hospital first."

"Who is in the hospital?" Dyanne asked with concern. "Anyone I know?"

"You might remember him, Randy Hayes. I played football with him in high school," Levi answered.

"Sure, I do, the cute blond you used to bring home every once in a while. He liked to pull my ponytail," Dyanne recalled. Levi reached over and ruffled her hair.

"Hey, I thought I was the only man in your life," Levi teased.

"You're the most important one right now, but hopefully, you won't be the only one in my life," she said as she laughed and reached over to clutch Levi's hand. "What's wrong with Randy?"

"Well ... he was ... shot last night," Levi stammered. He tried to say it in a nonchalant way, hoping it would keep Dyanne calm.

"He was shot! You mean with a gun?" Dyanne shouted. To say the least, his psychology hadn't worked.

"Yeah, with a gun. The bullet passed right through, and Doc Bernard said he would be just fine, but he'll be sore for a while," Levi replied, looking straight ahead.

"Doc Bernard. You mean he has the same doctor as we do?" Dyanne asked.

"Well," Levi hesitated, "he's been working out at the ranch, since he got laid off."

"You mean he got shot at the ranch," Dyanne said. "Boy, that ranch is getting to be a dangerous place to work at, somebody getting shot. I guess *somebody* needs to be more careful while they're hunting. You didn't shoot him, did ya?"

"No! I didn't shoot 'im. He wasn't shot hunting. It's not even huntin' season," Levi replied.

"I don't care if it's hunting season. Are you going to tell me what happened?" Dyanne asked, exasperated.

"I will, if you'll give me a chance," he replied anxiously.

"Okay, I will, I will. Explain." Dyanne stopped with silence, her arms crossed, her eyes staring out the windshield; only a rapid thumping from her right foot was heard.

Something told Levi she was a little perturbed as he started to explain. "I haven't told ya about our troubles the past coupl'a months because there was nothing you could do to help. So I figured, why should you worry about it and maybe not graduate?" Dyanne just looked anxious but kept her lips sealed.

"About two months ago, we started missing a few cows, forty or fifty head. I didn't think too much about it. It's hard to keep up with every cow. A couple of weeks later, our count was down another forty-six head I really got concerned. I knew we couldn't miss that many that close together," Levi explained as he pulled into the visitor parking area.

Not able to contain herself, she broke her silence as she stepped from the vehicle. "So what did you do?"

"I'm trying to tell ya," he replied. "So we started stakeouts all over the ranch." He opened the front door of the hospital and continued. "Ben Thompson and me—"

"Ben Thompson and I," Dyanne interrupted.

Levi gave her a dirty look. "Ben Thompson and I worked up some good locations on the big map in the study to place some lookouts. They were looking for anything out of the ordinary. Well, it took two months, but we finally caught 'em last night. Randy was the one who spotted 'em. He started following. He must have gotten too close, and they spotted him."

"Why didn't you just put two men at the opening where they were coming in?"

"There were no tracks around any of the gates, no fences cut. We couldn't find a clue."

"Well, are you going to tell me?" Dyanne asked.

"I don't know," Levi replied.

"Why not? Why won't you tell me?" Dyanne asked, steaming.

"No, I don't mean, I don't know if I'll tell ya. I mean, I don't know where they're coming in," Levi answered as he pushed the button for the elevator. "Randy is the only one who knows. I hope he knows."

"This is really getting intriguing. I can't wait to see Randy," Dyanne remarked.

Levi stopped at the nurses' station as they stepped off the elevator. "Nurse, do you know the room number for Randy Hayes, please?"

"Sure, it's … aahh, two-fourteen," the nurse said as she looked up the number in a small card file on her desk. Her head tilted back as she looked at Levi, and then she smiled in a flirty way. But not knowing who the girl was with this good-looking hunk, she didn't say anything more. Levi thanked her with a nod and a sexy smile and started down the hall. The nurse kept watching till he walked out of sight.

Dyanne asked with a grin, "Did you know that nurse, Levi?"

Levi, not thinking about anything but Randy, answered, "No, I don't think so. Why?"

"Oh, no reason, but you should take a break from the ranch once in a while." Dyanne proudly walked alongside her handsome brother, who looked at her with a confused expression.

As they entered the opened door to his room, Randy was sitting up in bed. "Hey, Levi. Who's that ya got with you? That couldn't be that scrawny little sister of yours," Randy asked with a happy and healthy smile. "Boy, I'd get shot every day for this kind of company." Dyanne smiled with a bashful grin.

"Well, she told me as we were coming up the elevator that she couldn't wait to see you," Levi said with a smile.

"Levi! I didn't say that," Dyanne said with a red face.

"You did so, Dyanne," Levi replied.

"Well, I guess I did say that. But I meant I wanted to hear the rest of the story," Dyanne explained.

"How disappointing," Randy said jokingly.

"Oh," Levi said, "I guess we both want to hear how those rustlers got across that box canyon so fast."

Randy smiled. "Well, let me tell you what they did. I followed those rustlers right up that gorge. You wouldn't believe how surprised I was when I got to the pond at the head of that canyon." Randy paused with a grin on his face. "The cattle, the rustlers, everything was gone." Levi and Dyanne were all ears. Then Randy continued. "All of a sudden, it hit me. All the tracks lead into the water. They were easy to see in the moonlight. It's the waterfall! There's an opening behind that waterfall, I thought. Sure enough, I ran old Lady right through that waterfall. I bet that old mare didn't know what was going on." Levi's face was all excited as Randy spoke.

"I'll be damned!" Levi was astonished and shook his head as he grinned. "There's an opening behind that waterfall?" he questioned, still shaking his head as Dyanne just looked on in disbelief.

"Yep," Randy replied, "it's a cave that runs all the way through that mountain."

Levi was still amazed. "It's hard to believe. I've been swimming in that pond all my life. I never knew it."

"Hey, ya know what? I was thinking how hard it was for Lady to walk in that cave, but now I know why. There were tracks in there," Randy explained as he remembered a few details.

"Tracks? Why would that—" Levi was interrupted. "Railroad tracks!" Randy shouted.

"Railroad tracks? Oh, tracks, you mean metal rails, like in a mine. Small rails, not very far apart?" Levi guessed excitedly.

"Yeah, that's it. They were mining rails. It was an old mine shaft. It even had shoring timbers. I remember now," Randy added. "I know that must be an old mine. It's probably been there for a hundred years. I wonder what kind of mine."

"Well, the old ghost town was called Dorado Ciudad. It means 'Golden City.'" Levi paused to contemplate and then said, "You know, I think I'll go over there and check out that old cave next week. I was planning to take a little trip up to the old line shack with Dyanne and do some fishing anyway. We'll be within eight or ten miles of the place."

"Wait a minute. I can't go on a trip," Dyanne interrupted, "It sounds good, but I can't leave."

"Ahh, why not? It'll be fun, just like the old times. We'll do a little fishing and some hiking and go through that old cave," Levi pleaded as Dyanne interrupted.

"I can't. I've got a girl friend coming in Tuesday."

"Girl friend," Levi said disappointedly.

"Yeah, Beth Cagle. She's coming in Tuesday from school," Dyanne explained, "She had a lot of stuff to send back, so she had to wait till Monday for the movers before she could fly home. She's even shipping a few boxes for me."

"I didn't know you hung around with her," Levi said.

"Well, we've been roommates this last semester, and I've really gotten to know her. She's my best friend," explained Dyanne.

"You wouldn't have anything to do with her in high school. You said she was stuck-up," said Levi. Randy just listened.

"Well, I really didn't know her then. She's really just shy. She doesn't talk much, but since we've been in the same room for four months, she's really opened up to me, and now we're best of friends," Dyanne continued.

"But isn't she a little too young for you to be hanging around with?" Levi asked.

"Young? We're the same age. As a matter of fact, she's five months older than I am," Dyanne explained.

"Really? I thought she was still a kid," Levi questioned.

"No, she's really not, and anyway, you and Brian have been best friends for years. I think it's kind of neat that his sister is now my best friend," she stated enthusiastically.

"Yeah, that's great, but it sure messes up my trip," Levi replied jokingly.

"How is Brian doing?" Randy asked, interrupting the private conversation, "I haven't seen him since high school. He sure was a good running back."

"He sure was. He shoulda played in college, and he says the same about you, the best wide receiver in the state," Levi said as he recalled his old days as quarterback. "But I guess he was just like me, had to think about that ranch too much. He's doin' fine. He stopped by one night last week just to visit a while. It was one night when y'all were out playing detective, hiding in the bushes," Levi said jokingly as Dyanne smiled, shaking her head.

"Well, Randy, I guess we'll see ya later. You look like you're doin' fine. Do you need anything? Can we pick up anything for ya?" Levi asked.

"No, I'm fine. I'll probably be outta here Monday or Tuesday."

"Oh, by the way, your parents should be in here this afternoon," Levi said.

"Yeah, I know. Ms. Nightingale told me she had a call from my mom at the nurses' station while I was sleeping. Thanks a lot, but ya didn't have to buy 'em plane tickets," Randy said appreciatively. "The nurse said Mom was all excited. She's never been on a plane before. You can hold 'em out of my pay."

"Oh no, that's part of your hazardous benefits, which comes with the job," Levi replied, laughing.

"I'll check on ya tomorrow," said Dyanne with a smile as she trailed Levi out the door.

As they started down the hall, Levi stated, "I think Randy's gonna be fine, don't you?"

"Oh sure. He looked great," Dyanne remarked.

"Double meaning there," Levi said with a smirk, and Dyanne smiled.

As the two were walking out the hospital entrance, the sheriff was coming up the walk. "Hey, Dyanne, how are you?" Ben asked.

"Oh, I'm fine. How are you, Mr. Thompson?" She had known the sheriff all of her life but was never really comfortable around that badge.

"Ah, Dyanne, you're old enough. Just call me Ben," he stated.

"Cops make me nervous, but I'll try, Ben," Dyanne remarked. Ben and Levi laughed. "Ben, have ya found out anything about those rustlers?" Levi asked.

"Oh yeah, they were some scuzzy barroom buddies. A couple of 'em used to work on the Rockford Ranch. Well, anyway, the Double R caught 'em stealing some of their cattle. So they fired 'em about four months ago. You know the one you found lying close to Randy," Levi nodded, "and that one we arrested were brothers. Their name was Tanner. Matthew, the one you found, was only twenty-eight years old, and he was the head honcho of the gang."

"Boy, I'll never forget that guy's face when I rolled him over," Levi said as the face flashed through his mind. "I figured him to be about 128. Well, I guess them working on the Rockford spread was how they discovered that old mine shaft, huh?" Levi thought out loud.

"Mine shaft?" Ben questioned.

"Oh yeah, Ben, that's what I was gonna tell ya. Randy was just telling us about finding an old mine shaft behind that big waterfall in the box canyon," Levi explained.

"I'll be damned, a mine shaft behind the waterfall!" Ben stated.

"I think it was one of those old gold mines we were talking about, back when the old ghost town was still booming. Of course, it wasn't from our side but from the Rockford Ranch."

"They probably didn't realize that mountain wasn't any thicker than it was. I can see their faces, looking for gold and finding water," Ben said jokingly. "Well, I guess Randy's okay if he's already filled ya in on all of that."

"Oh, yes, sir. He's doing fine, Mr. Thom ... I mean, Ben," Dyanne replied. Ben smiled. "That's good. He'll be okay for me to talk to."

"Oh sure. Go on up. He'll probably appreciate the company. We're going out to the country club. If you get a chance, stop by. I'll buy ya a drink," Levi said as they turned toward the parking lot. "We'll see ya later." Ben gave a short wave and went inside.

As they climbed into the Bronco, Dyanne commented, "Levi, you should go on up to the lake anyway. I know ya really want to go."

"And leave you at home alone? Your first week back from school? No, I don't think I should," but Levi thought about her suggestion very seriously as he backed out of the parking spot and pulled on to the street.

Dyanne could tell Levi really did want to go. "I'm not going to be alone. I'll have Maria and Manuel there. Besides, Beth is coming in Tuesday. We'll be together all week."

"Oh, speaking of Beth, not that I mind, but why is she coming to our house? She only lives next door," questioned Levi.

"The Cagles are going on a trip tomorrow and won't be back for a week," Dyanne explained.

"Brian didn't mention the trip."

"Well, he's not going, just his parents, but it's a good opportunity for her to spend a few days with me," explained Dyanne.

"Well, if you really don't mind, I might just go ahead and go up to the lake for a week," Levi said, thinking out loud.

"A week?" questioned Dyanne.

"Why? A week's not too long. It takes the better part of a day to drive up there," Levi replied.

"Well, the only thing I ask is that you be back by next Saturday," Dyanne requested.

"Why, what happens Saturday?"

"We're kinda thinking about having a party Saturday night, like maybe a graduation party. What do you think?" Dyanne asked.

"Graduation party! It sounds good to me. I guess I should have thought of it. You gonna invite all our old school friends?"

"Yeah, some old friends and a few neighbors too," she replied.

Levi was getting into it better than she expected. Because he had just been relieved of some big problems, a party sounded like a good idea. He hadn't really relaxed since their granddad had gotten sick two years ago.

"Then it's settled. I'll plan the party while you're gone to the lake," Dyanne said happily.

The parking lot of the country club was full, and many familiar people were entering the clubhouse. As they mingled, they spoke to lots of old friends they hadn't seen in quite a while. They hadn't attended the annual barbecue last year because of their granddad's death but had always made it in the past years with him. He had always been the life of the party, like a tradition. In spite of his age, or maybe because of his age, the granddad of the Calahan clan was well liked and always a gentleman.

Picking up a drink along the way, they made it to a huge patio overlooking the golf course. The lights were strung out overhead to a gazebo in the center, where a combo was playing. The dance floor surrounding the gazebo was packed with old friends. It was a very festive occasion. The couple was spotted by some close friends, and they stopped to talk. Levi felt a tap on the shoulder and turned to see his best friend, Brian.

The two boys had ridden a lot of miles together on horseback and had pretty well covered both ranches, acre by acre, over the past twenty years. Levi had also handed a football off to this favorite running back hundreds of times in high school. Although they were about the same size and had the same type of easygoing personality, Brian's light skin and blond hair made the duo look totally opposite. Maybe all these qualities played a part in this long-lasting friendship.

"Well, I was wondering if you would make it. How've you been?" Brian asked with a smile from ear to ear. He was really glad to see his old friend back out in public. Levi just wasn't the type to stay away from people very long. "Oh, I'm doing fine. You okay?"

"Oh, sure, I'm great. Walt, one of the sheriff's deputies, told me y'all caught those rustlers last night. Was it anybody we knew?" Brian asked.

"Nah," Levi said. "It was some guys from Borden County, somewhere around Big Spring. Their names weren't familiar at all. But I'm sure glad we got those bastards," Levi replied as he cupped his hand over his mouth so the ladies wouldn't hear his language.

"I heard that," another voice interrupted as a hand came over Levi's shoulder.

"Hey, Dave. How've ya been? I haven't seen you in a coon's age," Levi said with great feeling. Dave was another close friend. His family had moved to San Angelo when the boys were in junior high. He was a little stocky, but loving football as much as the other two, he had fit right in as left guard, always protecting Levi under pressure.

"Yeah, it's been quite some time, probably four or five years since we hunted those birds out at the water tank," Dave replied.

"I guess it was. It just doesn't seem like it's been that long,"

Levi recalled with a smile.

Dyanne walked up and joined the conversation. "Hi, Brian, Dave, y'all doin' okay?"

"Sure, Dyanne. How are things with you?" Dave replied.

"Everything's great."

"Hey, congratulations. You and sis finally got a couple of diplomas yesterday," Brian remarked. He smiled in a flirty way as he noticed Dyanne's maturing assets.

"Oh, thanks. Yeah, it feels great just to get out of school," she answered. She noticed Brian's appeal but then glanced at both guys. "Hey, Brian, aren't your parents here?"

"Yeah, they're here somewhere. I think they're at a table on the other side of the gazebo with Mari's parents," Brian answered.

"Thanks. I need to tell your mother that Beth's not coming home till Tuesday. I'll see ya later."

Brian watched as Dyanne walked away. "Wow, I don't know how you got such a good-looking sister," he said jokingly.

"Hey, that's my baby sister. Don't ya go gettin' any ideas," Levi joked back. "Those girls are cookin' up a party for next Saturday night. Y'all be sure and plan on it."

"Sounds good to me," Brian stated.

"Yeah, we'll be there," Dave added. "Hey, Levi, ya gonna enter the fast-draw contest?"

"No way. It's been two years since I've worked on that draw," Levi replied.

"Ah, come on, be a sport. You're a natural gunslinger," Brian said in a jovial tone. "My God, you won the tournament three years in a row. All you'll be doin' is maybe givin' someone else a chance."

"I can't enter. I don't have my gun and holster with me," he replied, hoping Brian would let it drop.

"No, no, it's not that easy. You can use mine," Brian added.

"But I've never shot your gun or drawn from your holster. I wouldn't be worth a damn."

"Ah, come on. No excuses. I know ya want to. It's in your blood," Brian pleaded. He knew how much Levi really enjoyed the competition.

"Well, okay. I hate to see a grown man cry. Let's do it," Levi consented. He had really gotten involved in the fast-draw competition in his early twenties and then slowly enticed Brian into the sport about four years ago. Levi was a natural. But both boys liked a good challenge, and they loved to compete against each other.

The three friends walked over to the registration table.

"Levi, how are ya? We've missed ya in the competition," said the middle-aged man sitting at the table.

"Hi, Mr. Barker. I'm doing fine. It has been a long time," Levi answered.

"Are you going to sign up for the competition tonight?"

"Well, I don't really think I should, but Brian's insisting. It's been fourteen or fifteen months since I've had a pistol in my hand. Whatcha think, Mr. Barker?" Levi asked.

"I think you've got a good chance. It won't hurt a thing for you to compete."

"I guess … sign me up," Levi said reluctantly. Mr. Barker slid over the registration form, and Levi signed on the dotted line.

"Brian, I guess I'd better try that gun of yours on and practice a few draws before this thing gets underway," Levi said. He was feeling a little insecure.

"Oh sure," Brian said. "Mr. Barker, would ya hand me that black bag by your feet. We'll see if the old master still has the touch."

Mr. Barker smiled and then pulled up several bags and soon came up with the right one.

"That's it," Brian stated, setting the bag on the registration table. "Okay, killer, show us how it's done."

Levi just grinned and shook his head as he took the set from Brian. He strapped on the holster, tying the leather strap to his leg as he looked up at his competition. "Brian, ya already have wax-tipped shells in here?" Levi asked as he flipped open the chamber.

"Oh sure. You know I'm not going to chance shootin' my leg off," Brian replied. Levi smiled as he put the pistol back in the holster and drew it out with lightning speed. Again and again, the pistol cleared the holster within the blink of an eye. 7

"Wow," Dave commented, "that's fast. He did that in less than a second." Dave's parents didn't belong to the club, so it was his first time to see the competition.

"Yeah, it was less than half a second," Brian remarked admirably. Dave, very impressed, just shook his head. Levi, still whipping the pistol from the holster, got into a crouching position. His legs slightly bent, Levi had reached the right mode to do well in the competition. His adrenaline was flowing. "Okay, I guess I'm as ready as I can get in such a short time, fellows," he said with a grin. "Vámonos."

The shooting had already started as the threesome walked up to the competition stand.

"What's the best time so far, Mr. Barker?" Brian asked.

"Thirty-one. Think you can beat it, Brian?"

"What ya think, Levi? You wanna go next?" Brian asked as he winked at Mr. Barker.

"You can if you want to, Brian."

"Nah, you've already got the gun on. Give me something to beat," joked Brian.

"How far back is he standing, Brian?" Dave asked.

"Eight feet."

"I guess the object is to hit that balloon when he shoots?" Dave questioned.

"Yeah. When that light comes on, the time starts. Levi can draw his gun and shoot the balloon. When the balloon breaks, it stops that timer." Brian was keeping his eyes on the clock. He always got excited when it came to competition, and he especially took delight in beating Levi.

"Boy, that timer must be fast," commented Dave.

"It's broken down into hundredths of a second," Brian continued. "The man who's got that thirty-one has thirty-one hundredths of a second.

"Boy, that's fast," Dave commented. "Do ya think Levi has a chance?"

"Sure. He may be a little rusty, but he's a natural."

The time came for Levi to draw. The crowd stood mute and motionless as the light came on. His hand moved with the swiftness of a bullet; the only evidence to prove the pistol had left the holster was the loud shot that rang out and the bursting of the balloon.

"The time is twenty-six hundredths of a second," announced Mr. Barker.

"You've taken the lead, Levi. You're in first place," Dave said with the enthusiasm of an eight-year-old. Levi smiled as he unbuckled the holster and handed it to Brian.

Brian moved toward the competition stand as he tied down the holster. "Yeah, I did better than I thought I could," Levi commented to Dave. "But Brian hasn't shot."

"Do you really think Brian could possibly beat your score?" Dave asked.

"Brian is good, and I think he can take this tournament if he concentrates," Levi explained in a whisper as a hush came over the crowd.

Brian got to a crouched position, and the light came on. Brian drew his gun, and almost at the same time, the balloon burst. The automatic timer stopped at twenty-five hundredths of a second.

"Brian won! I can't believe it!" Dave yelled as he and Levi ran over to shake his hand.

"That was great. Good shootin'," Levi commented as they slapped hands. The two friendly competitors just looked at each other for a second in a proud way as Dave chimed in.

"Boy, that sure was great, Brian. Congratulations." Dave felt like he had stepped back into the Old West.

"Thank ya, thank ya," Brian answered with a smile of satisfaction. "I've been practicing a lot, and I just barely beat ya. You're the one who really did fantastic, Levi."

"Well, now that that's over, let's go have a drink or maybe two," said Dave.

"That's a helluva suggestion, Dave. *Vámonos*," said Brian.

Walking through the crowded grounds, they stopped to say hello to half the people along the way. It was nice to be around so many people they knew.

Soon they reached the edge of the huge patio with a Saltillo tile floor, which had been transformed into an outside dance floor with multicolored lights strung overhead. A hundred or so lighthearted members were dancing to a country-and-western band playing Willie Nelson's "Blue Eyes Crying in the Rain"; but they knew that sooner or later, some south of the border, cha-cha-cha, and a little oom-pah-pah would be thrown in to spice up the festive occasion. A couple of minutes later, they had made it across the dance floor and up the steps to the inside bar.

"Set 'em up, bartender. Wild Turkey for me and my friends," Dave said the line from some old cowboy movie in an overexaggerated Mexican accent. The three laughed, and the drinking started. Levi hadn't been this loose in a long time. The boys were living in days gone by and loving every minute of it. Levi turned from the bar as Dyanne, Mari, and Anna walked up.

"Hey, what are girls like you doing in a nice place like this?"

Brian asked as the three guys laughed loudly.

"Hey, that's funny, Brian," Dave commented as the three continued to chuckle.

The girls took the joke as a joke and laughed with them as Mari asked in an exaggerated Southern accent. "Won't you handsome boys buy us ladies a drink?"

"Boys," the three guys chimed together. The six old friends grabbed a table and started to talk. It was fun to reminisce about old times. As the night progressed and the Wild Turkey and margaritas flowed, the stories moved from small tales to complete fiction. It did the whole group a lot of good to let their hair down.

"Last call" was heard from the bartender. "You mean it's one o'clock already? I can't believe it." As Brian was talking, the others looked around and noticed that the crowd had thinned. The check indicated that, besides a lot of talking, there had been plenty of drinking.

Levi quickly put his hand over the check. "Put this on my tab, and here's a tip for all your trouble." The barmaid was thrilled with the tip and couldn't resist a second look at Levi. His smile usually brought a second look. She gave him her sexiest smile, which most men would have taken as an invitation.

On the way out, Dyanne reminded everyone, "Don't y'all forget we're having a party at our place next Saturday."

The group acknowledged with a wave and yelled good-night as they headed for their cars. The Calahans pulled from the parking lot and started down the deserted dark highway toward home.

The long day was drawing to a close. The lights of the city were far in the background as Levi looked over at his baby sister curled up in the other seat. Dyanne was sound asleep, and Levi reminisced about the night. *She's not carrying on a conversation,* he thought, *but she's still a lot of company.* He made his way down the lonely stretch of road, which curved one way and then the other around the deep gorges and high-peaked hills of Central Texas.

Levi had also begun to feel the strain of the day and wished the road was a little shorter. The headlights soon spotted the massive entrance to the ranch. He sighed with relief as he pulled across the cattle guard.

Dyanne sat up as the rapid bumping shook the vehicle. "We're already home?"

Levi frowned. "Yeah, it only takes a couple of minutes when you're asleep," he commented.

"Oh, I'm sorry. I wasn't much company on that long drive, was I?" Levi stepped out and walked to the rear of the Bronco.

"I was just kiddin'. I don't know how you lasted through the party," he answered while opening the tailgate.

"Oh, Levi, don't bother with all that stuff right now. Just hand me that little blue bag, and I'll get Manuel to help me unload it tomorrow."

"That sounds good to me." He shut the tailgate, carrying only the blue bag, and they walked inside.

CHAPTER 3

THE TRIP

DAWN HIT EARLY with the bright sun pouring between the hilltops, early because the Calahans ended the night in the wee hours of the morning. But being very eager to start his trip, Levi wheeled out of bed with the vigor of a new colt anxious to see those greener pastures. Fully dressed and ready to go, he started down the stairs.

Dyanne was just in front of him, holding her head and slowly making her way down. "I can't believe you're up, sleepyhead. We've only had five hours of sleep," he stated cheerily as Dyanne glanced over her shoulder with partially opened eyes. She had just gotten out of bed, her entire body in shambles. She couldn't believe Levi felt that good. "Levi, you're despicable." The phrase came from their old TV cartoon days, of course.

Levi caught her before she reached the bottom of the stairs and ruffled her hair as he ran past. Dyanne screamed "Haaa!" in a playful tone.

Levi was already sitting at the breakfast table by the time Dyanne entered the kitchen.

"What took you?" Levi asked with a shit-eating grin.

"One of these days," she stated in a Jackie Gleason tone.

"I'm not really pickin'. I'm just in a good mood."

"I could never tell."

"Well, why are ya up so early?"

"You know why. I had to see my big brother off. I might even enjoy a few days of peace and quiet around here," Dyanne remarked with a little air of cockiness.

Meanwhile, Rosita, knowing how these two loved to pick at each other, continued setting the table and cooking breakfast. It felt good to hear the bickering between the two siblings she had cared for and loved all of these years.

She knew their pleasure as she served their breakfast. "Ah, Rosita, my favorite." Levi couldn't wait.

"Oh, these look great. It seems like years since I've had your pancakes, Rosita," stated Dyanne.

Rosita smiled. "It's been since Christmas, Miss Dyanne," she said in her broken English.

"Well, it was worth waiting for. They taste great."

There was a knock at the back door, and Levi swiveled to see through the half glass. "Hey, Manuel, come on in!" Levi shouted though the door and asked, "Would you like some coffee?" Manuel stepped inside.

"Oh, no, *gracias*, Mis-ter Lee. I was just wondering if you have some more things you want me to load in your trucka."

"I've got two bags in my room. If you'll wait a minute, I'll help ya bring 'em down."

"It's okay, Mis-ter Lee, me get 'em," Manuel said and headed for the stairs.

"I don't know what we'd do without 'im. That man knows more about cattle than anyone," Levi commented.

A few minutes later, Manuel returned with the luggage. Levi got up from the table and headed toward the study. "I'll get my guns and some shells. They may come in handy," he said jokingly.

"Okay, Mis-ter Lee," Manuel replied, carrying two pieces of matching luggage out the back door.

Levi took his last sip of coffee and then planted a kiss on Rosita's cheek. "Rosita, that was magnifico, perfecto."

"Oh, Mis-ter Lee," Rosita blushed bashfully. Levi headed through the door across the split-level rustic mansion and came to the room where he had spent many waking hours of late.

Once inside the room, he paused to check both gun cases for his needs. Walking to the right of the fireplace, he pulled out a Weatherby shotgun and matching rifle with scope. Both guns were beautifully carved. He scanned the cabinets once more and then reached in a drawer below, pulling out several boxes of shells.

Manuel walked in behind him. "Mis-ter Lee, I can help?"

"You sure can. I think the gun cases are in that big drawer at the bottom."

Manuel found the cases and placed the guns inside as Levi located his pistol, hanging in its holster on the other side of the fireplace. He paused for a second and then reached back into the gun case for the second holster. "I think I'm going to take my competition holster too. I should have some time to work on my fast draw, I hope." Levi smiled as he noticed Manuel's eyes. Levi looked down. He had laid one pistol and holster over each shoulder and loaded his arms down with shells. He looked better prepared than the Frito Bandito. The two men returned to the kitchen, loaded for bear.

"My God, you look like an army. Are you going to take over Mexico?" Dyanne asked. She smiled and opened the back door for the two men.

"I'll see you in a week, Rosita. You keep Dyanne straight, okay?" The two women smiled.

"Oh, wait, Mis-ter Lee, I have a lunch for you." Rosita scurried back to the counter and returned with a large picnic basket.

"Wow! Gracias. I think this'll last all week." Levi smiled as he walked out the door. Dyanne took the basket and followed him out to the Bronco.

"Hey, Manuel," Levi called, "tell Juan to go ahead and load Crimson into the trailer."

"Oh, Mis-ter Lee, she is already in the trailer," Manuel said proudly.

"*She's* already in the trailer? I hope you haven't done any surgery on my stallion, Manuel." Levi smiled with the statement, knowing Manuel's problem with gender pronouns.

"Que, Mis-ter Lee?" a confused Manuel replied.

"Never mind, Manuel. Mr. Lee is sick." Dyanne smiled as she shook her head.

"Mis-ter Lee is sick?" asked Manuel.

"No, no, Manuel, he's not sick, sick. He's … just forget it," Dyanne said as she laughed at the situation. Manuel was still confused as he placed the gear in the rear of the Bronco.

Levi laid his pistol in the passenger seat, and the long guns stood on the floor. "You sure ya don't want those in the back, Mr. Lee?" Dyanne mocked in a friendly way, but she was really worried about all that firepower in such close quarters.

"Yes, I'm sure. I don't want them in the back. I want 'em handy, in case I see something that needs shootin'," Levi replied.

"You mean like a vicious poor old jackrabbit or something?" Dyanne loved to tease.

"No, like a coyote or a mountain lion, thank you," Levi replied, duplicating Dyanne's smirky tone as he walked around to the driver's door.

A loud whinny came from the corral, only thirty feet away, as a high-spirited mare charged the fence. Her front hooves plowed into the ground, only to stop short of the gate as another loud neigh came from the stunning animal. Levi looked up at the mare and smiled. "I think Honeycup wants to go with us," he said as the others laughed. "She's sure gettin' big. She looks like she's gonna drop that new foal any day."

Dyanne studied the sorrel as Manuel agreed. "Si, Mis-ter Lee, he's gonna have that colt any time now."

"*He's* gonna have a colt! Dyanne, would ya explain a few things to Manuel about the birds and the bees or maybe just his use of

46

pronouns." Dyanne smiled and shook her head. Manuel was still confused but laughed along.

"Manuel, ya got all my fishing gear, huh?" Levi, still smiling, shouted as the roar of the engine started.

"Oh, *si*, Mis-ter Lee, I got ever'thinnn'," replied Manuel.

"Don't forget your lunch," Dyanne said as she handed the basket through the window.

"Thank ya, ma'am. Well, I'm leaving. Are y'all sure you can handle everything?"

"Will you go already? Manuel and Rosita and I can run everything. *Don't worry. Be happy.*" Dyanne leaned over and gave Levi a kiss. He smiled and drove off, waving.

Dyanne smiled. "I didn't think we'd ever get rid of 'im." She put her arm over Rosita's shoulder. "Now we can plan a *party!*" she yelled as the two women headed back inside. Manuel smiled, shook his head, and started for the barn.

A couple of hours passed, and the drive was getting to him. The ride wouldn't put you to sleep; it was too rough, but even the bouncing around could get boring pretty fast. The eleven miles of highway frontage on the Calahan Ranch seemed like a long distance. The thirty-three miles of rugged terrain and no road to the north end of the ranch were a long way. Driving just an old cattle trail plus pulling a trailer and then crossing over some washed-out ravines and climbing a few hills could run you down in a hurry.

Levi reached into the ice chest and pulled out a cold one. He then lit into Rosita's basket and pulled out a piece of chicken. "All right." He held the wheel and chicken in one hand and then took a swallow of beer as he continued his journey.

Another hour passed before the Bronco came to a halt. Levi, tired of the driving, got out to stretch his legs and walked to the side window on the horse trailer. "Hey, Crimson, are you gettin' tired of this ridin'?" Levi asked. Crimson whinnied. "That's what

I thought. Me too." He walked back toward the open door of the Bronco. "Well, I guess we might as well get this driving over with, huh, boy?" The boredom had Levi talking out loud.

As he reached the door, he stepped on a dried limb. The limb snapped loudly as a huge covey of quail came out from under his feet. Levi was startled. "Oh my God, it's good I've got a good heart," he said out loud with no one to hear.

He reached for the door once again as a roar came from his back side. He twirled around as he stepped into the Bronco. A cougar was standing only twenty feet away. The mountain lion had heard the covey and was expecting lunch when he plunged into the clearing. Momentarily, their eyes met as Levi received a piercing stare from the snarling cat. He lunged for his shotgun as the cougar leaped back into the brush.

"Boy, good heart or whatever, this trip could be very dangerous to my health." He shook his head and stood the shotgun against the passenger seat. He looked down at his pistol lying in the seat as a thought passed through his brain. He pulled the pistol from the holster. Then he popped a shell from it and picked it up. Sure enough, the shell had a wax projectile. He shook his head with a grin as he unloaded the rest of the shells. Opening the storage compartment between the seats, he pulled out a box of cartridges. He reloaded the pistol and looked at the row of bullets across the back of the gun belt. They were all real. He grinned with satisfaction and placed the pistol back in the holster.

His mind was still on that hungry mountain lion as he put the Bronco in gear and eased away. Leaning back, he took one more glance where the cougar had leaped through the brush. He shook his head and settled into the bucket seat.

Another hour had passed since Levi's encounter with the mountain lion. He had put the animal in the back of his mind and started reminiscing about the good times at the line shack he had shared with his granddad, and of course, Dyanne was always underfoot.

He was startled from his daze as a bolt of lightning crossed the sky in front of him. Levi looked around. The sky had darkened. He glanced down at his watch. It was only three o'clock. He eased off the accelerator and prepared for a real gully washer.

The rain had started pouring from the sky, and the clouds were coal black. His visibility was cut to just a few feet in front of the Bronco as he strained to see.

Levi knew he was less than a mile from the old line shack, so he kept moving forward as the Bronco slipped from side to side. The trailer was shifting even worse, and Crimson's eyes showed signs of fear as the big red stallion was knocked about.

All of a sudden, a huge smoky white circle formed before his eyes and moved rapidly toward the Bronco. It looked like a horizontal tornado ready to swallow everything. A gigantic bolt of lightning struck across the front of the Bronco and hit a huge oak tree, which split and fell across the road in front of Levi. He pulled the wheel as far left as possible as the Bronco turned and slid sideways, jackknifing the trailer. The land machine left the ground as the front tires shot across a washed-out ditch. The front bumper plowed into the soft, muddy bank as the vehicle reached the far side. Levi's body was slammed into the steering wheel, and his head crashed against the windshield, knocking him unconscious.

Although the vehicle was turned across the road, the trailer was upright and still on the trail. The swirling smoky white ring darkened to a grayish-black tint as it consumed the stationary vehicles.

CHAPTER 4

THE OLD WEST

LEVI AWAKENED TO a bright, sunny sky. He pushed his aching body back in the seat. He had a sore, stiff torso but was unscarred and had no permanent damage that he could feel. The sweat on his face dripped to his jeans. The cab was like an oven, as the sun built up heat in the closed vehicle.

He reached for the window button on the door. No power, he thought as he then reached for the key. The key was on. "Oh no," Levi remarked as he flipped the key off and then back on again. Nothing happened. The battery was dead. He flipped the key back off. *Maybe it will build back up if it sits a while, he thought as he looked around to get his bearings. No, better yet, I'm only half a mile or so from the line shack. By tomorrow, that battery will be okay.*

Levi opened the door and stepped out of the vehicle, but to his surprise, the mud he had expected to find coming up around his boots did not exist. The earth was dry, so dry that it fell freely as he scooped a handful, like sand through an hourglass. Levi's puzzled mind was also still in great pain. Maybe I'm still not thinking right, he rationalized to himself. As he looked around, everything was in order. He was sure glad to see the horse trailer still intact. Just thinking of Crimson, he moved as fast as possible up the bank and over to the trailer.

"Hey, Crimson. Hey, boy, how ya doing? That was a pretty bad storm, wasn't it?" Levi looked back at the ground, still not believing the powder-dry dirt at his feet. "Well, maybe it wasn't as bad a storm as I thought," Levi remarked out loud in jest. "I guess I'd better get ya out of that cage, huh, boy? I know you'll be glad to stretch your legs." He pulled the gate open at the rear of the trailer.

Crimson was a little jittery as Levi backed him out and off the trailer. "Easy boy, easy boy," he remarked as Crimson, not too sure-footed, came down off the trailer. "Good boy," he praised as he led Crimson to the storage compartment.

He pulled out a blanket and threw it over Crimson's back. Levi lifted the saddle and slung it over the blanket. It was a beautiful hand-carved Mexican saddle, and Crimson stood tall as Levi cinched the girth.

Tying Crimson's reins off at the front of the trailer, Levi started gathering all the items he might need for this first night at the cabin. He thought, *I guess I could wait till morning to radio the ranch. I'll have Manuel send the pilot up for a new battery.* Still disturbed by the condition of the soil, Levi reasoned to Crimson, "You know what, I was probably out for two days. That's why the ground is so dry," and he piled more supplies into the saddlebags. He walked to the Bronco's passenger door and grabbed his .270 rifle with a scope and his competition holsters. The rifle slid in the saddle holster. Then he buckled on his handgun holster and strapped it to his leg. He flipped the pistol out with lighting speed, just to get the feel of it. A couple of extra boxes of shells completed the haul.

"Well, Crimson, it's about three." As he spoke, he realized his watch was not working. Slipping it off, he laid it in the seat of the Bronco. "I guess I broke it too, boy." Then looking up at the sun, still to his east but high in the sky, he decided, "It must be about midmorning."

Levi swung up on the big red stallion. "Okay, Crimson, let's go." Levi had been to the line shack on the lake many times and had a good sense of direction. But for some reason, the trail didn't look the same. The general terrain hadn't changed, but the lay of the brush just wasn't right. The trail was too small, not like the width needed for his vehicle but much narrower. "Well, maybe it's just grown over. Everything grows so fast in the spring." He continued due north, knowing the cabin could only be a few minutes ahead.

Levi was startled as a shot rang out, and the bullet ricocheted off a nearby boulder. He sprang from his horse with swiftness born of instinct. He took refuge behind one of the boulders as he reasoned the situation. Is it someone hunting? he thought. *It's not any of my hands. They're all back at the ranch house. The rustlers, maybe one of those rustlers got stranded. I just surprised him, or maybe he surprised me.* Levi decided that was the case and started to make his way around to the back side of the man. It took three or four minutes as he climbed over boulders and through the brush.

Levi came upon the back side of a cowboy behind a large boulder. The man was looking down the trail toward the area where Crimson grazed. "Okay, you bastard"—Levi's adrenaline was talking—"lay that rifle down very slowly." The cowboy paid heed to Levi's commands. "Turn around real easy. Don't make any sudden moves." The man followed the orders to the letter as he slowly turned.

Levi had never pointed a gun at a human before and very nervously watched the stranger turn. He saw a silver beard and a well-weathered face as the man looked him in the eye. "Fellow, aren't ya a little old to be stealing cattle?"

"Stealing cattle! Me, stealing cattle? I'm not the thief around here," the old man replied.

"If you're not a rustler, tell me what you're doing on this ranch, old man," Levi questioned.

"What do ya mean? I work on this ranch. Ever'body knows me."

"You tell me who hired ya if ya work on this ranch," Levi challenged.

"Who else? Tom Calahan hired me."

The words hit close to home. Tom was his father's name. "Wait a minute. Who hired you?" Levi questioned.

"Tom Calahan. He hired me before the war. I've been here since '56," the old man explained.

"Before the war, in '56? What war are ya talking about?

Vietnam?" Levi questioned in disbelief.

"Viet-namm, what's that? I'm talking about the big war, sonny, between the blue bellies and the south. There ain't been no more wars," the old man explained.

"The Civil War in 1860? Old man, you know, you do look old, but let's not overdo it." Levi paused as he looked at the man's deeply wrinkled face. "Come to think of it, you do look that old," Levi joked, feeling more comfortable with the old cowboy.

"Listen, young fella, I've been cowpunchin' on this ranch for twenty years. You just ask Mr. Calahan or Tom Jr. They'll tell ya," the old man pleaded.

"Wait. Who is this Tom Jr.? I guess you're going to say Tom Calahan's son, right? Well, I hate to tell ya, but there's no such person, and Tom Calahan is dead," Levi stated.

"Dead! No! What happened? Was it the rustlers?" the old man asked excitedly.

"Tom Calahan has been dead for nineteen years. You really have your story screwed up, or you're not all here," Levi remarked, thinking the latter to be the real clue.

"Nineteen years? Ah, he ain't dead. I just saw 'im at the bunkhouse this mornin'. I knew ya must've been funnin'," the old man said with a sigh of relief.

"I don't know why you're sticking to that story, but if you've been here since '56, that's over thirty years, not twenty. I don't know what you're on, old man, but I don't want any of it," Levi stated as he shook his head. Now halfway relaxed with his gun, Levi pointed toward the cabin. "Okay, let's go up to the cabin. I need to radio the ranch. I guess I can radio the sheriff too and ask him what to do with ya."

The old man looked confused as they walked toward the cabin.

Levi whistled a short but high-pitched tone. The sound of speeding hooves coming up the trail got closer and closer as the big red stallion peaked the crest of the ridge. "Here, boy!" Levi yelled as Crimson answered the call.

"That's a fine-looking animal, Mister. I don't think I've ever seen anythin' like 'im around here," the old man remarked.

"Thanks. He's a Tennessee Walker." Levi's reply was short and to the point. He did not want to get too familiar with the outlaw.

"I don't know what you're talking about, this ray-de-o. There ain't nothin' in my cabin. But asking the sheriff about me is fine. I've known Sheriff Gore ever since I've been on this ranch, some twenty years," the old man explained.

"Old man, what's your name?" Levi asked. "I hate to keep calling ya old man."

"My name is Bartholomew Jones, but everybody calls me Buster," the old man replied.

"That's the first thing you've said that made sense, Buster. But the sheriff's name isn't Gore. It's Thompson, and it's thirty years you've been here, not twenty. If you're gonna tell this story, ya need to keep your facts straight," Levi stated with a little dry humor and no smile.

"Young fellow, I may be a little older 'an you, but I still know how to add. Fifty-six to seventy-six is twenty years. I may not read, but I can cipher," Buster explained.

The old line shack came into view as the two men rounded a clump of trees. "What's happened to the cabin?" Levi shouted but mainly asking himself.

"Whatcha mean what's happened to the cabin?" Buster asked.

"The cabin ... the cabin's different," Levi stated.

"I know what it is," Buster proclaimed.

"You do?" Levi questioned.

"Yeah, you're on the wrong ranch and in the wrong county," Buster replied.

"Buster, I'm beginning to agree with ya, and that's bad," Levi commented as the two men entered the cabin. "Where's my radio? All the furniture's different! The walls aren't finished!" Levi shouted in astonishment as he scanned the open room. "I can't believe this. There's no lights, the cabinets ... what's going on around here?"

He looked back at the old man, who was thoroughly confused with Levi's behavior. "I think that lightning must have done something to me last night," he said. Levi thought for a second and headed back out the door. Buster was right behind him as he rounded the corner of the cabin. "Well, there are no power poles here either."

"Young fellow, did ya say ya saw lightning last night?" Buster asked.

"What?" Levi responded as his mind was somewhere else. "Yeah, yeah, you know, during that storm, lightning almost hit me." His mind flashed back to the storm. The lightning striking in front of the Bronco and the weird smoky funnel that seemed to pass through just as the tree fell in front of him, it was all so vivid.

"Well," Buster said as he looked down and kicked the dry, powdery dirt, "there ain't been no rain around these parts in quite a spell."

Levi now realized there was a lot of truth in what the old man had been saying; he looked straight at him. "Buster, what year did you say this was?" Levi asked very calmly.

"This is seventy-six," Buster replied.

"No, it's not 1976. You've lost a few years, old-timer," Levi explained with a smile.

"It's 1876," Buster blurted out. "I didn't say 1976."

"1876?" Levi asked.

"Of course, 18 ... 76." Buster was still puzzled with Levi's weird expressions.

"I was afraid you were gonna say that," Levi remarked with a lost attitude.

"Are ya all right?" Buster asked.

"I'm not sure. I don't know what's going on or what's happening to me," Levi announced.

"Well, I guess if you're not here to steal our cattle, it would be okay if I fixed ya some coffee. You can put that gun away, okay?" Buster asked.

"Okay," Levi answered with a smile, and then he did a fancy twirl as he reholstered the pistol. Buster was impressed, and the two men walked back inside.

Buster took the pot from the hot wood-burning stove and filled two metal cups to the brim with coffee, which had a tarlike consistency. "You know, young fellow, I hate to keep calling you young fellow. What's your handle?" the old man asked.

"I'm Levi Cal ... Calman," Levi answered as he decided not to let Buster think he was even crazier than the old man already suspected.

"You know, Levi, you might want to ride into Dorado and let Doc Bernard take a look at ya. Not sayin' anythin's wrong with ya, mind ya. But maybe he could do something for ya," Buster mentioned hesitantly.

"Dorado Ciudad. You mean there are people there. I guess there would be in 1876. That would be something to see,"

Levi answered with enthusiasm. "My watch is broken. Have you got the time?" He looked down at his empty arm.

"No. My dad had a pocket watch, real fancy one, but I never knew how to use it, so I buried it with 'em," Buster replied. "But I can tell ya the time. It's past noon, but a few hours till supper." Levi smiled.

"Well, I can't think of any reason to get any closer than that. I guess I've got plenty of time to reach town before dark. So I guess I'll be on my way. I could be in Dorado, as you say, in an hour or an hour and a half, don't ya think?" Levi asked.

"Yeah, maybe two hours, no more," Buster answered with a little anxiousness in his voice. He had begun to feel more comfortable around Levi, but he would feel even better if Levi wasn't there at all.

Levi stood up and took one last gulp from the antique metal cup as he wondered why he asked Buster how long it would take to reach town. This man didn't tell time, but worse than that, he answered in hours. He doesn't know what an hour is, Levi thought as he shook his head and walked outside. He strolled over to Crimson and turned around. "I appreciate the coffee, Buster. I'll probably see ya again," he said as he mounted. "Hey, Buster, is this the trail into Dorado?"

"Yeah, take that trail and go about two miles. You'll hit the main road going into town. Just turn left," Buster explained.

"You mean I'll hit a road that runs north and south?" Levi questioned.

"Yeah, just about two miles ahead," the old man repeated as Levi rode off with a wave over his shoulder.

He headed down the trail; his heart filled with anticipation at seeing this old ghost town alive. His thoughts were very confused. How could he be alive in 1876? That is, if the old man wasn't completely crazy. *Of course, that lightning and the knock on the head could be my problem, he pondered. Buster sure convinced me he was okay. Well, when I get to Dorado, I'll know who's crazy.*

Levi was easing the big red Tennessee Walker down the trail at a slow pace. All the wild flowers were in full bloom, and the forest was untouched by human hands. After only riding about thirty minutes, Levi jumped in a small ditch and landed in the middle of a wagon trail. The center of the road was grown over with weeds. The ruts were thin and not very far apart, much narrower than a truck would make. His mind was reeling. There were so many questions. Was this possible? How could something like this happen? He seemed more convinced of the era with every minute that passed.

Just as Levi had Crimson turned south in the middle of the old wagon trail, he heard a shot crack the silence of the forest. As he tried to get a bearing on the sound, a loud scream from a feminine voice made goose bumps rise on his arm. *That scream came from the other side of that knoll.* Levi turned Crimson and jumped a shallow washout as the stallion headed up the small hill.

As Levi reached the ridge, he slowed Crimson to a walk. Spotting three men on horseback, he came to a stop. Levi could only see the backs of the three horsemen facing a pond. "Matt Tanner, you get off this ranch, and I mean right now." The voice belonged to a young woman. *One with plenty of spunk,* Levi thought.

Matt Tanner, where have I heard that name? He watched the intense situation.

The three horsemen laughed as the one called Matt slid down from his animal. "Or what's gonna happen, Elizabeth?" a deep, gravelly voice asked. The other two cowboys continued to laugh as the third man stepped closer to the pond. Levi spied a young woman treading water and looking for cover.

A small waterfall was running down the rocks in a white water stream, flowing gently into the clear water pool. He noted that the woman had crouched behind some small boulders in the middle of the pond.

"Matt, I'm warning ya. You better get off this property and take your two hyena brothers with ya," the girl yelled with force, but Levi felt a touch of fear in her voice as she spoke.

The two men on horseback continued to laugh as the third man pulled the hammer back on his pistol and aimed. The gun fired, and the bullet struck only a foot from the girl's head. Levi felt the pounding of his heart and realized the situation was dead serious, as the girl let out another terrifying scream.

The cowboys laughed as the tall, lanky Matt Tanner spoke in his scary deep voice, "Elizabeth, you come on out of that water so we can take a good look at ya."

The riders leered as the one standing holstered his gun. He reached down to unbuckle his gun belt as he spoke in his low, gravelly tone, "If ya don't come out, I'm coming in after ya. It'll be a lot easier on ya if ya get out on your own." The gun belt hit the ground. The young girl screamed again as her eyes searched in panic. Levi's heart was racing, and he could feel the pounding in his ears.

The three men had been so busy with the girl that they didn't notice Levi. Crimson advanced to the edge of the clearing behind them.

The young girl noticed Levi in the background. "Oh," she gasped.

The man standing whirled around as he reached for his gun. But his holster lay on the ground. Lucky for Levi, he was paralyzed. "Matt Tanner," Levi unconsciously said, being in total shock. The dead man he had rolled over, thinking it was Randy, now faced him alive. The man, not having a gun, just looked at Levi. The moment of pause seemed like hours. "You know me? Well, I don't know you, and right now, I don't want to know ya." The mesmerizing tone captivated Levi. "The best thing you can do for yourself is to get the hell out of here, you understand, asshole?" The other two men turned their horses toward Levi.

Levi's thoughts were racing. *The old man must have been right. It must be 1876, but this guy looks the same as he did in my day in time. It doesn't make sense. Maybe this was a blood relative, Tanner's great-great-grandfather or something,* Levi reasoned to himself as he regained his composure.

"I don't think ya heard my brother talking to ya," one of the riders threatened as he reached for his gun. With lightning speed, Levi's hand had drawn and fired before the cowboy's pistol cleared the holster. The bullet penetrated the muscle of the man's forearm, and the pistol fell to the ground.

The laughing stopped, and the trio stood motionless. Tanner glanced back at his pistol and holster lying on the ground. His thoughts of diving for his pistol were cut short as he heard the hammer click on Levi's revolver.

Matt's head turned quickly toward the stranger. "There's gonna be another day," he threatened as he walked back toward his horse. He stopped to pick up his gun, but Levi waved his pistol, indicating that he should keep on walking.

The youngest of the three brothers spoke out, "You mean you're gonna keep Matt's gun?"

"Shut up, Billy," Matt growled.

"Well, I'll tell you, Billy," Levi answered with a little more confidence. "If your brother wants that gun back, I'll leave it at the sheriff's office in Dorado."

The elder brother mounted as all three men stared hard at Levi. "You can pick up your guns there too," Levi added as the wounded cowboy looked silently at his pistol lying on the ground and then at the stranger on the vibrant red stallion. The leader turned his horse and spurred the animal. The other brothers followed suit as they glanced over their shoulders for one last look at the man with the quick draw.

Levi, trembling inside, watched the villains until they rode out of sight.

"Mister, I really want to thank you for what ya done, but what Matt Tanner said about gettin' even, he will," the young girl said loudly as Levi still faced the direction of the horseman, and then she added in a very concerned tone, "I don't want ta sound ungrateful, but the smartest thing you could do is to ride on out of here."

Levi turned to face the maiden in the pond as she came from behind the rocks. "Are ya trying to get rid of me?" Levi asked in a lighthearted tone as he saw the beauty in the pool.

"Oh, no," she answered.

Levi was speechless. Before him was a face as pure as heaven. It was surrounded by long blond hair, wet from the pond, and it has the most beautiful blue eyes he had ever seen. He was motionless. "Are ya all right?" she asked as she felt the sensitivity from his eyes.

Levi tried to compose himself. "What? Oh, yeah, I'm fine. Are you okay?"

"Yes, I'm fine, thanks to you. But don't you think the Tanners will be waiting for ya down the road?" asked the maiden.

"Well," he paused, "no, I don't think so. They've only got the one gun between 'em. They'll probably wait till they all have one before they come looking for me." Levi smiled.

"I don't think ya understand the danger you're in. You really don't have much to smile about. But I am very grateful for whatcha done. I don't know another man in Dorado that woulda stood up to the Tanners like ya did." She paused. "Well, maybe one," the girl added.

"Oh, who's that?"

"Tom Calahan." Levi's spine tingled as she spoke. "Not that he would still be alive, but he would've stood up to 'em," she replied.

"What do you mean may not be alive?" he questioned.

"Well, Mr. Calahan is a rancher like my dad and John Cagle. They're not good with a gun. They're just good at raising cattle," she explained as she looked down at her wrinkled fingers.

"I see. Hey, you'd better get out of that water. I'll move over by my horse so you can climb out of that pond," Levi said as he walked away.

The young woman climbed from the pool and started to dress as Levi spoke. "You said Mr. Calahan and your dad. I kinda figured you were a Calahan," he said.

"Why would ya think I was a Calahan?"

"Well, we are on the Calahan Ranch, so I assumed you—" Levi was explaining as the girl interrupted.

"Wait a minute. What makes ya say this is Calahan property?" the girl asked as she tiptoed around the pond from stone to stone. Levi could tell her voice was getting closer, so he turned as she came walking up.

The long blond hair was flowing in the breeze. She looked like an angel in her ankle-length blue and white striped dress. She stood five-seven in her bare feet and was the most beautiful woman he had ever laid his eyes on. He had always heard the old cliché "Beauty is in the eyes of the beholder." He now understood the meaning.

"This isn't the Calahan Ranch. My name is Morgan, Elizabeth Morgan, and this is the Morgan Ranch," she explained with a smile. "The Rocking M Ranch, and what's your name?"

"I'm Levi Cala … Calman," he stammered, realizing she may think he was insane if he said Calahan. He would need to do a lot of explaining, which would prove he was crazy.

"Calman, what kinda name is that?" she asked for pure conversation value.

"Well, what kind of name is Levi?" Levi added with a laugh.

Elizabeth laughed. "I know a Levi, Levi Calahan. He's a little shorter than you are," she stated as she looked up at Levi, "but he's only a year old." She smiled.

"The Calahans have a son named Levi? That's great. I'll bet he's a good-looking kid," Levi joked as he stared at Elizabeth.

"Do you know the Calahans?"

"No, not personally, but I've heard that name a lot." The two just looked at each other and smiled with a mutual admiration in their eyes.

"I guess I'd better be getting back to the ranch," she stated as she came out of the spell.

"Well, I guess I'd better get on into town myself."

"Oh, are ya going into Dorado?" She found this handsome stranger intriguing and well-mannered.

"Yeah, that's where I'm headed."

"Let's just ride together. You'll have to pass right by our place," she said with a smile.

"Sure, I'd like that," Levi remarked, looking very deep into Elizabeth's eyes. She smiled even bigger.

"Tu tienes muy bonitos ojos," he stated.

"Gracias," she answered as she grinned.

"You understood me?"

"Of course, all of our ranch hands are Mexican," she said as she turned toward her horse with a smirky grin on her face.

"I don't know if that's fair, Elizabeth," Levi commented with a smile as if he had gotten caught stealing candy.

"A girl always likes to hear a compliment. I'm glad you think I have pretty eyes. Didn't you mean it?" she asked.

"Well, of course, I meant it."

"If ya were talking to me and ya meant it, then I'm happy I understood."

Levi looked intensely at her. "I did mean it, and I'm glad you understood me." They both smiled. Levi's face was the same color as Crimson as they walked to the horses and mounted. They started up the small hill at a slow gallop, but as they reached the crest of the ridge, the horses were brought to a walking pace, and neither wanted the day to end.

"Where ya from, Levi?"

Levi was caught off guard. "Oh, you can call me Lee if you want to," he said as his mind raced for a good answer without repercussions.

"I think I like Levi better. It's a very unusual name, if it's okay with you," she questioned.

"Oh sure, I'm glad ya like it," he answered as they both smiled.

"You didn't say where you're from."

"Oh, that's right. I'm from Fort Worth," Levi answered with some hesitation.

"Fort Worth. You're from the big city, huh?" Elizabeth commented.

"Well, I guess it's a pretty nice-sized town."

"We used to go there about once a year," she pondered aloud as the horses walked side by side down the wagon trail. "We'd run our cattle up the Chisholm Trail—oops, I mean the Abilene Cattle Trail." She smiled and added jokingly. "Boy, I'm glad my dad didn't hear that slip of the tongue."

"What do ya mean?"

"Ahh, my dad's real funny about that."

"Real funny about what? What about the Chisholm Trail?" Levi had heard about the Chisholm Trail all his life and was interested in what she might say.

"Well, I'm sure ya being from Fort Worth, ya probably hear that argument all the time, but my dad says, 'Since Jesse Chisholm's never been to Texas and he sure ain't no Texan, I'll be damned if there should be a cattle trail named after 'im in Texas,'" Elizabeth replied with a grin.

"I didn't know that," Levi stated without thinking.

"You didn't, and you're from Fort Worth?"

"Well, I'm from a farm outside Fort Worth. I didn't get into town very often," he defended and in a sly attempt to change subjects added, "Why did they call it Chisholm to start with?"

"Boy, you don't get out much, do ya? Well, I guess ya know Jesse. Jesse Chisholm has a tradin' post on the North Canadian River."

"Oh sure," Levi answered positively.

"Well, he drove cattle up to the Little Arkansas River and then on up to Abilene, Kansas," she explained.

"So what does that have to do with Texas?"

"Boy, ya must really live a long way from town. Well, ten years ago when the Texan herds started using that trail through Oklahoma and Kansas, they started calling it the Chisholm Trail."

"So the name just followed it back down to here?" he

questioned.

"Not just to here. It goes all the way to the valley at the Mexican border," she answered.

"Well, I can sure see why your dad would get upset about that. So ya called it the Abilene Trail?" Levi asked.

"No, the Abilene Cattle Trail is what the government named it, which makes my dad happy," Elizabeth explained. "He really thinks the trail oughta be called McCoy Trail, after Joe McCoy."

"McCoy, who's that?"

She just looked at Levi and shook her head as the horses eased along. "I can't believe you're Texan, and ya don't know Joseph McCoy."

"Oh, Joseph McCoy. Sure I've heard of him, I didn't know Joe was his, his ..." Levi stopped as Elizabeth was looking at him with both hands on her hips but with a smile.

"I'll tell ya about 'im anyway. McCoy started coming down to Texas and rounding up the strays or what they used to call wild cattle. You know, nobody used barbwire around here a few years back, so a lot of cattle got free, and then they went wild. But anyway, McCoy started driving all those cows up north. Then he built some catch pens at the railhead in Abilene and made a fortune." Levi enjoyed the story, but most of all, he enjoyed looking at her as she talked; he couldn't get over how beautiful she was. Elizabeth could tell he was attracted to her, and she knew she was definitely attracted to him. She was a little nervous, and that's probably why she continued to talk. "But it also started the ranchers around here moving their cattle up to Abilene." She paused for a second. "Seems like there were thirty-five or forty thousand head drove up there the first year," she explained as the horses almost came to a halt. The couple was now paying more attention to each other than to where they were headed or where their horses were not going.

"Boy, I feel like I've had an in-depth history lesson."

"Oh, I'm sorry, I didn't mean—" she started to apologize as Levi interrupted, and the horses came to a complete stop.

"No, no, I didn't mean that was bad. I really think it's interesting." He smiled and paused as he looked at Elizabeth. Then in a quieter tone, he said, "I really did enjoy the class. I could listen to ya all day long."

Elizabeth's head bowed as her face turned red. She knew Levi was flirting with her as she tried to cover her shyness with a smile. "Hey, there're two riders coming," Levi stated with some excitement in his voice.

Elizabeth looked up. "I'm sure that white horse belongs to Tom Calahan. It's okay." A cold chill ran up Levi's spine as he thought, *It looks like I'm going to meet one of my ancestors.*

"Yeah, that's who it is, and that's Tom Jr. with him," she added.

The horses came at a fast gallop, and the cowboys pulled back on their reins, almost standing in the stirrups to bring their animals to a stop.

"Howdy, Elizabeth," a friendly voice came from the elder man, who sat on the back of the huge white stallion.

"Hi, Mr. Calahan. Hi, Tom. I want y'all to meet a good friend, Levi Calman," said Elizabeth.

"Welcome to our community, Levi. You said Calman?" the elder Calahan asked.

"Yes. Calman, C-A-L-M-A-N," Levi spelled, "and thanks for the welcome." He looked over the two tall men, studying their family features. *Here I am, talking to some of my great-great-great ancestors, and I can't tell 'em. I guess I could, but they'd probably have me committed or shot,* he thought as they continued to talk.

"Well, anyone Elizabeth would call a friend is sure welcome around here," Mr. Calahan added.

"And anyone named Levi can't be all bad," Tom Jr. added as he looked down at Levi's boots.

"What he meant by that is he has a new son named Levi. That's a pretty uncommon name," Mr. Calahan added.

"Your son is the one named Levi? Elizabeth told me about 'im," Levi remarked.

"Yeah, he's our first," the proud father remitted, "If ya don't mind me asking, what kind of boots are ya wearing? I've never seen anything like 'em."

"They're … ah, ostrich."

"What? Ostrich? Like the bird?" Mr. Calahan joined in.

"Yes, sir. They came from the bird," Levi answered.

"Boy, they sure are different. I like 'em," Tom Jr. commented.

"Yeah, but around these parts, you've got to wear something tough. You just can't beat cowhide," Mr. Calahan remarked.

"Well, I wouldn't say anything against cowhide, but this ostrich leather is much softer to wear and will outlast cow leather by three times. Believe me, it's really tough stuff," Levi defended.

Mr. Calahan smiled. "Well, maybe we all learned something. I wouldn't disagree with a man wearing such a fancy gun anyway." Mr. Calahan laughed. Levi smiled as Tom Jr. looked up, still admiring the boots.

"Levi, what brings ya to our little town?" Mr. Calahan asked.

Before Levi could come up with an answer, Elizabeth interrupted, "I'll tell ya what he did today. He ran the Tanner boys right off our ranch."

Mr. Calahan looked at Elizabeth with concern. "What happened? What were the Tanners doing on your ranch?"

"Well, I'd gone up to the pond, just west of that rocky ford by the north road, where I always go swimming. All of a sudden, the Tanners were there. I don't know where they came from. I just looked up, and they were just settin' there on their horses. Ya can't hear too good with that waterfall in your ear. It startled me so. I screamed and reached for my clothes. Then Matt fired a shot between me and my clothes."

There was a tremble in her voice, and Levi could tell it was upsetting her to recall the incident, so he took over the story. "I think it was about that time I came riding up, and I think it shook 'em up a little, so they rode off," he explained.

"I've never seen the Tanner boys shook up, as you say, or backed down from any number of men. They're the meanest boys I've ever seen," Mr. Calahan stated.

By this time, Elizabeth had composed herself and was eager to finish her tale. "Levi's not telling the whole story. Clyde went for his gun, but Levi drew first and shot it out of his hand. Then he told 'em to leave. That's why the Tanners rode off."

"Ah, ha … boy, I'd sure like to've seen that," Tom Jr. stated with a bald grin on his face. "I bet that would've beaten it all. Can't ya just see Matt's face, Pop?"

"Levi, I don't want to ruin your day, but those Tanners won't let that go. You better watch your back as long as you're in these parts. I don't know if ya shouldn't stay out of Dorado Ciudad, especially at night," Mr. Calahan warned.

"Well, I need to go into town," Levi explained. "But I will keep my eyes open, and I do appreciate your advice, Mr. Calahan."

"Hey, my name's Tom. I don't know where Elizabeth gets that Mister bit, but I wish both of ya would just call me Tom."

"Okay, Mr. Cal—I mean, Tom. We'll sure try, and it was nice meetin' ya both," Levi replied. "And thanks again for that advice."

"Well, Tom, I guess we'd better get to the house, before the womenfolk send out a posse. It was nice meeting you too, Levi. You'll have to get Elizabeth to bring ya by our place and meet our Levi," Tom remarked.

"Oh, I sure will, Tom. Thanks. I do want to meet 'im. If Elizabeth didn't forget me, maybe we'll ride over one day soon."

"Let's go, boy," Tom said as the two rode off the same as they rode up, in a fast gallop.

"That was two real nice people," Levi commented as he turned Crimson west and started down the road. "Is your place very far?"

"No, it's just up the road, where ya see those high posts sticking up."

"Oh yeah. There's a big entrance on both sides of the road," he stated.

"Yeah. The one on the left is the Cagle Ranch."

"The Cagles? Really?" Levi stated with excitement in his voice.

"Yeah, do ya know 'em?"

"Aaaa, no, there's some Cagles next door back home, probably some distant kin."

"Well, I don't doubt you've probably heard the name John Cagle, even as far away as Fort Worth. He's the most outspoken man in these parts but a good community leader and the most charitable man around," Elizabeth stated.

"Wow, you're sure on his bandwagon," Levi commented. "You could probably get him elected to Congress."

"Well, he deserves it. He's been a good neighbor, and he's really tried to do something about this cattle rustling," she said as they reached the gate. She swung low from the saddle and opened the latch.

"Oh, you're too fast. I should've got that for ya."

"Thanks, but I'm not helpless. I've been unhooking this gate from my horse since I was eight years old." Elizabeth smiled sort of uppity as she rode through the gate.

"Well, I guess I'll be going into town. I sure hope I'll see ya again."

"You'll do no such thing," Elizabeth proclaimed. "You're coming with me to the house for supper. Besides, I want ya to meet my dad. You'll like 'im."

"I don't want to put your family out, Elizabeth. Are ya sure it's okay?" Levi really didn't want to leave her, and he was glad she felt the same.

"Of course, I'm sure. Dad likes to meet people," she said with a smile.

"I feel funny just barging in on your parents like this," Levi said as he rode through.

Elizabeth just smiled at him and shook her head as she reached down to shut the gate. "Levi, ya don't mind meetin' my dad, do ya?" she asked teasingly as she continued smiling and looking at Levi. "You know, I think you're bashful."

Levi just smiled. The two rode on down the wagon trail toward the house. "These ruts sure seem to be close together," he commented.

"I think it's just a standard width. The deeper old ones were made by the chuck wagon. We haven't used it lately, but I know those ruts are too deep to come from the carriage," she stated as she wondered why the ruts are there. "You know, those ruts had to be there when I left this morning. I just hadn't paid any attention to it."

"Oh, those ruts have been there for at least a week. When did it rain last?" he questioned.

"Well, I guess it's been a week or so," Elizabeth pondered.

"Anyway, I've always thought about a chuck wagon as being pretty big, but I guess they must be pretty narrow, huh?" Levi asked.

"Well, I think of it as being big, but you can see it for yourself. It's just ahead, there by the barn. It's a Goodnight wagon too. My dad's very proud of it," she stated.

"What do you mean it's a Goodnight wagon? You mean you sleep in it?" Levi asked, a little puzzled.

"Are ya makin' fun of me?" she asked.

"No, no, I'm not. I really don't know what ya mean," he answered.

"Well, okay," she said as she looked at him with doubt. "I can't believe you've never heard of Charles Goodnight."

"I haven't, I promise. But that's what ya mean. This Charles

70

Goodnight is the manufacturer of the wagon?" Levi asked.

"Not exactly," Elizabeth wondered if he's for real but continued her explanation. "He just took the old wagons left over from the war and made all those compartments and storage areas inside. Then he calls it a Charles Goodnight wagon. It was shortened to Charles wagon, and now most everybody calls it a chuck wagon."

"So I guess the chuck wagon was the first van conversion job," Levi said as he stepped down from his horse to look the wagon over. "There're people who do this where I'm from too." He smiled as he studied the wagon.

"Really? I thought he was the only one who did that," Elizabeth replied.

"Well, they look a lot different," Levi commented.

"From what you said, they must be wider between the wheels."

"Yeah, that's right and has a wider wheel too. It makes them look a lot different," he answered.

"Well, that's good. They probably ride a lot better and safer. These turn over pretty easy, but it's still a good wagon. Don't let Dad hear ya say anything bad about Charles Goodnight."

"Oh, don't worry, I won't. I don't have a thing against 'im." Levi smiled.

As the two turned toward the house, Levi grabbed the dangling reins from both horses. He walked alongside Elizabeth down the dirt road umbrellaed by some large old trees. He felt very comfortable with her and had begun to feel at home in his new surroundings. He had been at this old homeplace many times through his youth. But he had always thought the old homestead was built by the Calahans. "Well, this place really has a woman's touch. I can tell your mother must really have a green thumb," Levi commented.

"Well, thank you. My dad said she really did enjoy the plants and the flowers, but she died when I was born," Elizabeth said as her head nodded. "All these plants are mine." She came back with a smile as a little sadness showed around the edges and then added, "Dad's always saying I'm just like her in so many ways he can't believe it." She regained her composure.

"I'm sorry about your mom."

"Oh, that's okay. It was many years ago," Elizabeth replied.

The two reached the porch as an elderly man with snow-white hair stepped out of the doorway onto the porch. "Hey, Dad, I want ya to meet somebody. This is Levi."

"How are ya, Mr. Morgan? I'm Levi Cal … Calman. It's a pleasure to meet ya, sir."

"Ah, just call me Ben or Pop. Ever'body in these parts just calls me Pop Morgan."

Levi knew right off that he liked the elderly gentleman, who was old enough to be Elizabeth's grandfather. "Did ya say Calman, son?" Mr. Morgan asked. "I don't think I've heard that name around here before." The old gentleman spoke slow but with character.

Before Levi could answer Mr. Morgan's comment, Elizabeth spoke up, "Levi's from a small place outside Fort Worth."

"Fort Worth, that's a good town. We used to drive our cattle up that way by the Western Trail," Mr. Morgan commented.

"You used to? Where do ya take 'em now?" Levi asked.

"We don't," Mr. Morgan commented as his head lowered.

"What Dad means is since the rustlers moved in, we haven't shipped any cattle," Elizabeth added.

"How long's this been going on?" Levi asked.

"About two and a half or … maybe three years," she stated. "We've lost about three thousand head since it started."

"Damn, excuse me, but that's a lotta cattle," Levi commented.

"Yeah, we know," Elizabeth remarked as her dad stood close with his eyes fixed on the floor.

"I don't guess y'all got any ideas who might be behind it, do ya?" Levi questioned.

"No, Dad thinks it's someone from another town. Dorado is a small place, and all the people around here are real good friends," Elizabeth answered.

"What do ya think about the Tanner boys, Mr. Morgan?" Levi asked.

"Oh, no, no, Matthew Tanner and I go back for thirty-five years. He's a good friend," Mr. Morgan commented in his slow but very assured tone.

"Dad, Matt and Clyde and young Billy came up on the pond this morning where I was swimming. They were acting pretty wild," Elizabeth explained.

"Well, they're just boys, and boys will be boys," Mr. Morgan stated.

"Dad, if Levi hadn't come along when he did, there's no telling what they might've done," she explained.

"Did they really get out of hand?" Mr. Morgan asked surprised. "What'd they do?"

"Matt fired some shots into the water right by me. Levi rode up, and Clyde tried to shoot 'im, but thank God Levi shot first," Elizabeth explained.

"Really." Mr. Morgan looked at Levi and then glanced down at his pistol and then back to his face. "What happened then?" he asked, listening much more intently.

"Well, Clyde was wounded in the arm. Levi told 'em to leave, so they hightailed it," she said.

"Well, it sounds like it's good ya rode up when ya did, son. But I don't think they would've done anythin' too bad. Those boys have known us all their lives. I know ya only got a look at their bad side." Elizabeth noticed the subject was upsetting her dad, so she came to his aid.

"Those boys grew up in a very strict, religious home. Their paw wouldn't let them get too far out of line. Let's stop talking about the Tanners and go inside. I'm starving," she said. She grabbed Levi's arm and then her dad's as they started up the steps. "Let's eat."

The house was modestly furnished, but everything was in the right place. "Let me see how supper's coming," Elizabeth said as she walked out of the room.

"You've got a nice place here, Mr. Morgan," Levi commented as the elderly gentleman walked over to a large padded rocker.

"Thank ya son, but all the credit goes to that girl of mine. She must have gotten it from her mother. She was a strong-willed woman too," Mr. Morgan stated. "Take a chair, and rest your bones." Levi walked over to the sofa and sat down.

"Thank ya."

"What's got ya out in these parts, son? You're a fur piece from home."

Before Levi could answer, Elizabeth walked back into the parlor. "Carmita says supper's on its way, gentlemen."

Levi smiled as he stood and then looked at Mr. Morgan. "Oh, I just decided I needed to see a little more of our state. There're so many things to do and places to see," he explained. They walked toward the other end of the room, where Carmita, the housekeeper, was setting the dining table. The room wasn't very large. The table for six sat comfortably in the surroundings with candles glowing.

"Carmita, esta Señor Calman," Elizabeth said.

"Buenos tardes, Señor," the very pretty but very shy senorita said.

"Hola. Mucho gusta, Señorita," Levi's Spanish rolled out, much to everyone's surprise.

"How did a man from Fort Worth learn Spanish?" A very impressed smile was on Elizabeth's face as Mr. Morgan asked the question.

"We've probably got more Spanish-speaking people all over

Texas than we do who speak English. Everybody around here needs both," he stated.

Carmita smiled her acceptance to the handsome stranger.

"The only thing wrong," Elizabeth said jokingly, "is Carmita is a señora. Her husband is Ricardo, our foreman. So don't get any ideas, Levi."

Levi just shrugged his shoulders and smiled. Unbeknownst to Elizabeth, his thoughts were all on her, not her housekeeper.

The sun was setting, and the room was dark, except for the dim glow from the candles. The three sat down to eat the home-cooked Tex-Mex meal. Levi appreciated the freshly made flour tortillas and the tasty food. Carmita walked through the living area, lighting the kerosene lamps. Levi had forgotten where he was and looked on mesmerized.

"Hand me your plate. Do you like a lot of gravy on your potatoes?" Elizabeth asked.

"Si, gracias."

"You can speak English to me," Elizabeth answered. Her dad smiled.

"Is this a chicken-fried steak?" Levi asked, looking at Elizabeth.

"Well, it's a steak that's battered and fried. It's the same way we do chicken," said Elizabeth with an enthused, schoolgirl look. "I guess it could be called a chicken-fried steak. That's a good name, don't ya think so, Dad?"

Mr. Morgan laid down his fork as he thought about the question. "Well, I guess it sounds better than 'battered fried steak,' but it may be a little confusing to the chickens. A chicken steak?" Mr. Morgan answered.

"No, Dad, a chicken-fried steak. Well, I like it. That's what I'll start calling it anyway," said Elizabeth. "Do ya want sugar," Levi's eyes raised to meet Elizabeth's, "for your tea?" Levi smiled as Elizabeth's face wore a bashful grin, and she lowered her head. It was easy to forget where he was around Elizabeth.

"Do ya have any sweet and loooo—" He saw Elizabeth's puzzled expression and shook his head. "Yeah, I do want some sugar." He would have to be careful. Elizabeth smiled as she handed Levi the sugar, and Mr. Morgan looked as if nothing was going on. But the old man wasn't born yesterday. He understood the game very well, and he liked this new young gentleman who entered his home. Most of all, he liked the new life and radiance the stranger had brought back to his daughter.

"Everything was great," Levi stated as he moved his plate back a few inches and patted his belly.

"Would ya like some pie and coffee?"

"No, thank you, Elizabeth. I couldn't hold another bite. I feel like I should run around the block a couple of times already," Levi commented.

"What should ya do?" Mr. Morgan asked with a confused look.

"You know, run around the"—Levi stopped as he realized they may not understand *city block* and then continued his sentence—"house. Run around the house, and burn off some calories." Levi smiled as he patted his belly again to explain the calories.

"Burn what?" Mr. Morgan asked.

"Oh, the, the fat. Run off the food so I don't gain any weight," Levi answered with a smile. *It loses something in the translation,* he thought.

"Ah, I get it," Mr. Morgan said. But by the look on his face, Levi could tell the line was a little out of place.

Elizabeth was stacking the dinner plates. She had been listening to the conversation but had no comment. She was just happy to have both men at the table with her.

Carmita started clearing the table as everyone stood. Levi picked up a couple of bowls. "What are ya doing?" Elizabeth asked.

"You fed me a great meal. The least I can do is help ya clean up the mess," Levi answered.

Mr. Morgan turned with a confused look and walked away from the table.

Elizabeth smiled. "I've never met a man like you, but Carmita and I can handle the dishes. Why don't you and Dad go out on the porch? It's probably a lot cooler. I'll be out there in just a minute."

"I think I'll turn in, baby. I'm tuckered out," Mr. Morgan said as he turned toward Levi, "It was nice meeting ya, son. I want to thank ya again for helping my little girl out today."

"Oh, it was my pleasure, sir, and it was nice meeting you too," Levi answered. He assumed this was a hint because of the late hour. "Well, Elizabeth, I guess I'll be riding on into town. I sure have enjoyed y'all's hospitality."

"You're not leaving. Dad, tell Levi there's no sense in him going into town tonight. He can ride in, in the morning, when he can see the road," Elizabeth stated.

The old man stopped as he reached his bedroom door and turned. "Levi, ya heard her. Once she's got her mind set, ya might as well do what she says," he replied. He grinned and walked on into his room and shut the door.

Elizabeth walked over to Levi and grabbed him by the arm. "Let's go out on the porch. You didn't really want to leave tonight, did ya?" she asked with a grin.

Levi took her hand. "No, I didn't want to leave, but I thought it might be more appropriate."

"More appropriate." She smiled. "Levi, you're so different from anyone I've ever met." Still holding hands, Elizabeth looked up into his eyes. Standing on her tiptoes, she reached up and kissed him gently on the lips. Their eyes still lingered as Levi leaned over and kissed Elizabeth a little harder and a little longer and with a lot more emotion.

"I shouldn't have done that," Levi said as he straightened up and stepped back.

"You didn't start it. I did." Their hands still clutched. She led Levi to the swing at the end of the porch. "That's a beautiful moon," she stated.

"And you're a beautiful girl," he added.

"I wasn't hinting for a compliment."

"That wasn't a compliment. It was just a fact. You're probably the most beautiful woman I've ever seen in my life," Levi said as Elizabeth gazed starry-eyed at him.

She had never heard anything spoken to her in this tone before. The two sat down on the swing. Levi's arm caressed her shoulder as she snuggled in close. "I've never felt so comfortable around a girl in my life," he commented.

"I know. I feel the same," she added.

As the two sat there in silence and looked at the stars, Levi's thoughts went back to the problems Elizabeth and her dad were having. "Elizabeth, you don't really feel that the Tanners could have had anything to do with the rustling?" he asked.

"I know ya saw those boys in a bad light today. They really haven't been that bad lately. If ya could have seen 'em just three years ago, you'd think they were angels now."

Levi interrupted, "You mean they used to be worse? Elizabeth, I really feel those guys were fixin' to do you some real harm today. They weren't playin'."

"Yeah, I got a little frightened," she recalled. "They were acting pretty rotten, even worse than when they were growing up. But ya know, the last few years since they've gotten some responsibility, they've been acting halfway decent."

"Responsibility? What's changed? Their dad put 'em to work?" Levi joked.

"Well, yeah. Since Mr. Tanner had a stroke two or three years ago, they've had to really go to work. They've really changed, and their silver mine is doing real good. They're doing a better job at the business end than their father did."

"I thought your dad said that Mr. Tanner was a tough businessman?" Levi asked.

"Well, he was. But beef prices fell a few years back, and the boys cost 'im quite a bit, being in and out of trouble. The ranch had been going down, and when he had the stroke, they took over. They've been doing real good ever since," Elizabeth explained.

"Doesn't that seem a little strange that their dad was always on their case, he has a stroke, and now they're doing good?" Levi questioned.

"I don't know, maybe you're right. I know it would break Dad's heart if Matthew Tanner was involved in any of this," she stated. "They've been friends … I know … thirty-five or forty years, since they split this tract of land."

"You must have about fifty thousand acres then," Levi commented.

"That's right. How'd ya know that?" Elizabeth asked with a surprised look.

"Wellllaa, I think, aahh, the size of all the tracts the government granted around here was hundred thousand acres, wasn't it?" he questioned as he thought, *I've got to keep my foot out of my mouth.*

"Yeah, but ya sure seem to know a lot of things," she said.

Levi smiled. "But ya gotta admit, there's been a lot of things I didn't know anything about."

"That's true. Maybe ya got some kinfolk that live around here," she pondered out loud. "Oh, and another thing, you knew who Matt Tanner was. You called his name when ya saw 'im at the pond today. I'd forgotten that."

Levi got a serious look on his face as he sat up straight in the swing and turned to Elizabeth. It looked like confession time, but cold feet set in as he began to speak. "I, I … Do ya trust me?" he asked in a quiet tone.

Elizabeth paused and looked straight into his eyes. "Sure, I do."

Levi smiled. "A hundred percent?" he asked as his hand clutched hers.

Still looking into his eyes as the smile faded, she seriously replied, "A hundred percent."

"Good. I can't tell ya anything yet, but please bear with me. I'll explain all I know as soon as I can. I'm going to catch those rustlers for you and your dad," Levi assured her. "It's going to be a long day tomorrow." The pair stood still hand in hand. Levi pulled her close as she looked up and kissed him as if to say, "No questions asked. I trust you completely." Then they walked inside. The kerosene lamps were put to rest in the parlor, and Elizabeth showed Levi to the spare room. Silently brushing his fingers across her lips, Levi stepped into his room. She stood by the closed door for a few seconds and then thoughtfully walked to her own room.

CHAPTER 5

DORADO CIUDAD'S ALIVE

THE MORNING GAME late for Levi. He was normally an early riser, but the day before had been an unusual one. He had tossed and turned all night, feeling exhausted. He lay in bed as the events of yesterday came back to haunt him. Levi could feel his heart as it picked up a more rapid beat. He had so many questions and absolutely no answers.

The aroma of bacon frying and coffee brewing assaulted his nostrils, and he knew it was time to face the new day. He sat up in bed and looked around the room. An old washbasin and pitcher sat on a small table next to the window. He slid to the edge of the feather mattress, and his feet felt the warmth of the knotty pine floor. Levi walked over to the stand and poured some water into the basin. He stared at himself in the mirror that hung above the basin. Then reaching into the saddlebag for his shaving kit, he pulled out his electric razor. "Click, click." He forgot for a second, and then he smiled and shook his head. Dropping the electric razor back into the kit, he pulled out a double edge he always carried to trim his sideburns. *This will work for the present, I mean, the past. Ha! What if I'm here to stay? I'll just have to play this time change by ear. A time change, that's a joke. The only time change I'm familiar with is spring forward and fall back,* he thought. He splashed on his aftershave and headed toward the kitchen.

"Good morning." Levi looked around as he entered. Everyone was there. Mr. Morgan was sitting at the table. Carmita was at the stove, and Elizabeth was pouring coffee for her dad. She looked up with a big smile. Levi could tell she was glad to see him, like a good close friend she hadn't seen for a while. She too had had a long night. So much on her mind and so many questions about the new stranger in her life had made it impossible to sleep. But she, like

Levi, was full of pep and vitality on this bright, sunny morning. Her whole world had been changed too. She had a new outlook on life. A knight in shining armor had appeared in her quaint little world. "Good morning," she replied.

Mr. Morgan looked up. "Good morning."

"That coffee sure smells good." "Sit right there," Elizabeth gestured as she spoke. "I'll get your coffee."

"Thank you," he answered as their eyes met.

"Do ya take anything in it?" she asked.

Levi, still looking into her eyes, said, "No, nothing, thank you."

"Cuantos huevos?"

"Carmita wants to know—" Elizabeth stopped as she saw Levi's knowing face with a smile on it.

"Dos huevos, por favor, señora," Levi replied.

Carmita smiled to acknowledge, and Elizabeth smiled with satisfaction. Mr. Morgan understood it all but didn't show it as he took another bite.

"Well, son, what're your plans for the day?" Mr. Morgan asked.

"Well, sir, I think I'll head on into Dorado and look around a little. Maybe I can ask a few questions about this rustlin'."

"Necesito café," Carmita responded.

"Oh, Levi, we're just about out of coffee. If I get ya the money, would ya mind picking up a bag when you're in town?" Elizabeth asked.

"Sure, I'll be glad to pick it up. Oh, I'm going to stay in town tonight. I don't want to wear out my welcome around here. But it's not that far. I'll run it back out here. No problemmm." Levi smiled.

"Oh no, you're not staying in town. Let me get ya some money. You just come on back out here for the night. We insist."

Levi found it hard to resist Elizabeth's smile. Both Mr. Morgan and Carmita were in complete agreement.

"Well, if ya let me buy the coffee," he bargained with a smile.

Elizabeth smiled. "Okay, you win."

"You got it. I guess you use the drip kind, right?" he asked.

"What?" she asked puzzled.

"Oh, never mind. I'll get it," Levi responded quickly, removing his foot from his mouth.

"Just take the road west, straight into town," explained Mr. Morgan.

"You shouldn't have any problem finding your way to town," Elizabeth stated.

"Oh no, I've been there mannn … once before," he responded.

"Oh, when was that?" she asked.

"Ohhh, it's been a long time. Seems like it's been a hundred years. Wellll, when I was ten or so, I came here with my dad for something," Levi tried a little double talk as Elizabeth and her dad listened to his explanation. "Boy, this breakfast really hit the spot."

"Did ya get plenty?" Elizabeth asked, helping him change the subject.

Levi set his cup down as he stood. "Oh yeah, I'm full as a tick."

"Good, I'll walk ya out to the barn," she replied.

"Great. Oh, wait just a minute. Let me get my saddlebags," he said.

"Why do you need your saddlebags? I thought I would wash out your dirty clothes while you were in town," she stated.

"Hey, that's sweet. But I don't want ya to go to all that trouble. I can get that done in town."

Elizabeth looked at Levi. "It's no trouble. I want to do it," she said. Her hand grasped his arm. "I wouldn't do it if I didn't want to. Besides, today's washday. The women have already got the fires going out back."

"The fires going! What ya gonna do, burn the dirt off?" Levi questioned with a grin.

"No, silly, they have the cauldrons boiling, you know," she answered lightly, figuring Levi was teasing with her. Levi smiled as he walked out the side door of the kitchen, handing Elizabeth the saddlebags. "I'll see ya this afternoon," he stated. He caught the potent smell of steaming starch, and his head cleared. It was like a strong sniff of ammonia. "They really are boiling something back there."

"Of course, they are. Don't tell me you've never watched your mother do the washing before." Levi started toward the back corner of the house with Elizabeth underfoot. "Well, probably not the same way you do it here. Things are always done a little different everywhere."

As they stepped around the corner, Levi saw several of the ranch hands' wives standing around, stirring large black kettles. The sun was already high in the sky, and the sweat poured from their brows. The cauldrons sat on the ground, over a stick-burning fire. "One of those pots must have starch in it?" Levi questioned.

"Yeah, the third one." Elizabeth paused. "Are you kidding with me?

Oh, I know."

"You do?" Levi answered, surprised.

"Yeah, the woman who does your laundry must take it to her house," Elizabeth replied with certainty.

"Yeah, that's right."

"I know most of the people in town do the same. It's hardly worth all this trouble, unless ya have a big group, like ours. That first pot has a little lye in it, and the second is just hot water for rinsing. Then the third one is just for the things that need starching. We always rinse everything a second time in the creek. It gets that lye out a little better."

"That looks like a lot of work. I guess I'd better get on into town, before these women try to put me on the payroll." Levi smiled as he grabbed Elizabeth's hand.

"What do ya hope to find in Dorado, Levi?" she asked as she

skipped a step to keep up with the long stride of her newfound hero.

"I don't really know, pretty. I really don't know what to look for, but when I find it, I'll know it," he answered.

The two reached the barn where Crimson was quartered. "What did ya call me?" Elizabeth asked as Levi threw the blanket across Crimson's back.

Levi looked down at Elizabeth and smiled. "I called you pretty. Is it okay?"

She swooned like a schoolgirl. "Oh yes, I like it. It's okay," she responded.

"Well, it just seems to fit ya." Levi had a bashful grin as he tried to explain.

"I don't need an explanation," she replied.

Their eyes never wavered as she stepped toward him. He pulled her close and kissed her. Elizabeth stepped back with a smile. "Hurry back," she said.

"You can bank on it." He mounted the big red stallion and rode out the open barn and started down the road. He turned and smiled a heart-stopping smile, which she was getting addicted to.

"Levi, you be careful." He waved as Crimson turned and galloped down the trail. Reaching the entrance, he leaned down and shoved the latch open like he had done it many times before. Shutting the gate, he turned Crimson toward town.

The massive stone entrance to the Cagle Ranch stood tall, with the ranch's name and brand carved deep into a heavy timber that stretched high across the wooden gate. A lone rider was coming up the Cagle trail as Levi was passing the entry.

"Howdy!" the young man shouted as he reached down for the latch.

Levi stopped. "Howdy."

Latching the gate, the young man rode toward Levi. "You must be Levi Calman?" he asked as a gentle smile was produced as approval.

"Wow, things sure get around fast in these parts," Levi replied with a surprised smile.

"Well, it's a small place. We don't have a lot to talk about. I guess a stranger is always news," the young man responded. The tall thin light-haired man rode up to Levi. "I'm Pete Cagle. This is our spread on the south side." His hand went out to Levi.

"Glad to meet ya, Pete, and you're right, I am Levi Calman. Are ya riding into town?"

"Yeah, I am. I'll ride along with ya, if ya don't mind," Pete replied.

"No, the pleasure's mine. I'd appreciate the company." Levi smiled as he answered his new companion.

"How'd ya know my name?" Levi inquired.

Pete laughed. "Ah, it's nothing. Aaahh, Jr. brought over a couple of strays this morning. He was tellin' me and Pa about your run-in with those Tanner boys yesterday."

"Jr.?" Levi questioned.

"Yeah, Tom Jr., aahhh, Tom Calahan. He met ya yesterday," Pete explained.

"Oh yeah, Tom. The Jr. threw me," Levi answered as the two horses picked up their pace.

"We all appreciate what ya did for Elizabeth yesterday. She's sorta special around here," Pete remarked.

"Yeah, she is special." Pete picked up on Levi's thoughts. Levi, not knowing that Pete had thoughts of Elizabeth himself, had no reason to hide his feelings. "But it wasn't anything anybody else wouldn't have done," Levi replied.

"Well, maybe not anything anybody else wouldn't have liked to have done, but to be able to stand up to the Tanners like that," Pete reacted excitedly. "Wow, that would've been tough on anyone around here, even the sheriff. Those boys ain't just good with a gun. They're also downright mean, and that gives 'em the edge, a big edge over a normal man."

"Ah, I think you give 'em too much credit," Levi commented.

"Listen, I know 'em, and you're gonna have to watch your back. They'll come after ya just to save face. I've known the Tanners all my life. They ain't gonna cut you or anybody else any slack." Levi could tell Pete's concern was sincere.

The conversation lightened as a large Texan rabbit appeared in the middle of the road, only forty or fifty feet in front of the horses. "I'll bet that's the same old jackass rabbit that wants to race me every time I start down this road. He'll stay straight down that right rut till I almost catch 'im. Then he's gone lickety-split." Levi was taking in the whole scene with a grin from ear to ear without a word as Pete continued with his story. "Hey, let's just mosey on up as close to 'im as we can and then just take off. Maybe that long-legged horse of yours can catch 'im. You willin'?"

"I'm willin'," Levi agreed as the horses closed the gap on the jackrabbit. The challengers were only a few feet behind when the speedy long-eared varmint accelerated, and the race was on. The contest only lasted a few seconds and a hundred yards or so when the competitor peeled off into the brush, disappearing as fast as he appeared. The boys were both laughing as hard as they could when the horses were pulled to a stop.

"There's that jackass rabbit yonder on that knoll. See 'im?" Pete yelled.

"Yeah, he's probably thinking, 'How do I get those grown men to play with me?'" Levi said as they both kept laughing. "Those jackrabbits are fast." They resumed their pace.

"Is that what ya call 'em back home, just 'jackrabbit'? I never heard anybody say just jackrabbit," Pete commented.

"You mean everybody calls them a jackass rabbit?" Levi questioned.

"Sure, that's all I ever heard," Pete replied as their voices sputtered, and the pace intensified.

"It must have been shortened before it got to where I'm from," Levi commented as they reached the edge of town.

Levi, trying not to act astonished at seeing the hustle and bustle of his once known ghost town, tried to listen to Pete as their horses trotted down the main street of Dorado Ciudad. Pete's laugh brought Levi back from his daze.

"Yeah, I sure woulda liked to see ol' Matt's face when ya drew down on Clyde. I'll bet that woulda been something to see," Pete concluded.

"Yeah, I wish you'd been there, Pete. I sure could have used a backup."

"Noooo, noooo, not me. All I do is punch cattle and race jackass rabbits," Pete proclaimed as they both laughed. The horses pulled up at a hitching rail, and the two new friends dismounted in front of the sheriff's office. "Whatcha stopping here fer? That's the sheriff's office."

"I thought I might just check with the sheriff about all this rustlin'," Levi explained.

"Rustlin'? Oh, ya mean at the Morgan spread?" Pete asked.

"You mean it's just at the Morgan Ranch? Nobody else is losing any cattle?" Levi questioned.

"That's right."

"I knew the Morgans were losing a lotta cattle, but I didn't realize they were the only ones," Levi commented aloud as his suspicion hardened.

"Yeah, that's what's so odd. That moron of a sheriff's not gonna tell ya a thing 'cause he doesn't know a thing to tell ya. That sheriff hasn't got a clue, and he's been working on that rustlin' case for over two years."

Levi could tell that Pete was getting pretty worked up over the job the sheriff was doing or maybe not doing. He retrieved the

Tanners' pistols from his saddlebags, and then he stepped up on the boardwalk as Pete was still standing by his horse.

"Levi, I'll catch up with ya later. I gotta take care of my dad's errands."

"Sure, that sounds good, Pete!" Levi shouted as he opened the door to the sheriff's office.

As Levi walked in, he heard a friendly voice. "Come in, come in." He saw a sloppily dressed middle-aged man with a huge beer belly sitting behind a dust-covered desk. Both feet were resting on the top, and his head laid against the wall, where the hair oils had stained a large circle.

"I'm looking for the sheriff," Levi stated, thinking the disarrayed man may be the town drunk.

"You found 'im. I'm Sheriff Gore, Amos Gore. What can I do for ya, young fellow?" he answered in a pleasant tone.

"Well." Levi, totally surprised, tried to carry on the conversation. "Sheriff, I was hoping ya might help me answer some questions concerning the cattle rustlin' at the Morgan Ranch."

"Oh, ya must be that Calman fella, aahh, Levi Calman," the sheriff replied.

"Yeah, that's right. I don't believe how fast things get around in this town." Levi smiled in amazement.

"There's not really that much gossip. There's just not that much for people to talk about."

"Yeah, someone else told me the same thing. It must be true." Levi grinned.

"Tom Calahan stopped in early this mornin' to fill me in on that fracas ya had with the Tanners yesterday. He was speaking on your behalf," the sheriff explained.

"Maybe he didn't feel that I would come by to explain what happened," Levi pondered out loud.

"No, that wasn't it, son. He thought, with ya not being from around these parts, I might be more inclined to believe the Tanners if they filed a complaint against ya," the sheriff explained.

"Oh … well, I guess I should thank 'em for that." Levi was a little perturbed that everyone knew more about him than he did. *Well, there were still a few things no one else knew,* he thought.

"Tom Calahan is a fine man, son. He didn't have to come by here at all."

"I wasn't taking anything away from him, Sheriff. I just thought for once I could tell something myself." Levi smiled as he shrugged his shoulders, and the sheriff smiled back.

"Whatcha got there? Something for me?" the sheriff asked as he looked down at the pistols in Levi's hand.

"Oh yeah, these belong to the Tanners. I told 'em they could pick 'em up here."

"Boy, you must be pretty good with that gun to take these from the Tanner brothers. They're just about the toughest men in this town," the sheriff commented as he took the pistols from Levi. Levi just smiled.

"Well, gettin' back to your original question. I really hadn't found a clue. I and my deputies have ridden every foot of fence line on that Morgan Ranch. Not only were there no fences down but we also even looked for splices, thinking someone might hide their spot so they could use it again. We didn't come up with a thing. If I didn't know Pop Morgan so well, I'd probably doubt if he really had the cattle to start with."

"Sheriff, what about the Tanners? I know those boys are rough, but Mr. Morgan seems to think the sun sets with the father. Do ya think they may be connected?" Levi asked.

"No," the sheriff said. "I know those boys have been pretty bad, and they use to have a big chip on their shoulder. But when Mr. Tanner had that stroke about three years ago, those boys did a complete turn." "

Yeah, I heard they did a one-eighty."

"Huh?" the sheriff asked with a puzzled look.

"Oh, I said I had heard they were going straight maybe," Levi explained with a strange-sounding reply.

The sheriff, still puzzled by Levi's comment, continued, "You should just see the difference in their place."

"Are ya saying the place looks better, or the Tanner Ranch is doing better?" Levi redundantly asked.

"Well, both. When their mine started paying off, they got their herds back in shape, and now they're doing real well." As the sheriff answered Levi, it brought some guilt in the sheriff's mind. "Those boys have done so good for Mr. Tanner. It makes me feel guilty just thinking bad about 'em."

Boy, have they got this town fooled, Levi thought as he listened to the sheriff. "What have they done for their dad?" Levi asked.

"Well," the sheriff paused as he collected his thoughts, "they fixed that old house, added some rooms, painted everythin', put up a new sign at their front gate, even changed the name of the ranch from the Circle T to the Matthew Tanner Ranch. It was just as though they finally appreciated the old man and wanted to show it to 'im before it was too late." The sheriff paused. "No, son, there's just got to be another answer."

"I guess you've asked Mr. Tanner if he's got any ideas about these rustlers," Levi inquired.

"Oh, no. He's been bedridden since he had that stroke. He couldn't help us at all."

"How often do ya see 'im?"

"Oh, not very often."

"Does anyone go out to the Tanner Ranch and visit?" Levi questioned.

"No, I don't think so. I know I should go see 'im more than I do. It's probably been six or eight months since I've been out there myself. But those boys really watch after 'im. The last time

I was out there, those boys were right by his side the whole time, never let 'im out of sight, watched over 'im like a mother hen," the sheriff explained.

"Well, it sounds like you've been doing all your homework, Sheriff. If ya don't mind, I think I'll just do a little looking around on the Morgan Ranch. Hopefully, something'll turn up. The Morgans are just too nice a people to go down the tube," Levi said.

"Go where?" the sheriff questioned.

Levi frowned to himself. *Why do I keep using all the strange language?* "Oh, it's just an expression. They're too nice to lose their ranch," he explained with a funny look on his face.

"Oh yeah, that's right. Son, as long as it's okay with the Morgans for ya to snoop around on their property, it tickles the shit out of me. But if ya run across anythin', let me know. Don't do nothin' without gettin' with me first … okay?" the sheriff impressed on Levi.

"You got it. I'll keep in touch," he said as he reached out to shake the sheriff's hand.

As Levi walked from the office to the boardwalk, the sheriff followed. Levi stepped off the walk and onto the street. He looked back at the sheriff. "Nice meetin' ya," he commented as he turned and started across the dusty dirt street.

Levi hadn't noticed, but across the street on the corner, Clyde Tanner was coming out of the saloon. Clyde emerged through the swinging doors, rolling a cigarette. He glanced up and spotted Levi coming across the street. Blowing the cigarette from his mouth, his left hand rubbed across his bandaged right forearm provided by this stranger. Clyde stepped back against the wall. The sun beamed straight down, and Levi was squinting as he made his way across the street. Clyde realized that he was standing in the shade. That would give him an edge, and the whiskey shots had rendered the courage. Clyde was primed to draw against the man who had humiliated him. He stepped forward to the edge of the wooden sidewalk. "Hey, you son of a bitch. Your life is mine!" he yelled. As

Levi looked up, he focused in on a man clearing his holster with a revolver aimed at his direction.

The sheriff had also spotted the man in the shadow who had yelled in his direction, but his hand was paralyzed, his arm glued to his side as he watched the man draw.

Levi never knew when his hand reacted to his brain. He only saw the man's pistol fire into the ground, and the gun fell down the steps and into the street. The man was carried backward by the impact. The shell from Levi's revolver had driven the man to the wall, and then he fell forward to the wooden planks of the boardwalk. Levi's stomach muscles tightened as his gun returned to the holster.

"Are ya all right?" the sheriff asked as he ran up to Levi, putting his hand on Levi's shoulder.

"Yeah, I'm okay. How about him? Is he okay?" Levi responded.

"No, I don't think so," the sheriff replied. "I'll check 'im out. Wait here."

The sheriff ran over to the boardwalk and up the steps. As he reached the body, Billy Tanner, the younger brother, came running out of the saloon. "What the hell's goin' on?" Billy yelled when he saw Clyde lying on the porch.

Billy drew his gun as the sheriff bent down over Clyde. Another shot rang out, and Billy grabbed his arm. His pistol fell to the deck as the sheriff jumped up.

"What the hell are ya doing, Billy? Who were ya gonna shoot?" the sheriff yelled.

The storekeeper from next door had run out onto the boardwalk after the first shot. He was standing only a few feet away and replied to the sheriff's question, "He was fixin' to shoot you, Sheriff, right in the back."

The sheriff had turned quickly, just in time to see Levi holstering his pistol. "Thanks, Calman," he responded as Levi came up the steps.

"Okay, Billy. Let's go," the sheriff said, and he grabbed Billy by the arm.

"Where're you takin' me?" Billy asked.

"Wait a minute, Sheriff," Levi said. "He didn't mean it. It was just a normal reaction when something like that happens to your brother. You can't really blame 'im."

"Don't do me any favors, dead man. You can't shoot down a Tanner and get away with it," the young Tanner threatened.

"Okay, Billy, come on. I'll take ya by the doc's office, and then you're gettin' out of town," said the sheriff. "Thanks again, Levi. I guess I'd better get this bastard over to the doc's before he bleeds all over the sidewalk."

The sheriff turned to Billy and said, "You should thank that man. He just pleaded your case and kept ya out of jail. Your brother drew on him. Clyde started the whole thing. I was watching everything that happened," and he tugged Billy away.

"I'll be back with my brother Matt. You won't be standing long, you son of a—" The sheriff jerked Billy and continued to drag him down the street as the young rebel screamed back at Levi.

The barber came from his shop. He hurriedly slipped on his black coat and hat, activating his second job as the town mortician.

Pete Cagle stood in the crowd as Levi stepped from the boardwalk. "Boy, that was some kind of shootin'. I ain't ever seen anything like it. You must be the fastest man alive," Pete said excitedly as he walked toward Levi.

"I don't feel too good about it," Levi commented as they walked through the supportive crowd.

The citizens of Dorado were all on Levi's side. He could sense their support as he sauntered through. "You only did whatcha had to … No one could blame ya … It was pure self-defense." He could hear the people talking, but he knew the young kid, Billy Tanner, blamed him. Matt Tanner would also, just as soon as Billy could make it to their ranch. Matt Tanner was a tough thing for

94

Levi to deal with. He was still a face on a dead man he couldn't forget, those glassy eyes staring up at him. Levi relived the incident in living color, time and time again, as they walked back to their horses.

He shook off the trance as he heard Pete talking. "Ya just have to stop blaming yourself. I saw the whole thing, and there wasn't anything else to do."

"Oh, I know, but I've never done anything like that before. It makes me a little sick to my stomach," replied Levi.

"I'm sorry, I didn't know. The way ya handle that gun, I woulda thought ..." Pete didn't finish his sentence; he just stopped talking and walked alongside Levi. Sensing Levi's feelings, he thought it might be better just to be there.

Reaching the horses, the two mounted and started down the street. "Oh, wait a minute, Pete, let's stop at the store. I've got to take some coffee back to the ranch," Levi remembered.

"Sure thing, up there on the right, where those two men are loadin' that wagon," Pete replied. The two rode to the hitching rail and dismounted. A farmer was loading some supplies in the rear of an open wagon.

The storekeeper, easily recognized because of the white apron, came down the steps with a large bag of flour on his shoulder as Pete and Levi were starting up. "Yes, sir, can we help ya, Pete?" the question came from a slightly heavy middle-aged storekeeper.

"You sure can, Mr. Warner," Pete replied. "My friend here is looking for some coffee."

"Sure, y'all go right in. Martha'll fix ya right up," Mr. Warner replied. "What was all that shootin' we heard down the street, Pete?"

Pete leaned over to whisper as Mr. Warner bent to listen. "My friend here," he said proudly, "just killed Clyde Tanner."

"What!" the storekeeper replied in a louder than normal volume.

"Shhh, not so loud," Pete replied as he looked around to see how far away Levi was standing. "He's kinda touchy about it." It was his friend who just shot one of the fastest guns in town.

"Ya say he just took Clyde Tanner?" Mr. Warner asked in a quieter voice.

"Yep. Clyde drew down on 'im. Then Levi drew faster than greased lightnin'. He shot Clyde before he could pull the trigger, the fastest man I've ever seen," Pete remarked.

"I'll be damned. I'd never believed anybody was that fast, except maybe Matt," Mr. Warner replied.

"Hey, Pete, come here!" Levi shouted discreetly.

Pete jumped, thinking he got caught talking too much. He turned and walked quickly inside. Levi continued, "Mrs. Warner said it only comes in five- or ten-pound bags. Which would the Morgans use?"

"Oh, I'd get the ten-pounder or maybe two. You go through a lot of coffee with all those cowhands," Pete responded.

"Yeah, I guess, especially when you're an hour and a half from a convenience store," Levi laughed for his own benefit. Pete laughed too. Levi looked at Pete a little peculiarly, knowing full well he couldn't completely appreciate his remark. Levi shook his head at Pete and smiled.

"If this is for the Morgans, you can probably get by with one ten-pound bag," Mrs. Warner remarked.

"Are ya trying to lose a sale?" Levi asked jokingly. "Nah, we'll take two ten-pound bags." He reached into his pocket and pulled out his money clip. "What do I owe ya for the coffee ... beans?" Levi stammered as he read the label lying on the counter. "We're not buying ground coffee?"

"Well, we do have small bags that we grind but ..." Mrs. Warner looked confused.

"No, no, he wants the beans. It's for the Morgans, and they

have a grinder," Pete explained to Levi. Pete wondered why Levi was not more familiar with the customs.

"Well, that'll be four dollars and sixty-two cents," Mrs. Warner said.

"For twenty pounds of coffee!" Levi stated.

"We had a price increase with this last shipment," she explained.

"No, I didn't mean that. I meant … I think that's a good price … I mean, isn't it?" Levi asked, embarrassed. Levi pulled a twenty off of his clip of folded money. Pete watched as Levi laid the bill on the counter. Before Mrs. Warner could focus on the bill, Pete grabbed it.

"Here's a five, Mrs. Warner," Pete said. "Levi, never break a big bill. It spends too fast," he replied. He smiled and handed the bill back to Levi. Levi could read some serious questions in Pete's eyes as he took the twenty.

Mr. Warner finished with his customer and returned inside. "Let me tie those bags on behind your saddle, Mister," he said. "

Thanks, that'll be great," Levi commented, his eyes still fixed on Pete. He was sure Pete was curious.

Knowing Pete would be curious, Levi handed the twenty-dollar bill back to him. He looked at Pete and smiled. "It's a souvenir." Pete looked down at the bill and then back up at Levi and smiled. He knew Levi trusted him completely. Levi stepped to the side and patted Pete on the back as they stepped out onto the boardwalk. Mr. Warner, with both bags on his shoulder, walked by them and headed down the steps to the hitching rail. Pete reached into his pocket and pulled out a few bills. "Here, take your change. You may need it." Pete smiled. Then Levi smiled and reached for the money. The two bounced on down the steps and mounted their horses.

"Thanks, Mr. Warner!" Levi shouted as the duo turned and headed up the street. Mr. Warner nodded as they rode away.

Levi knew at this time Pete had accepted him as a friend with no questions asked.

The two rode for several miles in silence. Just for conversation, Pete asked, "What kind of horse is that animal? That's got to be the tallest horse I've ever seen."

Levi smiled. "He's a Tennessee Walker. Whatcha think about 'im?" Levi responded.

"Ah, he's a beautiful animal. I'll bet he has the longest legs and the biggest hooves I've ever seen. He looks like he could walk across mud without sinkin'," Pete commented teasingly.

"I don't want to brag, but he's probably the fastest animal you'll ever see," Levi bragged.

"With feet that big, no way he's as fast as this quarter horse," Pete challenged.

"Are ya kidding? Look at the difference in those legs, Pete. There's no way that horse can keep up with Crimson," Levi egged.

"Oh yeah? Do ya see that clump of trees down yonder on the right?" Pete asked.

"Oh, no. You see those big boulders at the top of that hill?" Levi asked.

The top of the hill was a good mile away. He knew the quarter horse was fast on short runs, but Crimson could take him on a longer course. Pete, not knowing the difference in the two animals, agreed on the finish line. The men looked at each other without a word. The two horses left the mark. The race was on. Pete pulled out in front with a quick start, a trait well-known in the quarter horse. As the two passed the clump of trees, Pete led by a length. They rounded a small curve and then up a shallow grade on a long straight away to the top of the hill. A third of the way up, the long-legged animal caught up with the Texan-bred quarter horse. Pete was amazed as he watched the big red stallion pull away with ease. Crimson was ahead by three lengths by the time they reached the top of the hill.

The jockeys came to a halt as the horses panted vigorously. "Boy, that horse can run," Pete commented, a little short-winded himself.

"Well, I took advantage of ya, Pete," Levi confessed, and Pete looked surprised. "I knew your horse could take Crimson on a short run. It takes a while to get those long legs stretched out, but once ya do, he's gone." Levi smiled.

"You got me. I thought when we passed those trees, I had it made," Pete said. "It was still a good race." The two settled down to a slower pace. They both had questions, but not a word was spoken the rest of the way. Before long, they reached the entrance to the Cagle Ranch. The trip back seemed a lot shorter. The race had made for a fun time, and getting to meet a new friend made the trip pass even easier.

"Pete, it was sure nice meetin' ya. I'm glad we had that little trip together," Levi commented. He avoided all the questions he thought Pete might have floating around in his head.

"Lee, I can call ya Lee?" Pete asked.

"Sure, I've got some other good friends that call me Lee." Levi smiled.

"Well, that's what I want to tell ya. I am a good friend. If ya ever need to talk about anything ..." Pete paused. "Lee, Matt Tanner's not gonna let this slide. If ya left town right now, nobody would think bad about'cha. The Tanners have twenty or more hands working on that ranch. Most of 'em are better with a gun than cattle, and if Matt pushed 'em ..." Pete paused.

"Thanks, Pete, but I'm not leaving. I feel that was a fair fight. Besides, he drew on me. I can't just leave with my tail between my legs, like a whipped dog. If Matt Tanner has a problem with it, I'll be right here."

"I'll be here too," Pete stated as he entered the gate and waved as he rode down the trail.

Levi, thinking that it had been a long day, rode over to the Morgan gate, reached down, and opened the latch. He ambled inside. It's old hat, he thought, as he swung low and latched the gate. He turned and started down the wagon-rutted old road and began to think a little deeper. *I feel like I've done this all my life. All of my life? he pondered, What life? Which life? What am I doing? Why am I here? Will I ever go back? Will I ever see Dyanne? My God, poor Dyanne. What will she do? What will she think happened to me? Can she make it okay? God, I hope so. I'm not sure if I could leave Elizabeth anyway. I wonder if I could take her back to the 1990s. No, she'd probably be like a bird without wings.* So many questions and absolutely no answers. Levi rode up to the hitching rail and slid down from Crimson's back. Elizabeth had spotted him through the window and ran out to meet him. As he finished tying off Crimson, she ran down the path and straight into his arms. "I sure have missed ya. I've already gotten used to having ya around," she said as she graced him with a large smile.

"Oh, ya have?" Levi responded with a smile. "To tell ya the truth, I've missed you more than that." Then he leaned over and kissed her.

Remembering where she was, Elizabeth jumped back and straightened up. "We'd better go inside. Dad's here," she said.

"Oh, great. Are ya trying to get me into trouble?" he said jokingly. They started up the steps to the front porch.

"Are ya hungry? We've fixed a good meal."

"Oh, let me get the coffee!" Levi shouted as he jumped from the steps and jogged back to Crimson.

Elizabeth walked back down the dirt path as Levi untied the leather straps that held the bags. "Sure, I'm hungry," he proclaimed. "What are we having?" He grabbed both bags and started toward her.

"Well, we're having chicken-fried chicken." Before she could say another word, Levi laughed out loud. Taking both bags in his right hand, he pulled her close with his left, and the twosome started back up the steps. For a moment, he had forgotten his day, and his mind only held thoughts of this beautiful and precious woman who had come into his life. Maybe he had come into hers too.

"How did it go in town?" Mr. Morgan asked as the two entered the screen door.

The moment had passed. Reality set in as Levi recalled the day. "Not too good, I'm afraid." His head dropped as he answered.

"What happened?" Elizabeth questioned.

"I shot Clyde Tanner," Levi answered.

"Oh no, Levi. You're not hurt, are ya?" she asked with deep concern.

"He didn't say he got shot. He said he shot somebody. He's not the one that hurts," Mr. Morgan said in a quiet tone to calm Elizabeth.

She looked at her dad as a slight grin came across his face. Then she looked back at Levi. "What happened?" she asked.

"Well, I was in the sheriff's office asking a few questions. I walked outside and was crossing the street when Clyde yelled at me and drew. There just wasn't anything else to do."

"So ya drew and hit your target. How far away was he?" Mr. Morgan asked excitedly.

"About forty-five or fifty feet, I guess. But I missed my target. I was aiming for his arm. I didn't mean to kill 'im." Levi shrugged his shoulders and walked across the parlor. He stood behind a high-back chair, grasped the top carved wood with both hands, and stared into the cold black fireplace.

Elizabeth placed her hands on Levi's shoulders and laid her head on his back. She understood his emotion. Taking a life wasn't an easy thing for him to do. She was glad and felt a lot of compassion for him.

"Well, I feel sorry for old Matthew. He never could control those boys," Mr. Morgan said, saddened. "Maybe that will straighten out the other two."

"I don't think so, Mr. Morgan. Billy came out of the saloon right after the shootin', and he thought the sheriff had shot Clyde.

He drew down on Sheriff Gore," Levi said.

"Oh, my God! What happened?"

"Well, I had to shoot him too," he explained. Not much aroused Mr. Morgan, but his eyes opened wide as he listened to the reply. Levi continued to stare into the fireplace, not taking the situation near as well as Mr. Morgan seemed to.

Elizabeth was beside herself. "You mean Billy's ..."

"No, no! I just got 'im in the arm. He's okay."

"Thank God. I didn't think there were going to be any Tanners left," commented Mr. Morgan. He smiled at Levi, trying to break up the tension shared by the two youngsters. "I'm not making light of it, but it was something that would have happened sooner or later. That man was bad all the way to the bone."

The consoling and understanding from Mr. Morgan had really helped Levi. Knowing Ben Morgan and Matthew Tanner were old friends had made it even harder for Levi to talk about the incident. He really appreciated Mr. Morgan's support.

"That's enough talk about a bad subject. Carmita, can we eat?" Mr. Morgan shouted to the dining area, where she was setting the table.

"Oh, *si, Señor*. Everything is ready," Carmita answered.

Levi turned and smiled. "I thought this girl only spoke Spanish?" Carmita smiled. Mr. Morgan laughed, and Elizabeth joined in.

The two girls headed for the kitchen and started bringing out the food, while Levi walked over to the table and lit the candles. Mr. Morgan took his chair at the head of the table.

"Here comes the food, gentlemen," Elizabeth stated.

"I want to see this chicken-fried chicken," Levi commented, and Mr. Morgan grinned.

The air in the room was much lighter than it had been just minutes before. The three dug into their chicken-fried chicken, and Carmita started her nightly ritual of lighting the coal oil lamps in the parlor. This lighting ceremony fascinated Levi even more than the crude kitchen. It amazed him that this kitchen could run as smoothly as it did. The food seemed to have more taste as well. He had a few more hurdles to cross, but he was definitely getting used to this new life.

"Everything tastes great. You sure did fix a perfect meal," Levi stated. He fixed his eyes on Elizabeth.

"Thank ya, sir," she answered. "But I'll have to give most of the credit to Carmita."

Carmita looked up from her chore and shook the match. "Oh no, Señor, she prepared this food herself. She prepared everythin' for you," Carmita explained in her heavily accented English.

"Did ya really?" Levi asked. "Not that I had any doubt that ya could." He tried to explain.

Mr. Morgan looked at him and laughed. "You can't get out of that line. You'll just make it worse," he said.

Elizabeth looked at Levi with a serious expression, but a smile came shining through. "So ya didn't think I could cook, huh?"

"No! No, I mean, yes, sure, I did. I don't know what I meant," Levi stammered. "Well, as I said before all of this hassle you're givin' me started, everything tastes great."

Elizabeth smiled. "How about more tea?"

"Just a half a glass," Levi answered.

"Dad, how about you?"

"No, darlin', I think I've had enough. Something's makin' me feel real hot," Mr. Morgan replied.

"You feel bad, Dad?" Elizabeth asked.

"No, I just feel hot around the neck and my head."

"Does it seem to take all of your energy, Mr. Morgan?" Levi asked.

"Yeah, come to think of it, it sure does."

"Well, with the redness in your cheeks and what you're saying about the heat, I think you probably have high blood pressure, don't you think?" Levi commented and then paused. "I think ya should probably check with the doctor."

"What do ya mean high blood pressure?" Mr. Morgan asked as Elizabeth listened with interest.

"Well, it's when the pressure on the heart is too high." Levi could tell they didn't understand and explained a little further. "You know, when the heart beats, it creates so much pressure. Then in between beats, it's supposed to rest. When the pressure doesn't go down enough, ya feel hot, and you'll tire out real easy. It can also cause a stroke."

"Ya mean that's what happened to Matthew Tanner?" Mr. Morgan asked.

"Well, I don't know if that was his problem. Maybe he's overweight, or there're other problems," Levi answered.

"What d'ya mean other problems?" Elizabeth asked.

"Well, like stress," Levi said.

"Huh?" Mr. Morgan questioned.

"You know, your nerves. Like maybe he was under a lot of strain, like those boys keeping him upset all the time. That can create stress, and that can cause a heart attack or a stroke. Just like this cattle rustling. It's got ya under a lot of stress. I know you're not going to like the cure, but naaah, I'd better shut up," he concluded.

"No, no, please tell us. If it can help Dad, we need to know," Elizabeth pleaded.

"Well, you're not really overweight, and ya seem to get a lot … or enough exercise anyway. So probably it's just all that coffee and all that tea. They both have a lot of caffeine," Levi answered.

"Caff what?" Mr. Morgan asked with a baffled look on his face.

"Caffeine. It's really bad on your high blood pressure. You just need to cut back. Why don'tcha try maybe one cup in the morning and just one glass of tea in the evening or just drink water at night and see if ya don't get better. Oh, and don't drink any booze," Levi added.

"Any what?" Mr. Morgan asked, a little bewildered.

"Liquor. Ahhh, whiskey, you know?"

"Confound it, son, you're taking this doctor thing too far," Mr. Morgan expressed.

"Dad, it won't hurt ya to try it for a few days. It might even help. I don't wantcha to end up like Mr. Tanner," Elizabeth implored.

"Okay, okay, I'll try it. He sounds like he knows what he's talking about," Mr. Morgan conceded. Elizabeth looked at Levi and smiled as if to say she was proud of him. She was happy that her dad consented. Inside, she contemplated her dad's last words. Levi did seem to know a lot more than a farmer from Fort Worth should.

"Well, if y'all don't mind, I think I'll turn in," Mr. Morgan commented.

"Not at all, Mr. Morgan." Levi felt anticipation at the thought of the front porch with Elizabeth. Mr. Morgan stood slowly, with one hand still on the table for support.

"Dad, can I help ya. Are ya all right?" Elizabeth was concerned as she took his arm.

"No, no, I'm okay," he mumbled. He looked fatigued as he straightened up and walked across the parlor. Without turning, he quietly said good night and went to his room.

Elizabeth turned to Levi as the door to her dad's room closed. "I'm really concerned about him. Do ya think he'll be all right?"

"Sure, he will." Levi was thinking to himself how weak Mr. Morgan really looked. "He's a tough old bird. He'll be just fine." Levi comforted her and reached over to take her hand.

Elizabeth grinned, but deep down, she also knew her dad was

looking frail. "Why don't you go out on the porch? Let me help Carmita with the kitchen, and I'll be right out," she suggested.

"No, Miss Elizabeth. There's not much. You go. I finish up," Carmita replied.

"Carmita, ya old smooth talker. Elizabeth, you heard her. She said ya could come outside with me." Levi grinned. He pulled on Elizabeth's hand and started out the screen door.

"Carmita, are ya sure?" Carmita was grinning as Levi tugged Elizabeth through the doorway.

"Would ya like to sit on the swing?" she asked.

Still holding her hand, Levi smiled and without a word pulled her close and kissed her. She put her arms around his body. A long kiss prevailed in silence, and then backing off, they strolled toward the old wood swing hanging at the end of the porch. The two sat down, and the swing started to move. There was a light breeze in the air, and only the crickets could be heard.

The silence was finally broken as Levi tried to express his feelings. "This is sure nice. It's probably the most peaceful time, the most comfortable time I've ever had in my life."

"I feel the same when I'm with you. I feel so secure. That's what it is. It's peaceful, all inside. It's such a good feeling. I hope my parents had this kind of companionship. I think they must have. I think that's why Dad never remarried," Elizabeth stated.

"How old was your mother when she died?" he asked. Elizabeth snuggled back into his arms and laid her head on his shoulder.

"Mother was thirty when I was born. Dad had sent his only hand into town to fetch the doc, but it was a real bad winter. The doctor had a lot of problems in town. Most of the townspeople were down with the flu. There were several cases of pneumonia. Mother had some kind of complication. By the time the doctor got here the next morning ..." Elizabeth's voice trailed off.

Levi felt the tremble in her body and heard the sadness in her voice and quickly changed the subject. "So you've been raised right here all your life." Thinking that sentence didn't come out just right, he decided to try another as she nodded a reply. "I bet you know this neck of the woods pretty good."

"Yeah, I sure do. I know every rock and every tree on this ranch," she proclaimed. Her voice came back with spirit. "Why?"

"Well, I'd like to look around a little bit tomorrow. Maybe you'd like to come along and show me some of the ranch."

"Would I—" Before she could finish, Levi interrupted, "Harelip, harelip," and burst out laughing.

He was still laughing as Elizabeth set up. "What did ya say? What's so funny?" she asked. She turned toward him smiling and thinking maybe he's gone crazy.

"Ah, it's an old joke," he continued to chuckle, "maybe you've heard it." *Maybe it's not that old*, he thought. "Well, this guy is real poor, and he only has one eye. So he carved an eye from a piece of wood, see. But everybody made fun of his homemade eye. He's really paranoid about this eye. So he goes to this dance, and he sees this girl sitting across the room. It's kind of dark. So as he walks up close, he notices she has a harelip." Elizabeth was smiling and paying close attention. "But she's not bad looking, so he walked on over and says, 'Would you like to dance?' and the girl says, 'Would I?' and he says, 'Harelip, harelip!'" Levi laughed through the whole story.

Elizabeth was just shaking her head from side to side but with a smile. "Boy, you've really got a sense of humor."

"Well, didn't ya think it was funny?" he asked, still chuckling.

Elizabeth turned and slid back up to him and laid her head back on his shoulder. "I guess it was pretty funny," she replied as she snuggled in. The two gazed up through the clear dark blue sky as the moon appeared to be only a few miles away. "Azure," she whispered.

"You mean *azul*, the blue skies," Levi responded in a peaceful tone.

"No, azure, the blue in the sky," Elizabeth replied.

"How do ya say it? A-zure. They didn't teach me that in my Spanish class," he commented.

"That's not Spanish. That's English. Azure. It means the blue in a clear sky."

"Wow, they never taught me that word in English either," he proclaimed.

"Well, it might have a Latin background, but it is English, and I did learn it in college," she stated.

"You've already been to college, and you're only twenty-one?" Levi was amazed.

"Well, I was out of school at sixteen. Then it took a year to convince Dad to let me go back east. Then two years in college. I graduated last year when I was twenty, and now I've been out for a whole year," she boasted.

"That's fantastic. I'm really proud of ya. How did you get out of school when you were only sixteen?"

"Well, I started when I was five. You know, my mother was the schoolteacher at one time, and we had several copies of all the books here, so Dad used to read to me a lot. I guess he was doin' what he figured Mother woulda liked. Anyway, eleven years later, I graduated."

"Oh, that's right. Just eleven grades," he blurted out.

"What do ya mean just eleven grades? How many did you go?" she inquired.

"Ohhh … I just went eleven, but it's been so long," he responded. "I guess ya went to one of those finishing schools back east, huh?"

"I did not. I went to Cornwall University," Elizabeth replied with an uppity grin.

"Boy, I'm impressed. Hey, wasn't Cornwall just for men?" Levi questioned.

"It used to be, but it turned coed the year before. I started in seventy-three. The girls who started that first year, seventy-two, they could really tell some stories. Seventy-three wasn't so bad, and then my second year—seventy-four, seventy-five—was even easier. Now if I ever need to, I can teach school," she added with a little touch of bragging.

"All right, what would ya teach?" he asked with enthusiasm.

"What do ya mean?" she questioned. "I would teach at the school."

"No, I mean, what subjects? What grade would ya like? You know," he explained.

"There's only one room. It's all subjects and all grades," she answered, somewhat confused by his question.

"Oh …" He paused. "That's right. The school I went to was a little bigger. The teacher moved around from room to room, and each room had different ages," he explained.

"Oh, that's good, when ya have a bigger school. Do ya really want me to go with you tomorrow?" she inquired.

"Sure, I'm hoping I can show ya something you haven't seen before, if I'm not too early," Levi stated.

"You mean, if you're not too late, don't ya?"

"No, I know I'm not too late. It'll be there for a long time, but … it may not be there yet. Just trust me." Levi grinned to himself. Elizabeth was trusting but confused. "I'll show ya tomorrow," he added.

Levi's train of thought changed. "Say, how old is your dad?"

"Well, he was born in, let me think, aahhh, eighteen hundred and five, and this is seventy-six, so he's—" Before she could finish, Levi interrupted.

"He's seventy-one years young."

"Why do ya ask?"

"Well, nothing, I guess. He seems to be about the same age as my granddad was," Levi replied.

"That's probably true. He was fifty when I was born. He was

one of those confirmed bachelors until Mother moved out here in fifty-one. She had a contract to teach school, but when her two years were up, she was going back to Boston."

"But the old confirmed bachelor had other plans, huh?" Levi commented as he smiled.

"Yep, they got married on July the twenty-first of '53, and I was born January the nineteenth, eighteen and fifty-five," Elizabeth stated.

"So you're forty-one," Levi teased as Elizabeth sat up and turned toward him.

"I'm twenty-one. I know I don't look forty-one, Levi Calman," she replied in a sassy but cute way.

"It wouldn't matter how old ya were. You're the most beautiful girl I've ever seen." Elizabeth leaned forward as she stared into Levi's eyes. He moved in closer, and she melted into his arms. Almost like being drawn by a magnet, his lips sought hers, and they kissed. At first, it was gentle and then became a passion born of the soul. The kissing continued for several minutes as the heat between them came to a smolder. Elizabeth pushed back. Her eyes made contact with Levi's, and her heart beat rapidly. Her breathing had deepened.

"I guess we better go inside. Tomorrow is going to be another long day." Levi could almost feel the heat from the flush on her cheeks and neck as he leaned back and stood. He decided that this was her first encounter with such passionate feelings.

He sensed her emotion to be something close to his own and readily agreed. "You're right, maybe we should call it a night."

Still holding hands, they strolled to the center of the front porch and opened the screen door. The only sound besides the creaking of the door was the chatter from the crickets as the man in the moon looked on. The couple walked inside, and the lamplights faded quickly only seconds later.

CHAPTER 6

THE EVIDENCE

THE SUN HAD gotten there first, and the coffee's scent had made it to Levi's nose, causing the muscles in his body to flex. He jumped to his feet, wanting to start this day as never before. Walking over to the old marble-top stand, where his shaving kit lay, Levi started his morning ritual—brushing his teeth and shaving and then combing his hair. But this morning, it didn't seem to be a chore. He did it all with vigor, even humming a peppy tune. One might assume he was in love.

Enthusiastically, he grabbed his freshly washed jeans, which were folded and placed on the dresser. He appreciated his electric drier as he felt the jeans' cardboard texture. Without changing his happy mood, he slipped them on. He opened the wardrobe to find the shirt Elizabeth had taken with the jeans. The shirt looked clean and wrinkle free. Levi pried it from the hanger as his fingers felt the stiffness, and his nose smelled the heaviness of the starch. He proceeded to open a path down the sleeve, so his arm would slide through. Prying the buttons from the cloth and starting them through the closed-up buttonholes seemed to be the toughest part. The socks slid on with very little pain. The boots, normally the more physical part of dressing, ended up the easiest. With the ease of a knight in armor, he headed for the kitchen. He knew the coffee and the girl of his dreams would be waiting. "Good morning, good morning," he said with a vibrant smile as he entered the kitchen door.

There was a glow about Elizabeth's face as Levi entered. "Good morning," she replied.

"Mornin'," Mr. Morgan replied cordially but not with near as much enthusiasm as Elizabeth.

"Grab a chair, son."

"Thanks," Levi responded as he pulled the chair back.

"Are ya ready for coffee?" she asked.

"I sure am. I could smell that coffee before my feet hit the floor," he replied.

As Elizabeth poured the coffee, Carmita served his food. "Buenos dias, Señor Levi," Carmita said in a friendly voice.

"Buenos dias, Señora Carmita," Levi replied, and they both smiled.

Elizabeth was happy; Carmita liked Levi. Her approval of him meant a lot. It was not only for her amo, but also her *óptimo amigo*. She knew Carmita was also happy for her.

"I think I'm going to ride into town this morning. Would ya like to come along?" Mr. Morgan asked as he looked over at Levi.

"No, sir. I appreciate you asking, but I thought I might take a ride up to the north range and then head west down the fence line, just to see if I could spot something different," Levi answered.

"Well, of course, I sure wish ya luck, but I just don't have much hope anymore," Mr. Morgan responded.

Levi smiled. "Don't give up, as John Paul Jones once said, 'I've not yet begun to fight.'"

"Yeah, you're right. But he was sinkin' British ships. Come to think of it. Somebody's tryin' to sink my ship," Mr. Morgan remarked.

"I'll find the culprits, Mr. Morgan. You know, John Paul Jones found some renegades among his own men. He had to jump ship and hide out for a couple of years. He even had to change his name."

"He did?" Mr. Morgan responded as the women listened on. "But I don't think we can survive a couple more years."

Levi smiled. "Maybe you won't have to wait that long. All John Paul had to do was to Americanize."

"He did what?"

"He Americanized," Levi said still smiling. "He added Jones to his name and then came back even stronger."

"Well, if that didn't beat all! I didn't know that," he stated. His face perked up, and he dug in for another bite.

Things quieted down for a few minutes while everyone finished their food. Mr. Morgan leaned back.

"Well, if y'all don't mind, I think I'll get an early start into town."

"Are ya going in for supplies, Dad?"

"Not unless ya need something. I'm just going in to talk to Mr. Sims at the bank."

"Well, we could use a sack of potatoes and a sack of flour. Anything you can think of, Carmita?"

Carmita just shook her head.

"Carmita, will ya tell Ricardo to hitch up the buggy, while I go put my boots on?" Mr. Morgan asked.

"Suurre, Mr. Morrgan," she replied. She very promptly headed out the back screen door, and Mr. Morgan started the other way.

"I could've picked that up yesterday," Levi stated.

"No." Elizabeth smiled. "I just don't like Dad riding anymore. It's much easier on him if he takes the buggy," she explained in a whisper.

Levi nodded his head and smiled. He then stood and took his last sip of coffee and looked at Elizabeth. "Well, I might as well get Crimson saddled and get on the trail myself," he stated.

"What do ya mean yourself? Are ya forgetting someone?" she asked, a little worried.

"No, I just thought it might be a little risky and ..."

"Risky, ya mean dangerous! Well, I want ya to know I'll do anything I can to protect this ranch. If it requires a little risky business, then it's my duty. Besides, you need me as a guide. Ya told me so last night."

"Okay, okay, ya know, you sure are pretty when you're excited." Levi smiled. "I just thought … I just don't want anything to happen to ya," he stated. He placed both hands on her shoulders and pulled her close.

Elizabeth smiled as Levi stepped back. "I'll go saddle the horses, and if ya got a canteen, let's take it with us." He turned toward the door and headed down the back steps toward the barn.

Ricardo had just finished harnessing a mare to a two-passenger—three, if you're really friendly—black buggy with a small area on the back for storage, like a "Sunday-go-to-meetin' rig."

"Ricardo, buenos dias," Levi greeted.

"Ah, buenos dias, Señor Levi," he replied with a smile.

"Donde me y Señorita Morgan's caballos?" Levi asked.

"Ah, the corral, *Señor*," Ricardo replied.

"If ya like, I'll run them to the barn," Ricardo suggested in his broken English.

"Great, that'll be *bueno, gracias*," Levi replied.

Ricardo, out to please, took off in a run toward the barn and then remembered that Mr. Morgan's mare was not tied.

As Ricardo looked back, Levi spoke. "I'll tie her off." Ricardo smiled and continued on his way through the barn and into the corral.

Levi walked over to the rear of the buggy, where a round block of iron laid. The piece of iron was attached to a four-foot rope. Picking up the block, he carried it to the front of the horse and dropped it on the ground. He tied the rope through a ring at the bit of the harness and then headed to the barn.

Ricardo had herded the horses in and was in the process of saddling Elizabeth's mare as Crimson stood nearby. "Señor, your animal, he is *magnifico*," Ricardo said.

"Gracias, gracias," Levi replied with the pride of a new father as he reached for the bridle.

"Wait, *Señor*, I will do it," Ricardo stated.

"No, that's okay, Ricardo." Levi smiled. "I can do it, *gracias*."

They were both coming from the barn leading the horses as Elizabeth and Mr. Morgan came from the house. Mr. Morgan boarded the carriage as Elizabeth untied the hobble and carried it to the back of the buggy. "Dad, be careful," she said as he drove away. He smiled and waved, but no vocal reply was given.

"What have ya got in the saddlebags?" Levi asked.

"Well," Elizabeth replied with a lighthearted smile, "you said bring the canteen, so I thought maybe some cold chicken-fried chicken would be good too."

A look of satisfaction crossed Levi's face. "That's a good idea. I like the way you think," he responded. "I knew ya were good for something."

Elizabeth smiled. Oddly enough, she understood this different kind of humor that came from this stranger, who she did consider perfect. She threw the saddlebags across her horse and quickly tied them down with a leather strap. She mounted as her vigorous and well-bred mare took a few steps forward.

Levi was already in the saddle. "You ready?" he asked. She nodded.

"Vámonos," he added as the two horses start off down the trail.

A couple of hours had passed, and a lot of ground had been covered. A picturesque view of some pretty large hills and trees came in view as they crossed a rocky stream. The scenery kept changing, and the sights got more beautiful as they traveled on. Levi had covered this territory many times before but had never stopped to smell the roses. Love would do funny things to one's mind.

"Why don't we stop at this pond and water the horses?" Levi suggested.

"Sounds good to me."

"Where's that canteen? I think I could use a drink myself," he stated as he swung down from Crimson's back.

"We've got the stream right here at the neck of the pond. The water will be cooler than the canteen, don't ya think?" she replied.

Levi smiled. "Yeah, you're right. Lead the way," he said as he dropped the reins to the ground, and Crimson took a few steps forward to quench his thirst.

Only a few paces away from this wide spot in the stream, the springwater was trickling down among the rocks. "This water's not cool. It's cold," he stated as he kneeled and took a big gulp from his cupped hands.

"I always stop here. That little old trickling stream just sounds peaceful, and it's always cold and wet." She smiled. "What do ya hope to find? What are ya looking for?" she asked. "You said ya hoped to show me something. Ya must have something in mind."

"Well, do ya know where there's a box canyon and a good-sized creek coming down through it?" he asked. He knew a question like that would be giving Elizabeth room for more questions.

"Sure, I know where it is. But how did you know?" she asked. "Well, let's go straight there."

Levi reached for her hand. "If we find what I think we'll find, then maybe there'll be enough evidence so that you'll believe what I have to tell ya," he answered.

"Levi, I can't believe you'd say that. You should know I trust ya with all my heart. I would believe anything ya tell me." Elizabeth clutched Levi's hands and spoke with deep sincerity.

"Pretty, I love you too very much, and I don't want to jeopardize that trust. Something I need to tell ya, you may have a hard time understanding. It might cause doubt in your mind, and believe me, that's an understatement."

She looked at Levi and smiled. "Okay."

"Well, *vámonos, Señorita*," Levi said with a smile and a Mexican accent. The two remounted and headed on down the small cattle trail, weaving their way through the rocky terrain.

Levi took the lead, not following behind Elizabeth as he had done the first part of their trip. He figured Elizabeth needed to feel confident that he knew as much about the ranch as she did. *Even if she is open-minded and well educated, and she does trust me completely,* he thought to himself, *it still doesn't mean she would believe any of this story I'm going to tell her. Nothing like this has ever come up before. She doesn't even have television to be exposed to any ideas like this. I know she's gonna think I'm crazy. I'd probably have a hard time convincing H. G. Wells under these conditions.* Many thoughts poured through Levi's mind as they trudged on toward the canyon. The heavy flow of the white water coming from the creek sounded loud enough to be a roaring river. The two of them reached the mouth of the canyon. The winding trail alongside the creek was well-worn. Levi was feeling more confident that the man-made opening would already be in place behind the falls. Elizabeth had also noticed that the trail was well used. The gradual incline and rough terrain had made for a slow ride up the dead-end canyon. The loud roar of the waterfall had cut conversation out completely as the two reached the small pond at the base of this majestic waterfall.

"Are ya ready?" Levi yelled over the roar.

With a surprised look, she shouted, "Ready for what?"

Levi stepped down from his horse. Elizabeth followed suit. He then laid back against a large rock and proceeded to remove his boots.

"Levi, are ya goin' swimmin'?" she asked. He smiled as he placed the boots in his saddlebags and then walked over to Elizabeth.

Placing his hands on her shoulders, he pulled her close so she could hear him over the roar. "I'm going to check something behind that waterfall. Wait here."

Elizabeth just nodded to confirm the request. Levi started across the pond. The water only reached a few inches above his waist as he faded into the falls. The time seemed to stop as Elizabeth waited for Levi. *What could he be doing in that water? How could he stay so long?* As the thoughts ran through her mind, she stepped into the water and moved as fast as possible toward the falls.

She decided to dive for his rescue when Levi appeared through the flowing curtain. "Levi!" she yelled and fell into his arms.

"I was afraid," she cried softly into his ear as Levi held her tight.

"I'm okay, I'm okay," he whispered as the spray covered a warm kiss. "Hey, pretty, I found what I wanted to show ya!" Levi yelled as he turned toward the falls.

She placed her hand on his cheek and turned his face toward her as the spray covered them both. "I like that name," she said, looking deep into his eyes.

"It's a natural for you. When anyone looks it up in the dictionary, there should be a picture of you." She smiled and pulled him to her lips as their bodies were drenched from the falls.

"You found something in there?" she questioned in a loud tone and wiped the spray from her eyes.

"Yeah, it's a cave!" he shouted.

"It's a what?" she yelled back.

Levi pointed to the horses. He grabbed Elizabeth's hand, and they moved toward the bank. As they reached the edge of the pool, away from the waterfall, Levi explained, "There's a cave behind that curtain of water. I'm sure that's how they're takin' your cattle."

"Who's takin' the cattle? The Tanners? You're sayin' they're rustlin' our cattle through a waterfall!" Elizabeth shouted.

"I don't have any real proof yet, and I don't know how they're gettin 'em off their ranch." Levi said under his breath,

"Boy, if they just had an eighteen-wheeler rig, I'd sure know."

"If they had a what?" Elizabeth asked.

"Aaahh, I said those cattle-stealing pigs, I don't know how they're getting rid of 'em," he explained, and then in a serious tone, he said, "Elizabeth."

"What happened to 'pretty'?" she interrupted jokingly.

"Okay, pretty." He smiled. "While we're this close to the Tanner Ranch, I want to look around a little. Would ya be okay for just a little while?" he asked.

"You mean wait here? I will not. I'm going with ya," she pleaded.

"All right, all right," he yielded. "We might have a little trouble with the horses, so hang on to those reins real tight, and watch your step. There's a foot or so step up into that cave, okay?"

"Okay, I'm right behind ya."

Levi, leading the way, had crossed the pool and was being pounded by the rushing falls as he disappeared. Then Crimson followed his master without hesitation as Levi held a firm grip on the reins, and they both faded out of sight.

Elizabeth was only steps behind Crimson, and she too followed with no hesitation. Her horse showed some reluctance and reared her head as the water pounded her, but Elizabeth held tight, and the mare calmed with the firm control of her mistress.

The cave was not very deep, and after twenty or thirty yards of darkness, the sunlight could be seen down the narrow tunnel. The ceiling was high enough for the horses to stand tall, but Elizabeth's horse was still skittish. The roar of the falls was amplified and echoed through the cave. Levi led the way through the knee-deep water. The tunnel widened, and the stream only flowed ankle-deep as they reached the entrance. He swung up on Crimson as Elizabeth stepped from the cave.

"You're not going to put on your boots?" Elizabeth asked as she mounted.

"No, I think I'll wait till we go back through," he explained in a whisper.

Elizabeth took heed. "Well, you're right so far. This is Tanner property," she commented in a lower tone.

"Yeah, that was the easy part. Now we've got to find something incriminating. Vamos," he said as Crimson took a fast start.

Elizabeth followed as Levi started down the shallow-graded path beside the newly discovered stream. As they reached the bottom of the hill, Levi turned north, following the most beaten path. The rocky terrain hid a lot of secrets, but the path was clear enough for his eye to see he was on the right trail. They rounded a bend, and a small meadow appeared. A pretty substantial catch pen blocked the trail.

"Hey, hey, hey, as Yogi would say. I think we've found a clue," Levi stated, mimicking the famous voice.

"It's just a corral. That doesn't mean anything," Elizabeth commented.

"You've got to admit this is not a normal place for a corral," Levi remarked in the Yogi Bear accent, sounding a little cocky and proud of his discovery.

"You sure sound funny, but you're right. This ain't a good spot for a corral," Elizabeth acknowledged.

"Wait a minute. I didn't say this wasn't a good spot for a corral. I just said it wasn't a normal place for a corral. It's in a good location for what I think it's used for," he stated.

"Maybe they don't use it anymore," she commented.

"Are ya kiddin'? This pen couldn't be two years old. It's in perfect shape. Look at that," Levi added.

"At what?"

"That campfire. I'll bet it's no more than a week old," he stated very confidently.

"It doesn't mean anything. Anyone coming up here to check on the herd would start a campfire, maybe not to cook but at least to keep away the wolves and the coyotes," she reasoned.

"Yeah, I know what you're saying, but what I'm saying is why is there a catch pen up here to start with? There's no reason to have one so far from the main activity, unless no one is supposed to see it."

"What do ya mean?" she asked.

"They've got to be up to no good with a pen up here. Maybe it's here to keep it from their dad. Y'all keep tellin' me that the old man wouldn't put up with any foul play." Levi kept talking as he swung down from Crimson's back. "So ... they rustle your cattle and bring 'em through that old mining tunnel, and then they're kept in this pen till they can."

"Watch your step," Elizabeth spoke out. Levi was paying no attention to where he stepped, while his mind was in deep thought.

"Oh yeah, thanks," he said as he stepped to the side, dodging some large piles of cow patties. "Okay, what do ya think? They leave 'em here till they sell. Doesn't that make sense?"

"Well, it does make sense, I guess," she stated. "But who would they sell 'em to? There's no one around here, and they sure couldn't risk 'em on a cattle drive."

Levi looked around and wandered over to the railing. "You can sure tell this pen's been used a lot. Just look at all the tracks," he commented as he lifted his foot to the fence rail. He quickly pulled it back from the rough wood, forgetting for a moment he was without boots.

"Levi, is that branding iron broke?"

"What branding iron?" he asked as he looked around.

"Right there, hanging on the side of that post," she answered as she pointed toward a corner post on the catch pen.

"It sure looks broke. Half of the ring's missing. How could they do that? They sure must have some tough cows," Levi jokingly commented as he walked over to the post. He looked the iron over. "No, it's not broke. It was made like this. They sure have an odd-looking logo."

Elizabeth had slipped down from her horse as Levi walked up with the branding iron. "That's not the Tanner brand. They've always used the circle T. Are ya sure it's not broken?" she questioned.

"No, it's too smooth. Even if it was their T, it would be too long." Levi pressed the iron in the sandy soil as he spoke. "Besides, I've never seen a branding iron this large."

"You're right, that's what's wrong. It's bigger than a normal-sized iron," Elizabeth agreed.

"Ya know," Levi paused, "if ya put ..." He bent to a squat and filled in the Morgan logo, the Rocking M, at the opening in the stencil.

"*TM*," Elizabeth blurted out.

"No. *MT*, Matthew Tanner," Levi proclaimed as he looked up at Elizabeth.

"But that's not their brand. How could they get by with that?"

"I think the sheriff told me the Tanner boys changed the name over the entrance of their ranch," Levi recalled.

"That's true. When Mr. Tanner had that stroke, the boys changed it to the Matthew Tanner Ranch. It used to be called the Circle T, but nobody mentioned the brand was changed," she stated.

"Well, this looks like a homemade brand," Levi speculated.

Elizabeth laughed. "You're right, Mr. Garza didn't make it. He's our blacksmith in Dorado and does real pretty work."

"I think I'll take this branding iron back to the ranch and show your dad," Levi stated as he walked over to Crimson. Levi mounted with the iron in one hand and looked over at Elizabeth.

"Didn't someone say it was about three years ago when old man Tanner had that stroke?" he asked.

"Yeah, it's been about three years," she confirmed.

"Ain't that about the same time y'all started losing cattle?" Levi asked as the two started back toward the cave.

"Yeah, it sure was. I remember when Dad found the first bunch of cattle missing. He went into town to talk to the sheriff. But Mr. Gore had ridden out to the Tanners with Doc. Mr. Tanner was real sick. Dad rode out there too. That was the same time," Elizabeth recalled.

As they reached the trail leading back to the cave, Levi spotted thirty-five or forty head grazing in a meadow just below.

"Wait here for a minute. I'm gonna check the branding out on those cattle," he stated as he started down the hill.

Elizabeth scanned the open hillside as a lookout would. It was open country, and the meadow could be seen from a half mile away. But the questions raised were strong enough to entice the devil down that hill. Her post was soon forgotten, and she turned her horse down the open slope. Levi had reached the small herd and was checking brands as Elizabeth rode up. "Why didn't ya wait? We could be spotted from a long way off. At least ya could've gotten away if some of 'em came ridin' up." Elizabeth scanned the valley and then the ridges as she listened to Levi preach in her direction. "Well, while you're here, you might as well take a look at these brands." Elizabeth slid down from her horse as the horse took a few restrained steps down the vertical grade. "They're fresh. They haven't completely healed. Except for the M and the bottom of this circle," he explained.

"That's our Rocking M, all right," she confirmed, while looking at the bottom of the makeshift brand. "These are our cattle." She ran back to her horse and remounted. "Let's go get 'em!" The overwhelming evidence had broken her whisper.

"Wait a minute." Levi tried to hold a low tone. "Where ya think you're going?" he asked as he grabbed her reins.

"I can't believe those bastards have made me go through this torment for three years. Boys I went to school with and grew up with made Dad go through all the problems with the bank. I just want to kill 'em!" she cried.

"Hey, pretty, slow down. Calm down a minute. I've been saying they're guilty for fifteen minutes. What's got ya so worked up now?" asked Levi.

"Well, I guess it just sunk in. I just got convinced. I always had a little doubt, I guess," she explained. "I'm sorry, I lost my head."

"Are ya okay?" he asked as he stood by her horse, patting her leg but still holding the reins.

"I'm okay," she answered as she nodded.

"Okay, let's get off this property. It makes me nervous," Levi said. With some relief, the two started back up the long open stretch of hillside. They reached the flat and then blended in among the large boulders and trees as they made their way back to the cave entrance. They both dismounted, and Levi led the way back up stream through the dismal damp tunnel. As they neared the falls, the roar intensified. The large echo chamber amplified the rumble as Levi hurried into the pounding water. Elizabeth was only a few feet behind as he approached the edge of the pool. He placed his bare foot in the stirrup and swung aboard.

"I think I'll wait till I dry out a little before I put those boots back on," he commented.

"Good idea," Elizabeth agreed as she swung over the saddle. "You think I should fill this canteen?"

"I don't think I want to see any more water today," Levi commented as he turned her way and smiled.

The ride back was in a faster pace, and the two riders covered a lot of ground at the first hour. Not many words were spoken until they reached the small stream, where they had stopped a few hours before.

"Hey, pretty, let's stop, okay? We can let the horses drink, and I think I'm halfway dry. I'd like to get my boots back on."

"Sure," she answered as she stepped down. "Levi, you knew that cave was there, didn't ya?"

"Well, I, aaaahh, thought it might be," he answered, knowing more questions were to follow.

"Elizabeth," he said as he stood, after pulling up his boots.

"Maybe it's time I told you about me."

Elizabeth was looking straight into his eyes. "I wish you would. I just don't know what to think. Please talk to me. Maybe I should say something first. It may make yours easier. I love you very much, and no matter what you tell me, I'll still love you. Okay?"

"Okay," Levi smiled, "but what I'm going to say isn't bad. You're just not going to believe me. I think that's why I've been putting this off. I hate for you to think I'm crazy," he stated.

"I trust ya completely. Have a little faith in me."

"Okay, here goes." Levi paused. "Maybe you'd better sit down."

"Levi, just tell me. I'm not sitting down," she proclaimed.

"All right … boy, I really don't know where to start," he said with a concerned look. His mind searched for the right words. "I guess I should start with my name. My real name is Calahan, not Calman. It's Levi Calahan." Elizabeth looked on calmly without a word. "You know what 'the future' means?"

"What?" she answered, confused, with a blank stare.

"You know, the future, like what's going to happen next year or what are your plans for the future?" he asked.

"Levi, just tell me something. Don't ask me riddles," she answered, somewhat annoyed and puzzled. "Of course, I know what future means."

"Okay, okay, I'm trying. I'm from the future," he blurted out. Not a word came from Elizabeth. She just stared at him with a dumbfounded look.

"You know Tom Junior's little boy, Levi? He's my great-great-grandfather. I wasn't born till nineteen sixty-one, not eighteen something but nineteen sixty-one." Elizabeth still only stared at Levi. "I don't know how I got here.

I think I know why I'm here. I think I'm here 'cause I knew about that cave, and I knew about the Tanners. I knew you'd think I was crazy. Don't ya?" Levi asked.

"I think I will sit down." Elizabeth was in sort of a daze as Levi helped her over to the large rock where he had put on his boots.

"Pretty, I knew this would be hard for ya to swallow. That's why it was hard for me to tell ya. But if ya can just keep an open mind, I think I can give ya enough answers that you'll be convinced," he pleaded.

Elizabeth, collecting herself, straightened up and looked at him. "I've been thinking about what you're saying. Mind ya, I'm not saying I understood ya, but I'm not saying I don't believe ya either. Let me just think about it for a minute," she answered.

"Fair enough," Levi commented as he walked over to Crimson to give Elizabeth room to think. She stared at the ground, and then she stared at Levi and then back at the ground.

Levi started pacing like an expectant father. "Elizabeth, I can tell ya more things. I'm sure I can convince ya," he stated.

Elizabeth's eyes raised to find Levi perched at her feet and his hands on her knees. Then her head came erect, and she placed her hands on top of Levi's hands. "There're enough things already," she said with a smile. "I knew ya couldn't be from here. I do believe you."

Levi, still holding Elizabeth's hands, rose with her. Their eyes never wavered as he took her in his arms and caressed her for several moments.

"I'm sure glad ya didn't try to tell my dad this story. He'd probably have both of us put away." They both laughed still holding hands.

"Hey, how about a piece of that chicken-fried chicken? I think I just got my appetite back," Levi said as he rubbed his belly and smiled.

"That sounds great." Elizabeth had a new appetite of her own. She retrieved the food from the saddlebags. Soon chicken bones were being tossed, and the canteen was emptied. The short break was over, and they walked over to the horses, where Levi tied down the saddlebags.

Elizabeth stuck one foot in the stirrup and ascended into the saddle. "You don't have a wife waiting for ya in the twentieth century, do ya?" she asked as a concerned look came to her face.

Levi smiled. "No, ma'am," he answered as he crossed his heart. Elizabeth smiled also. He walked over to Crimson and mounted.

"Vámonos," he said as Crimson briskly started up a small incline.

Elizabeth was following close behind. "I don't think it's all hit me yet. I keep thinking of things to ask ya. This sure opens up a lot of questions for me," she remarked.

"Like what? What do ya want to ask me?" he questioned.

Elizabeth came up alongside Levi as they headed down the trail. "Well, like how are the women? How do they dress?" Levi smiled. "Do they act any different from me? Do they all ride better than me, or do they all ride sidesaddle?" she asked. "You know all the ladies in Europe ride that way."

"Wait a minute, wait a minute. Wow, how many questions did ya ask? I did catch that they were all about women." Levi shook his head. "Well, if they're out like this, they'd probably wear the same—jeans, a shirt, and boots. I've seen very few who could ride a horse like you can. They may act a little different, but the times are different," he answered.

"What do ya mean different?"

"Well." Levi paused, collecting his thoughts. "They can vote in elections."

Elizabeth's face had a la-di-da look. "That's good! I knew it was coming. You could tell by all of that equal-rights stuff they talked about in college when we were studying the Great American Conflict of 1860. Go ahead," she said.

"Yeah, we call that the Civil War."

"Really? Some people I know would say they were two different countries in that fight. But anyway, tell me more. I was only ten when they stopped fighting." Her inquisitive mind was anxious to hear more.

"Well, most women work outside the home. I mean, there're more women in offices than there are men," he stated.

"You mean the men stay home?" she questioned.

"No, no, that's not what I meant." Levi laughed. "More men work in factories and plants and do outside construction work, aaah, and outside sales," he answered.

"Outside sales?" she asked.

"You know, aaahh, like maybe you'd say a traveling salesman," he explained with a chuckle.

"Oh, kinda like John Gates," she compared.

"Like who?"

"John Gates. He's our traveling salesman. He comes by every few months and puts on demonstrations and sells barbed wire. Most of the people around here weren't in favor of barbed wire at first. He was almost a dead salesman, rather than a traveling salesman." She laughed as she told the story.

Levi smiled too as he listened. He was happy that they got along so well and could talk so freely. He was amazed that she has accepted him without any reservations. All of a sudden, his face lit up. "Gates! John Gates! I know him! Well, I mean, I've read about 'im. You really know 'im?" he questioned.

"Sure, I know 'im. He comes by every couple of months. What did ya read about 'im?" she asked. "He's just a barbed wire salesman."

"Well, he was a moneyman behind *Spindletop*." Elizabeth had an unknowing look about her. "That's one of the largest oil strikes ever," Levi stated. He recalled the information from a Texan history lesson. "I don't remember what year that oil strike happened, but we'll be around to see it. Then I can say, 'I told ya so.'" Levi laughed, and Elizabeth smiled. He sounded as though he wasn't planning to leave, and that made her happy. "Hey, maybe I'll be the one who tells him to put his money into an oil-drilling venture in Beaumont, Texas. That should at least make us a partner, huh?" The two pondered over good thoughts, and their troubles took a backseat for a few seconds.

"You know, I may not own the Calahan Ranch now, but there's a lot of people maybe I could encourage, you know, plant ideas for some of the things that will be invented. Elizabeth, you're not going to believe some of the … no, you're not going to believe *most* of the things that's happened in the last hundred years." Elizabeth looked on with contentment as Levi rambled on. "Every evening, when we're sittin' out in that swing, I'll tell ya about a hundred new things ya won't believe."

"Levi, it sounds like you're gonna miss a lot of things. It won't mean as much to me because I've never seen it. But you … you're gonna have an emptiness, and I won't know what to do," she stated sympathetically.

"Well, you're probably right. I might miss some of those things, but I've had a bad emptiness all my life," Levi paused, "which you've filled."

Elizabeth smiled as she heard Levi's words. The two continued to ride at a pretty good pace as she listened to Levi's carrying on. He filled her head with things she didn't really understand. The time passed fast, and soon they reached the ranch house.

Mr. Morgan was in the barn talking to Ricardo as the two rode up. "Elizabeth, I don't think we should say anything to your dad about me right now," Levi said under his breath. They stepped down from their horses.

"Huh? Oh yeah, I agree. Let's just tell 'im about the cave we just found and the branding iron."

"Okay but not in front of Ricardo. Call him over here," Levi whispered. They tied off the horses at the rail in front of the barn.

"Hey, what's that y'all are whispering about?" Mr. Morgan shouted with a smile as he walked from the barn.

"We've got something to show ya, Dad. Come over here."

Mr. Morgan handed a mended harness to Ricardo and walked toward the two. Ricardo continued his chores. "What's up? Did ya find something?" He noticed the serious look on their faces.

Levi reached back behind his saddle and untied the branding iron as Elizabeth began her story. "Dad, do ya know where the big falls are in the box canyon?"

"Sure," he replied.

"Well, behind that waterfall is a cave," Elizabeth started.

"Really," Mr. Morgan interrupted. "Are ya sure?"

"Dad, we went through it," she explained.

"I never knew that," he stated, astonished.

"Well, that's not all. Levi, tell 'im what ya found."

Levi, standing with the branding iron in his hand, started to explain. "Well, sir, as we came out of the cave on the other side of the mountain, we were on the Tanner Ranch."

"Yeah, that would be right," Mr. Morgan agreed.

"We followed some cattle tracks up a trail to the north about three or four hundred yards and rounded a bend, and there was a fairly new catch pen and a pretty good pile of new ashes. Somebody had been doing some branding," Levi stated.

He showed Mr. Morgan the iron. "Have you ever seen a Tanner branding iron like this one?" Levi asked as Mr. Morgan took the iron.

"Well, it's the circle T, but it's just not a full circle," Mr. Morgan confirmed.

"Well, ya see, it's a little bigger than a normal branding iron," Levi stated.

"Yeah, it is a little big," the elderly Morgan agreed.

"It has to be larger to halfway match up to a brand after it's stretched on a full-sized steer. Look how long the T is. It's out of proportion," Levi added.

"Yeah, but what does it prove? It doesn't prove anything," Mr. Morgan questioned.

"Wait a minute, Dad," Elizabeth butted in. "Let Levi finish."

"Okay, okay."

Levi squatted and took his index finger to draw the Morgan logo in the sand. "Here's your Rocking M, Mr. Morgan," Levi stated. He stood and took the branding iron by the handle from Mr. Morgan. Levi pressed the iron in the sand and pulled it back.

"*MT*, Matthew Tanner. But what is that? It's not the Tanner brand. They just use a circle T on their cattle," Mr. Morgan defended.

"Dad, we saw forty to fifty head with this brand on 'em," Elizabeth stated as she pointed down at the drawing.

"And the main thing, sir, was that the *T* was freshly burned, but the Rocking M was well healed."

Mr. Morgan turned toward the house. "Where ya going, Dad?" Elizabeth asked. She could tell her dad was upset.

"I guess there's only one place to go, baby. I'm going to get my gun and confront that son of Matthew Tanner's. He's got to be the bastard who's been stealing our cattle."

"Wait a minute, Mr. Morgan. I think we need to plan this out before we jump into the fire." Levi tried to console Mr. Morgan as they both walked toward the house.

Elizabeth was only a few steps behind and could hear her dad speak. "Have ya got something in mind, young fellow?"

"Well, yes, sir. I was thinking—"

"If you're thinking about Amos Gore, you can forget it," Mr. Morgan interrupted in a low tone.

Levi, trying to keep his cool, said, "No, sir … at least not right now. I was thinking about the other ranchers. I thought I might ride over and talk to Mr. Calahan and Mr. Cagle and get their opinion first. But the only way I can see going up against the Tanner bunch is to have every man with a gun from the Calahan and the Cagle ranches and all of your men too." Mr. Morgan began to calm down as he listened to Levi talk. "And then we get the sheriff to go along to serve the papers on those boys."

"Well, it sounds like you've been thinking this thing out. But

I'm not sure how my neighbors would feel about gettin' involved in my fight," stated Mr. Morgan.

"It's not just your fight, Mr. Morgan. These Tanner boys are a problem for everybody. You think they're going to stop when they steal everything from you? They'll find a way to start in on the Cagle cattle or the Calahan's," Levi explained.

"I suppose you're right. I guess I'll ride over and talk to Tom first," Mr. Morgan commented.

"Levi, would ya mind ridin' over with me?" he added.

Levi smiled. "Not at all." He now felt accepted as he answered Mr. Morgan's request. Elizabeth watched with pride as the two men she loved planned their strategy.

"Let me get my gun. I don't think I've had it out in years," Mr. Morgan commented. He walked toward the house.

"Now I know where ya get that fast-draw temper of yours," Levi said smiling as he waited alongside Elizabeth.

Only seconds had passed when a deafening blast echoed through the screen door. "My God, what was that? It sounded like a shot!" Levi yelled. He entered the doorway at a dead run toward Mr. Morgan's room.

"Oh, Dad! Oh my God, what's happened?" Elizabeth cried as she ran in Levi's steps.

Mr. Morgan was bent over the foot of the bed, holding on to the bedpost, when Levi reached his side. "Mr. Morgan! What is it? What happened?" Levi shouted.

Mr. Morgan tried to straighten as Elizabeth came flying through the door. "Dad, what is it?" she asked. But her heart was already relieved when she saw he was still standing.

"This damn pistol of mine. The chamber was stuck. I was trying to free it when ..." He limped around the corner of the bed.

"Oh, Dad, you're shot!" Elizabeth shouted as the blood soaked his jeans just below his knee.

"Let me help ya on to the bed, Ben," Levi said.

He put Mr. Morgan's arm over his shoulder and eased him on to the bed. Mr. Morgan just looked at Levi with a smile. Levi had finally called him Ben. "Just lie down, and I'll go into town and get the doc," Levi suggested.

At that instant, Ricardo came charging into the room. "I hear a shot, Señor," he said.

"Dad's gun went off, Ricardo. Would ya ride into town and get Doc Jones?" Elizabeth asked. Ricardo pulled off his hat and held it with both hands.

"Si, Miss Elizabeth, mucho pronto," he answered.

"Elizabeth, why don't ya get a towel or something to keep this blood off the bed," Levi suggested.

"Sure," she answered and scampered out the door. Carmita was coming in as Elizabeth was going out. "Carmita, heat some water. Did Ricardo tell ya Dad shot himself in the leg?" Elizabeth excitedly asked.

"*Si*, he told me. I will heat the water right away," she answered.

Levi was holding up Ben's right leg when Elizabeth returned.

"Right here?" she asked, placing the towel on the bed.

"Perfect," he replied. Laying the leg down, Levi reached into his pocket and pulled out a small knife. The blade was very sharp and cut through the jeans easily. "I think we'll cut these jeans off a little above the knee, and that should give the doctor room enough to work." "How does it look?" Elizabeth asked.

"Well, I don't think it's too bad. It went in here and out over here, so the bullet's not in there. It's not bleeding too bad. How does it feel, Ben?"

"Oh, it's okay. It doesn't really feel too bad."

"It's probably not gonna be sore till tomorrow," Levi speculated.

"Levi, why don't ya let Elizabeth show ya the way to the Calahan Ranch and—" Ben started talking.

"Wait a minute, Dad. I'm not leaving till the doc says you're gonna be all right. Ya just quit thinking about those Tanner boys for a little while."

"She's right, Ben. It's gettin' dark anyway. One more day won't matter. Those Tanner boys will still be around tomorrow," Levi commented. "I think that wound has bled enough. I'm gonna stick a tourniquet on your thigh, sorta loose till the doc gets here, Ben."

"Whatever ya think, son, go ahead," Ben replied. Elizabeth looked at Levi and raised her eyebrows and smiled.

"Get me the whiskey bottle, Prre—Elizabeth," Levi said as he rolled his eyes at her.

Elizabeth grinned and scurried out. She was back in seconds with the bottle of whiskey.

Levi took the cap off as Ben reached for the bottle. "This is for the wound," Levi stated as he poured a little on the bullet hole.

"Oh," he cried with a pained frown. "Don't waste it down there. Give it to me!" he shouted.

Levi smiled. "Well, I guess ya need it too." He handed Ben the bottle.

Ben downed a big gulp. "Uuuhh, that's whatcha do with whiskey," he stated.

"I think he's gonna be all right." Levi smiled.

Another hour passed before the doctor arrived. Elizabeth was standing at the foot of the bed when Doc Jones came through the door. "Oh, Doc, come on in. I think Dad's fallen asleep."

"Well, good. He must not be in too much pain. It looks like you've been playing doctor, Elizabeth. You did a fine job," the doctor replied as he undid the bandage.

"No, not me, Doc. Levi did that," she explained.

"Oh, so you're Levi. I fixed one of your casualties yesterday, didn't I?" he remarked with a smile. "It's a pleasure to meet you."
"Well, thanks, Doc. It's nice meeting you."

The doctor, still dressing the wound, looked down at Ben's drowsy eyes looking back at him. "Pop, you'd better keep this young fellow around. He could have saved me a trip out here. Levi, maybe you can keep an eye on this for me. If I don't hear from you tomorrow, I'll be back Thursday to check on Pop." He finished the new bandage.

"That's fine, Doc. I'll keep a close eye on it tomorrow," Levi replied.

The doc picked up his bag and walked back over to Ben. "Pop, you just take it easy for a few days. Let these young folks do all your walking, and I'll be back on Thursday," he stated. Ben nodded as the doc patted his hand and walked outside. Levi and Elizabeth followed Doc Jones out on to the porch.

"Elizabeth, he's going to be fine," the doctor said as he grasped her arm.

"Thanks a lot, Doc."

"Yeah, Doc. We really appreciate ya coming out," Levi added.

"Well, you already had it under control, but you're welcome anyway. I'll see y'all Thursday." With his old black bag in one hand, he walked down the front path to his carriage.

As the doctor rode out of sight, Elizabeth clutched Levi's hand.

"Why don't we sit out here for a little while?" she suggested.

"Sounds good to me," he responded. He walked across to the old wood swing, which had become a special place for them.

"I'll check on Dad and be right back."

"Don't be long," he said with a devilish smile. She opened the screen door and smiled back, shaking her head.

She found her dad fast asleep and Carmita cleaning up the mess the doctor had made. "Carmita, go on home to Ricardo. We can do this in the morning," she said in a whisper. Carmita smiled, picked up a few things in her arms, and walked out ahead of Elizabeth. Elizabeth eased the door closed and walked to the kitchen behind Carmita.

"Mr. Ben, he will be okay, no?" Carmita asked.

"Sure, he will. He's going to be fine," Elizabeth reassured her.

Carmita opened the back screen door.

"Hasta mañana," she said. "Hasta mañana," Elizabeth replied. She walked back through the dimly lit parlor and opened the screen door. It seemed to squeak louder than usual. Only the crickets could be heard on this bright, warm summer night. Levi lay back in one corner of the swing with his arm across the back.

Elizabeth walked up to the swing. "You look tired," she commented.

"I don't know why. It's been a perfectly calm day," he replied as he raised his head and sat up in the swing.

"You know, I love you," she said as she sat down beside him.

His hand tightened against her shoulder. "You know," he started as Elizabeth looked up and smiled, "I love you too." Their eyes fixed, and Levi pulled her closer as they kissed. Their blood ran very warm for several minutes; the two felt just perfect for each other.

Elizabeth straightened up. "Oh, we've got to slow down. That makes me feel weak all over."

"What do ya think you do to me?" Levi questioned.

Elizabeth smiled. "I hate to change the subject, but what will we do now? Dad's in no condition to stand up to the Tanners."

"Pretty, your dad doesn't need to be standing up to the Tanners. I'll ride over to the Calahans in the morning, and if Tom feels like I think he'll feel, we'll ride on over and talk to the Cagles. It'll all work out. I promise." Levi smiled as he reassured Elizabeth.

"Oh, Levi, I don't know what would've ever happened to us if ya hadn't come here," she cried softly as he hugged her tight.

"Well, I am here. So don't worry about it. Everything's gonna be all right." He smiled. "Now let's talk about something better, like us. Hey, you know what? Tomorrow if your dad's feeling okay, you can ride with me to the Calahans. We'll go by my Bronco. You'll see something that'll really be different," Levi added, and his face lit up.

"I've seen a lot of wild horses. What makes this one so different?"

Levi smiled. "This one's got four … wheels," he stated.

"What?" she questioned.

"It's not a horse. It's a truck, a vehicle," Levi started to explain. Elizabeth looked confused. "It's like a wagon, but you don't need a horse to pull it. It moves by itself and much faster too."

"Then maybe it won't still be there. Did you tie it up?" she questioned.

"No, it's not like that. You have to start it. It's pulled by an engine," he explained.

Elizabeth looked hard at Levi. "That's cruel. A horse would be better than an Indian. I think it would even go faster with a horse," Elizabeth stated.

"What? No, I didn't mean an Indian. I mean an engine, a motor, like a … steam engine, you know, like a train has," he explained.

"Oh, like a train engine. I know what you mean now. I wasn't thinking of something so big," she stated.

"Oh, I know. It's something you've never seen, so how could ya know what I was talking about. But it's much smaller than a train. You'll see it in the morning. I think you'll be impressed," Levi explained.

"Just thinking about it, I probably won't sleep at all," she pondered out loud.

"I'd sure like to take ya to my time. There's so much that's changed over the next hundred years," Levi reminisced.

"Yeah, I know, some of the stories Dad's told me and things I learned in school about the last hundred years, you know, like all of our conveniences," Elizabeth said sincerely.

Levi's eyes rolled back as he smiled to himself.

"Well, I guess it's about the same kind of thing, a lot of easier ways to do things. I was just thinking about all the little things, like the small appliances that help in the kitchen. But that would be hard to explain without going back to electricity," Levi rambled.

"Electricity! I've seen it. They had it on the streetlamps back east in the evenings," she replied proudly.

"Oh, okay. That makes it easier. That same electricity is now, I mean, will soon be in every home. You can walk into every room and just flip a switch, and the room lights up," he explained.

"Wow, I guess that is something to see," Elizabeth remarked.

"Well, that's just a straw in a huge bale of hay," he stated. "We'll have a lifetime together to talk about it." Levi smiled. "That is, if you'll have me."

Elizabeth paused with a sexy grin. "Oh, you know I will. You just try to get away," she smartly replied. Levi looked into her eyes and pulled her close. He began kissing her, and her arms fed around his neck as the passion ran unhampered.

"Oh, Levi, I love you so much," she whispered passionately in his ear.

Levi pulled back as he looked into her eyes. "I love you twice that much." As Levi remembered the heavy schedule for the next day, he said, "Well, Miss, if we're going to get up in the morning, I guess we'd better turn in."

"Yeah, tomorrow may be a long day," she confirmed. They both stood as Levi put his arm around her shoulder, and they walked back to the screen door.

When they reached her bedroom door, Levi leaned over and gave her a light kiss. "I'll see ya in the morning," he said.

"Good night," she replied. She walked inside, and Levi turned and strolled into his room across the hall.

CHAPTER 7

THE UNITING

THE ROOSTER CROWED in vain at five o'clock. The morning light was there when Levi awoke. The previous day had taken its toll. By the time he hit the bed, the old feather mattress carried him soundly through the night. He could smell the bacon frying and the coffee perking as his feet hit the floor. His morning was getting routine; only ten minutes had passed as Levi's door opened, and he stepped toward Mr. Morgan's room. The door was open, and the white-haired gentleman was sitting up with a cup of coffee in hand.

"Well, good morning," Levi said.

"Good morning," Ben replied in a jovial mood.

"Do ya feel as good as you look?" Levi asked.

"For some dumb reason, my leg's sore." Levi smiled. "But I feel a lot better than I did last night," Ben replied as his voice picked up, and he smiled at Levi.

"Well, that's great. I'll bet you'll be up and about in a week," Levi responded.

"A week! I'd better be out on my horse in two days," Ben remarked.

"Well, don't worry about a thing. I'm gonna ride over to the Calahans this morning and take that branding iron with me. That is, if ya don't mind me going without ya," Levi said.

"I'd rather be there with ya. I didn't want to put this off another day," Ben admitted. "I should be saying, 'If ya don't mind going without me.'"

"It's no trouble to me. I figured if the Calahans have no problems with it, then I'll see if they'll ride over to the Cagles with me. Don't ya think?" Levi asked.

"Yeah. Ya won't have any problems convincing either one about the Tanners. They've both been trying to tell me how bad those bastards are for years. I'm the one who's so hardheaded," Ben admitted.

"Wow, what did you say?" Elizabeth asked with a smile. "For Dad to admit he is hardheaded." She shook her head as she came through the door, carrying a breakfast tray.

"Never mind. You just serve the food," Ben said jokingly. "Levi, how ya gonna find your way to the Calahan Ranch? You ain't ever been there, have ya?" Ben asked.

"Well, sir, I thought if you were feelin' okay and ya didn't mind, Elizabeth could show me."

"Mind, I'll be glad to get her out of the house. This pampering is more than a man can stand." Ben smiled and winked at Elizabeth as he answered.

She put her hand on his shoulder. "Dad, are ya sure you'll be all right?"

"I feel fine. Besides, I got Carmita here if I need anything. You just go on. Take your time, and don't worry about me. I want to see those Tanner boys in jail, and the sooner, the better."

She bent down, kissed him on the forehead, and smiled. Elizabeth turned toward the door as Levi followed.

"Levi," Ben whispered with a motion of the hand. Levi walked back to the bed as Elizabeth started down the hall. "I know you love her, maybe not as much as I do, but—"

"Yes, sir, just as much," Levi interrupted.

"Good." Ben smiled as he took Levi's hand. "Take care of her for both of us. She's all I got."

"Don't worry, Ben. I'll watch after her with my life," Levi replied.

"Thanks, son. Go get those Tanner boys for me," Ben said. Levi smiled as he patted Ben's hand. He walked out slowly. He entered the kitchen and heard the sound of Elizabeth's voice. "Carmita, I think Dad will probably take a nap now, but check on 'im every hour or so."

"Sure, Miss Elizabeth. I watch out for him. No problem," Carmita replied.

"Well, Levi, I guess I'm ready," Elizabeth stated.

"Let me get my hat, and I'll be ready," Levi answered as he started toward his room.

"Levi, aren't ya going to wear your gun?" she asked with a grin on her face.

"Oh sure." He reached down to feel the naked spot. "I guess I haven't gotten used to strapping on that thing every time I walk out of the house. I may never get use to that," he remarked.

"Maybe ya won't have to much longer," she replied hopefully. Levi headed for his room and returned in seconds. He tossed his hat to his head and buckled the gun belt as he continued to walk. By the time he reached the back screen door, the buckle was secure, and the strap was being tied.

Elizabeth had already stepped off the small back porch and yelled for Ricardo.

"Yes, *Señorita?* Ya want me?" Ricardo asked.

"Ricardo, Levi and I are going to ride over to the Calahans. We'll probably be gone for four or five hours. Would ya mind helping Carmita look after Dad?" she asked.

"Oh, sure, *Señorita.* No prroblem," he answered. "You want me to saddle the horses or hitch up the buggy, Miss Elizabeth?"

She twirled around with a big grin to face Levi. "Levi, let's take the buggy, okay?"

Levi smiled. "Sure, that's fine, whatever ya want," he stated. His long stride speeded up to catch Elizabeth. "This ought to be great. I've never driven a buggy before." His boyish side showed through. Elizabeth was clearly thinking of the romantic side, and it showed in her smile. But they were both happy for this opportunity to spend more time alone.

Only a few minutes had passed when Levi came rolling out of the barn driving a one-horse-powered buckboard. "Whooa!" he yelled as he pulled the reins. The buggy stopped perfectly, and Elizabeth looked impressed.

She grabbed the seat-rail and jumped aboard. "Vámonos!" she shouted. Levi took off as if someone had just handed him the keys to a new Porsche.

Elizabeth put her hand through Levi's arm as the buggy pulled out of sight. The buggy reached the gate, and Elizabeth prepared to jump off. "Where're ya going?" Levi asked.

"I'm gonna open the gate," she replied.

"Wait here, I'll do it," he remarked.

"Levi, you'll do no such thing. You've got to drive that buggy through the gate. I'll open it. I'm a woman, not an invalid," she stated as she hopped down and opened the gate.

Levi quietly drove the buggy on through the gate. After latching it, she jumped back on to the board. "Levi, don't you get closemouthed on me. I'm just trying to do my part."

Levi looked over and smiled. "I've known a lot of women in my time who would be real proud of ya," he stated, and she smiled back.

Elizabeth had a passing thought. "Oh, did ya bring the branding iron?" she questioned.

"Yeah, it's back there in that burlap bag," he replied.

The buggy ride was just what they both needed. Elizabeth was snuggled up to Levi's arm as if they were just taking a buggy ride over to visit their neighbors on a cold, wintry day. It was a bright, sunny day, plus a beautiful, scenic ride down an old dirt road. It did put them in the right mood. Reluctantly, they remembered the reason for the trip, and it sure wasn't for socializing. Time passed by much faster when you're wishing it wouldn't end.

"That's the entrance. That big gate on the right," Elizabeth stated.

"You mean where it says 'Calahan Ranch' above the gate?" Levi smiled as he made the dig.

Elizabeth looked at him in a huffy way but just in fun as he continued his picking, "Who would've believed it? That's amazing. They would have the entrance right below that sign." Levi was still smiling as Elizabeth stared at him with a piercing look and an ever-so-slight grin. They were just kidding around in a flirty way.

"Whoa, boy!" Levi shouted. The reins tightened, and the buggy came to a halt.

"I'll get it," Elizabeth remarked as she looked at Levi.

"I wouldn't say a word. Who am I to stand in the way of the beginning of women's lib?" he remarked. Levi was still grinning as Elizabeth hopped from the buggy. He pulled on through the gate as Elizabeth did the legwork.

"What did ya mean women's lib?" she questioned as she climbed back on to the buckboard.

"Ah, a lot of the women in my time really go in for this 'women's liberation' stuff. It was shortened to 'women's lib,'" he explained.

"It doesn't sound like you approve," she stated.

"No, no, I really do approve. Most of the American men think it's okay, but it's just hard for us to take it to heart. Most of the guys think the women will be lowering themselves if they want to be equal to men. No, not really, the whole thing is equal pay for equal work. There're some jobs that are pretty equal, and there are some tedious things women are even better at," he admitted. "Whoever does the best job deserves the highest pay."

"But I can feel you still have a problem with it," Elizabeth guessed.

"Well," Levi smiled, "you're right. The problem is someone

always takes things to the limit or maybe just a little further than the limit. I've seen women stand around on construction jobs. Their partners are doing physical strength labor they're not capable of, and they draw the same money. It's just not right. You got to draw the line somewhere."

Elizabeth smiled. "Wow, you do get on the bandwagon about some things. I'm used to seeing women work hard. Some of these farmers' wives work in the fields right alongside their husbands. Of course, they can't stand up to the physical abuse that a man can. So I suppose I feel the same way you do about it."

"Is that the Calahan home?" The small-framed house was very neat but not what Levi expected from his ancestors.

"No, that's not Tom's house. I think that's Librado's home. He's the foreman. You can't see the Calahan house until ya round that next curve," she explained.

Sure enough, as the road straightened, from around the bend, an old hacienda came into view.

"All right. That's a nice-looking place. I wonder why it's not around in my time or even a little part of it," Levi thought out loud as they pulled up to the hitching rail.

The women were sitting on the veranda, swinging as Levi took Elizabeth's hand and assisted her from the buggy. He smiled to himself when he thought about Elizabeth jumping on and off the buggy, and now he helped her down. Elizabeth caught his grin and his drift as she shook her head and smiled and stepped from the buggy. Tom Jr. was in the house when he heard the commotion of the horse and buggy. He came out the screen door as Tom Sr. spotted his guest from the barn.

"Well, Elizabeth, I see ya got your young man out visitin'!" the elder Calahan yelled. He wiped his forehead on an old rag and then his hands as he walked vigorously toward them. "Levi, glad y'all came over to see us." He reached for Levi's hand.

The women got up, and Tom Jr. followed them as they walked

out to greet their infrequent company. "Mary, this is the young man you've heard Junior and me talking about," Mr. Calahan stated.

"Oh, nice meeting you," she said.

"The pleasure's mine," Levi responded.

"Levi, you've met Tom Junior," Mr. Calahan said.

"How are ya, Tom?" Levi asked.

"Oh, I'm fair to middlin'. Ya doin' okay?" Tom Jr. commented as he shook Levi's hand. "This is my wife, Karen. Karen, this is Levi Calman," he added.

"Glad to meet ya," she replied.

"Nice meeting you, Karen. I hear you've got a new cowboy in the family with my name," Levi stated.

"Yes, we do. That's very strange. It's such an unusual name too. Do ya have someone in your family named Levi?" Karen asked.

"Yes, my parents named me after my great-great-grandfather," Levi replied, laughing at his little inside joke.

"Wow, I thought it was very uncommon, but I guess it's been around for a long time, huh?" Mary questioned.

"Well, it is uncommon, but when I was born, it had been around for at least four thousand years. It was the name of one of the twelve sons of Jacob, about 1800 BC," Levi stated as he looked over at Elizabeth. She rolled her eyes back and shook her head with a very coy look.

"Where is little Levi? I'd sure like to meet 'im," Levi added.

"Little Levi, that's cute. I like the sound of that," Mary, the proud grandmother, remarked.

"I'll go get 'im. Consuela was feedin' 'im in the kitchen a few minutes ago," Karen replied.

"Don't disturb 'im if he's eatin'. I know I don't like anybody botherin' me, while I'm feedin' my face," Levi commented jokingly.

"Oh, I'm sure they're through," Karen replied. She started up the walk and onto the porch.

Levi turned toward the men. "This isn't just a social call, Tom. We found something yesterday we wanted to show y'all," Levi said discreetly so as not to get the womenfolk upset.

"Whatcha got?" Mr. Calahan inquired.

Levi started back toward the buckboard, and the curious men followed. "Elizabeth and I went for a ride yesterday, just to see if we could find anything that might be a clue concerning these rustlers," he explained. He reached the buggy, placed his right hand on the rear wheel, and turned to finish his story before bringing out the branding iron. "Well, we ended up at that big waterfall on the west end of the ranch. The brush was beaten down to the ground."

"There in the box canyon?" Tom Jr. asked.

"Yeah, that's it," Levi replied.

"Go ahead, Levi, what did ya find?" Mr. Calahan asked anxiously.

"Well, behind that waterfall was a cave," Levi added.

"What? A cave, behind that waterfall?" Tom Jr. questioned. "Why, I've swum in that pond all my life. I've been all in that waterfall. There ain't no cave behind that waterfall."

"There is too a cave back there, Tom. I went through it yesterday with my horse," Elizabeth confirmed as she stepped forward and joined in the men's conversation.

"Tom, how long has it been since ya were up there?" Levi asked.

"Oh," Tom paused, "if my memory serves me right, I reckon it's been six or seven years now."

"Well, now there's a cave behind that waterfall. It's a mine shaft with rails and shoring timbers," Levi stated.

"Levi, go ahead with your story," Mr. Calahan stated.

"Well, we went through the cave and came out on Tanner property," Levi started.

"Yeah, that'd be right," Mr. Calahan confirmed.

"So we started down a small trail till it forked. There were real heavy tracks up the north leg, so we turned up that path. Then we went over a little knoll and rounded a bend, and right there, hidden from everywhere—"

"What was it?" Tom interrupted excitedly.

"Let him finish, Tom!" Mr. Calahan growled.

"It was a corral." Disappointed, the two men just looked at Levi. "You know, a catch pen, way up there in the hills, miles from the ranch house."

"Yeah, we know what ya mean. There's nothing illegal with a catch pen away from the ranch house," Mr. Calahan remarked.

"Oh, but wait a minute," Levi stated. He turned and lifted an old tow sack from the back end of the buckboard.

He slipped out the iron as the Calahans looked on. "Ya found a branding iron?" Mr. Calahan questioned.

"Yep, but not just a branding iron. This one's sort of special," Levi commented as he pointed the iron toward Mr. Calahan. "Ya see how part of that iron is missing? Let me show y'all how it works."

"That iron sure seems to be bigger than most," Mr. Calahan said as Tom nodded to agree.

"Yes, sir, that's because it's used on full-grown cattle, not yearlin's," Levi stated as he smoothed a place in the dirt with the sole of his boot. He then pressed the iron into the soil as the two men looked on.

"It's just the circle *T*," Tom said as Levi pulled the iron away.

"But it's not a full circle, and here's why. This is the Morgan's Rocking *M*," Levi stated as he drew the brand, just the right sizes to link the iron to his finger drawing. Then he pressed the iron down in just the right place, making a circle *T* with an *M* on the stem of the *T*.

"A circle *TM*, what's that? I don't know that brand," Mr. Calahan stated.

"Oh, Dad, that's the new Tanner brand," Tom declared.

"What?" Mr. Calahan questioned.

"Yeah, that's what Matt did to their brand after Mr. Tanner had that stroke."

"Why, I've never seen that before," Mr. Calahan emphasized.

"That's why this iron is a little larger than a regular one. It's made so ya can brand over an old brand on a full-sized steer. You know how the brand sort of stretches as the cow grows," Levi explained.

"Boy, if that don't beat all," Tom shook his head.

"Tom, you've seen this brand before?" Mr. Calahan questioned.

"Sure, Dad."

"When did ya see it, Tom?" Levi questioned.

"Oh, I saw it at least a year ago," Jr. recalled.

"Why didn't ya ever say anything about it?" Mr. Calahan asked.

"I thought everybody knew it. I was thinking the Tanner boys did it out of guilt." Tom paused. "Ya know, they were always givin' 'im a hard time. I figured they probably caused that stroke," Tom remarked.

"Ya know, Tom, ya might have something. What if Mr. Tanner found out the boys stole some cattle from his best friend, Mr. Morgan, and confronted 'em, with it," Levi suggested.

"Yeah, maybe there was a fight. Ya know that would sure help explain why a solid man like Mr. Tanner had a stroke," Tom theorized.

"Boys, let's don't stray from our problem and start playing doctor. I'm convinced that the Tanner boys are guilty of stealing Rocking *M* cattle. Now what do we do? We know Amos Gore can't go ridin' out to the Tanner Ranch and arrest Matt, even if we convinced 'im Matt was guilty. The Tanners have an army up there," Mr. Calahan rationalized.

"Well, I've been thinking about this all night. If y'all are with us—and the way ya said, 'Our problem,' I guess ya are."

"Sure, we're with ya," Mr. Calahan interrupted, and Tom agreed.

"What's your plan?" he added with a smile. Tom also had a proud smile as the group united.

"Well, I think you're right about the sheriff, so what I'm thinking is we should have a talk with the Cagles. If we all see eye to eye, then we take every man available from all three ranches. Then we ride into Dorado and explain everything to the sheriff. I feel, with a posse of twenty or twenty-five men already formed, it'll give the sheriff some real confidence. It'll also be hard for 'im to turn his head."

"You're right, I think you've got a good plan there," Mr. Calahan remarked.

"Well then, what are we waitin' for? Let's go see the Cagles," Tom stated. The three looked at each other and smiled.

Mr. Calahan turned toward the women standing a few yards away. "Ladies, we're gonna take a ride over to the Cagles. We need to have a talk with John and the boys. We'll be back in a couple of hours," he explained.

Elizabeth asked, "Should I come along?" She knew Levi didn't have a horse. "

Well, of course, you're welcome, Elizabeth, but if ya don't mind, we'll just saddle an extra horse for Levi. Then we can shoot straight across the pasture. We'll be back a lot faster," Mr. Calahan replied.

"Sure, Elizabeth, why don't ya just visit here with us? We don't get to see ya as much since you've grown up," Mary stated. The Calahan men headed for the barn to fetch their horses. Levi started to follow as Mary turned and directed her next sentence to him. "She'd play over here all the time when they were just young'uns. Ya know, our younger son and Elizabeth were the same age."

"I didn't realize y'all had another son, Mrs. Calahan." Levi sounded surprised. "What's his name?"

"Oh, I'm sorry, I figured ya knew. His name was Levi." A cold chill went up Levi's back as she spoke in the past tense. "He drowned a few years ago," Mrs. Calahan stated as a tear trickled down her cheek. Trying to control her emotions and to hide her tears from Levi, she turned and started toward the house. Elizabeth stepped in front of Mary as she walked dazed. Elizabeth pulled her tight and hugged her. The tears rolled as Mrs. Calahan was reminded of her loss.

Karen stood and watched her mother-in-law weep in Elizabeth's arms for a moment. She turned to Levi. "It's only been three years since Tom found his brother in the pond. It's still very upsetting for us all. He and Tom were real close. That's why we named the baby Levi."

"I'm sorry, I didn't know. Was he swimming alone?" Levi asked in a soft, concerned tone.

"No, he was dressed. The best Tom could figure, his horse probably spooked. He must've hit his head on a rock or something."

Karen's composure was shaken as the old memories flowed back. She used the back of her hand to wipe the tears from her cheeks, like a field hand would do when his palms were grimy from the soil.

"Where? What pond? Where did it happen?" Levi asked excitedly as he fumbled his thoughts.

From the corner of his eye, he saw Mr. Calahan and Tom coming from the barn, leading the three saddled horses as Karen replied, "It's the small lake, by the line shack."

Really, down at the far end, Levi was thinking, "The opposite side from the shack?" he questioned.

"I don't know, we never talked about it much," she replied.

"Levi, you ready?" Tom yelled.

"Well, we'll see y'all ladies later," Levi stated as he turned and jogged toward the barn.

"We saddled this filly for ya. She can't eat out of the same trough as that stallion of yours, but she's got a lot of spunk in her," Tom stated as he grinned.

Levi smiled as his foot jabbed the stirrup, and his leg cleared her back. "She's a fine-looking mare. She doesn't have to play second fiddle to any horse," he commented. The high-spirited animal started off in a sprint. The fast pace subsided as the three reached the first cross fence. Tom did the honors and leaned down to unlock the gate. Leaving the gate ajar, the three men continued their journey. Twenty minutes or so had passed when the men reached a small gate in the fencerow. "This gate was put in by Dad and Mr. Cagle about fifteen years ago. So all of us boys could visit without going on the main road." Tom laughed as he told his story.

"That's great. Y'all have been friends a long time, huh?" Levi asked.

"Oh, yeah, I and John Cagle and Pop Morgan and Matthew Tanner changed this part of the country from mining gold to raising cattle many years ago. That's the whole problem with this rustling business. I almost wish Matthew hadn't lived to see this mess. It's really gonna be hard on us, especially Pop, riding in on Tanner property and arresting the sons of an old friend," Mr. Calahan stated.

"Yeah, Mr. Morgan sure didn't want to believe it at first, but as soon as he was convinced, he was ready to get 'em right then." Levi laughed. "Yeah, it really made him hot."

"I reckon so. He's the one who's lost so much from this whole thing," Mr. Calahan commented. "I guess he's ready for this fight, huh, Levi?"

"Well, not exactly. He got so mad yesterday he went inside to put on his gun." Levi paused and smiled. "This really isn't funny, but his gun went off and shot 'im in the leg. It was just a flesh wound, but he's madder and twice as cantankerous as he was yesterday," Levi replied.

"But he's okay, huh?"

"Oh yeah, he was fine this morning when we left."

Both men chuckled and shook their heads. "It's probably just as well. Pop's getting a little too old for this kinda party anyway," Mr. Calahan remarked.

The two boys laughed as Tom latched the gate behind them. The pace got even slower as they left the flat pasture trail and started into some narrow winding passages through some large boulders. "This is some rough terrain, but we'll break out into some pastures shortly," Tom commented.

"Yeah, this rocky ground sure doesn't help these horses be too sure-footed," Levi replied as the other two agreed.

"Talking about this rocky terrain, I'd sure like to ask ya a few questions about your brother's accident. If ya don't want to talk about it, ya just tell me to shut up, and I will," Levi stated.

"No, no, it's okay. What do ya want to know?" Tom asked.

"Well, Karen told me ya found your brother at the pond by the line shack," Levi started.

"Yeah, that's right."

"Was it on the east side, on that rocky trail?" Levi asked.

"No, he was lying right in the edge of the water by the cabin."

"I stopped by that old cabin a few days ago, met an old man that worked for ya," Levi began.

"You mean Buster?" Mr. Calahan interrupted.

"Yeah, that's his name," Levi remembered.

"Boy, it's a wonder ya didn't get ya head shot off. Old Buster watches that part of the ranch pretty good, and he doesn't cotton to strangers." Tom grinned.

"Well, he did get a shot at me, but everything turned out okay. But what I was about to say," Levi paused, "as I recall, that end of the lake is flat, not a rough rocky terrain where someone—for

153

sure someone as used to riding as your brother—might fall from a horse," Levi stated.

"Well, you're right. We looked all over, and there just wasn't anything around to cause that bruise on his head either," Tom replied.

"Karen also said it happened about three years ago. That was about the same time the rustling started. Ain't that right?" Levi questioned.

"Yeah, you're right," Tom recalled.

"Tom, wasn't it just a few days after Levi's funeral when Pop rode over and told us about his cattle missin'?" Mr. Calahan recalled. "I thought, 'What else could possibly happen?'"

"Yeah, Dad, you're right. It was just a few days later. You think there might've been a connection, Levi?" Tom asked.

"Well, everythin' sort of points that way to me."

"I've been kinda feeling sorry for those Tanners, but if we find out there's some connection here, there won't be any mercy on my part," Mr. Calahan threatened.

"Tell me something. How'd ya find your brother? Did ya just go looking for 'im?" Levi questioned.

"What'd ya mean?"

"You know, like, maybe he was gone all day, didn't show up for supper, and ya went looking for 'im," Levi questioned.

"Oh, no, it was like midafternoon. Stockings showed up at the barn that afternoon," Tom began.

"Stockings was Levi's horse," Mr. Calahan explained.

"Yeah, Levi named 'im that 'cause he looked like he had on four white stockings up to his knees when he was born." Tom smiled, thinking back on the day in the barn when his brother first saw that new colt. He recalled the fuss Levi had made over the animal with the long white legs, remembering his persistence in naming the new foal Stocking Legs and his dad compromising to just Stockings. Tom came out of his trance with the sound of his name.

"Tom, Tom, are ya gonna finish telling Levi, or ain't ya?" his dad prompted.

"Oh, sure I am. I got sidetracked. Anyway, whenever Stockings showed up without Levi, I saddled up and went looking for 'im," Tom began.

"Boy, it's amazing that with a ranch this large, ya ever found 'im," Levi commented.

"Well, it wasn't that hard. See, I knew old Stockings could find Levi if I'd just take him along." Levi smiled and nodded as Tom continued. "But that old horse stayed right with me till we got through the east section, and then he took off like greased lightning. I'd just about given up on him when he took off. He went straight to 'im and stood right there till I went and got the wagon and brought Levi home. He followed along behind the wagon all the way back." The tears fell from Tom's cheeks as he told the story, and Mr. Calahan followed suit.

"I hate for ya to go through this Tom, but this may be very important," Levi said.

"No, go ahead. If ya can come up with something that might clear up some of the questions I've been asking myself for three years, I want to know it," Tom replied.

"Yeah, go ahead, Levi," Mr. Calahan added.

"Well, it sounds to me like that horse would've never left his master in the first place. I think that horse would've stood right there until he starved to death. Second," Levi paused, "ya said he didn't move from your side till ya got through the east section. Didn't ya mean ya went through a gate, and then he broke lose?" Levi questioned.

"Yeah, that's right. He didn't try to run until we went through that gate," Tom answered quickly.

"I think your brother could've come up on the Tanners by accident. Not thinking about anything being wrong, he rode in on 'em, just to see what was going on with some of his neighbors. By the time he figured out what they were doin', he was already in the middle of it. They either had to cut 'im in or ..." Levi theorized.

Mr. Calahan blurted out, "They'd never get Levi to join in their shenanigans. He'd tell 'em where to go."

"Yeah, that's what I figured. I'd say Matt figured the same way. He didn't have a choice," Levi remarked.

"That sounds pretty right, Levi, but you're forgetting we're not missing any cattle. What would they be doing on our ranch?" Tom interjected.

"Well," Levi paused as he collected his thoughts, "I don't think it happened at the line shack or on the pond. Let's say your brother just went for a ride, maybe counting newborn calves or something. I know sometimes when I want to be alone, I could ride for hours. No tellin' where he might've been when that happened."

"You're right. Levi would do that. You remember, Dad, he used to end up a lot of summer afternoons swimming in that pond, where Levi found Elizabeth and the Tanners," Tom agreed as his dad listened and in deep concentration nodded his head.

"Ya said there wasn't anything there for 'im to hit. Maybe it wasn't a rock, maybe that bruise came from the butt of a gun. Maybe it was a rock in someone's hand, or maybe it was an accident. Then they had to cover it up. It's hard to say," Levi speculated.

The new insights and their speculations had their adrenaline flowing, but unconsciously, they had almost brought their horses to a standstill.

"Tom, ya said Stockings wouldn't leave your brother's side till ya brought 'im home," Levi questioned.

"Yeah, that's right. Even when I went back to get the wagon, he wouldn't budge," Tom replied.

"Don't y'all think it's strange he left 'im and came back to the ranch?"

"I don't. That horse came back for help. Levi had that horse since he was twelve years old," Mr. Calahan remarked.

Levi paused as he looked at Mr. Calahan. "Well, what about the cross fences? Tom said he had to open a gate or two on the way back to the line shack," Levi questioned.

"Well, he could've jumped 'em," Tom replied in his dad's defense.

"I'd think if he jumped 'em, leaving your brother, he woulda jumped 'em going back to 'im," Levi replied.

"Maybe you're right. It's hard to figure what a horse will do. What ya think happened?" Mr. Calahan asked. He bowed to some strong questions from Levi that he could not answer.

"Well, I think your son ran upon the Tanner brothers somewhere, doing something they didn't want 'im to see. They probably got into a fight. Levi got hit. Maybe he was accidently killed. In their eyes, it was just a bad mistake. But something would've had to be done to hide their crime. So they took his body back to his own property, close to the cabin, where someone would find 'im," Levi said, still speculating.

"Why would they care if he was found? Why not just take 'im back, as ya say, to his own property and then hide his body so no one would know?" Tom agreed by a nod as his dad questioned Levi's theory.

Levi's face lowered in deep thought, staring down at the withers without seeing the saddle horn. All of a sudden, his head lifted. "The obvious! They didn't want anybody snooping around. They knew ya wouldn't just quit searching if ya didn't find your son on your own ranch. You'd go wherever it took."

Levi's thoughts struck home as Mr. Calahan's face captured the pain he felt in the truth Levi spoke. Without a word, Mr. Calahan turned his horse toward the Cagle's ranch house and picked up speed.

The convincing words of Levi's theory, along with the facts they already knew, made it that much harder for the men to stick to their plan. The Calahans' torment had them almost to the point of calling on the Tanner fortress without a posse. Fortunately, their common sense prevailed.

The ranch house came into view as they topped a knoll overlooking the Cagle domain. The silence was broken as Levi lightened the subject. "Boy, what a view—the house, the barns, those corrals, and that fruit orchard lying in the valley. It's a beautiful sight."

"Yeah, it really is," Tom replied as the three horses gained speed, coming down the hill. The riders were spotted as they topped the ridge. Recognizing their visitors, the Cagle clan had already started to assemble as the riders approached. "Hey, Tom, this ain't Sunday. What brings ya visitin' in the middle of the week?" a jolly old character joked.

Levi watched as a grin came over Mr. Calahan's face. The elder Calahan stepped from his horse. Levi knew his insides were being pulled apart, but the show must go on.

Mr. Calahan's hand went out to the head of the Cagle household as he spoke. "John, you old sidewinder, I ain't seen ya in a month of Sundays. Whatcha been up to?"

"Not a damn thing, 'cept chasing those grand young'uns around, just tendin' my flock," John Cagle replied as his eyes glanced over to the stranger in Calahan's company.

"Oh, John, I want ya to meet a friend of ours, Levi Calman." Levi and Tom swung down from their saddles. Levi stuck out his hand as the elder Cagle smiled and offered a firm handshake. Levi could feel the sincerity and strong will John Cagle radiated. "How'd ya do, Mr. Cagle? Nice meetin' ya," Levi responded.

"Ah, ya just call me John, and it's a pleasure meetin' ya, son. Pete's been taking about'cha for several days. You are pretty tall, but I was 'specting someone about seven foot from the stories spread around here." The old man laughed as his loud voice came from deep inside. "I'm just funnin' ya, son. Don't take me too serious. You've met one of my boys." Levi shook hands with Pete, and both boys smiled. "These other two are Paul and Samuel. Boys, y'all shake hands with Levi Calahan, I mean, Levi ... Calman." Levi was startled but caught himself and smiled. The two young men smiled and shook hands with Levi as Mr. Cagle continued to talk. "I'm sorry, son, I put ya in such bad company, but you even look like a Calahan. But I do apologize for the insult," John remarked with a shit-eating grin.

"Well, I know you fellers didn't ride all the way over here for a cup of coffee, or did ya?" John asked as he walked a little ways from the house. The boys too had sensed that Levi and the Calahans were not there for a social call. The group gathered under a big oak a few yards away from the dirt walkway that led to the house.

"No, I wish it was social and we just wanted a cup of coffee, but it looks like we're gonna need to ask ya for a lot more than coffee," Mr. Calahan stated.

"Ya just name it, Tom, and ya got it," John replied. All the sons seemed to share their dad's feelings. Mr. Calahan smiled for a second. "You'd better hear our askin' before ya commit, John."

"This does sound serious, Pa," Samuel, the youngest of the Cagle men, blurted out.

"Quiet, son, let Tom say his piece," John said in a somber tone.

"I think Levi can explain it better. He's the one who's been doing some Pinkerton work. Levi, tell John and the boys whatcha found," Mr. Calahan requested.

"Sure thing, Mr. Calahan. I guess y'all know about my run-in with the Tanner boys and that I've been trying to find out what's been hap'ning to the Morgans' cattle. Well, yesterday mornin', Elizabeth and I made a little run up to the northwest corner of the Morgans' ranch," Levi told the Cagles his story about the findings on Tanner property. Then he brought out the homemade branding iron he found by the Tanner's catch pen. The Cagle family was convinced that the Tanner brothers were guilty after Levi had given a complete account of their detective work.

"Well, it seems to me you've got a good case against those boys, son. What da ya want us to do?" John asked as he stood from a long squat.

Levi had been drawing in the sand, while everyone had gathered in close. John made a few groans as he stood because of the extra weight he carried, and then he leaned back against the tree as the conversation continued.

"What da ya think can we do? Have you got an idea?" Samuel asked.

"I guess ya know that the Tanner Ranch is like a fort," Paul, the elder son, stated.

"Paul's right. I'll bet Matt has twenty-five men staying on that ranch, and they don't punch cows either," Pete remarked.

"Well, I guess we've all heard that whole bunch is hostile, but none of 'em like to fight as much as Matt Tanner himself. I and Levi and Tom were talking about this at the house a little earlier. We're kinda figuring if y'all and all y'all's hands, Pop's cowhands, and we and our bunch all rode in and talked to Amos at the same time, he'd build up enough nerve to go arrest Matt and Billy," Mr. Calahan explained.

"Those gunmen Matt's got on his payroll may hightail it if it looked like an even fight," Tom remarked.

"Yeah, that's right. When we all show up, they'll probably take off like a ruptured duck, ha haaa," Samuel stated in a boisterous manner.

"Can't ya just see their faces if we all came ridin' in?" Paul commented.

Everyone chuckled and stood tall as they thought of the sheriff and their twenty odd men riding on to the Tanner's domain. All of them thought of the gunmen scurrying around, trying to escape, all but Levi. He had been listening to the group describe the band of gunmen employed at the Tanner fortress. He didn't feel it was time to pack the food for the picnic the others were convinced they were taking.

"Hey, fellows, wait a minute. Don't get me wrong. I'm gonna

be at the front of the pack, but don't let our big posse fool ya. Matt hasn't hired all those gunslingers because they run from a fight. They're probably just as mean as he is. They're all sittin' back drawing that easy money, and they ain't gonna give it up without some strong convincin'," Levi preached.

Everyone had a moment of realism as Levi spoke. A few faces were looking at the ground, and a little dirt shuffling was managed by the edge of some boots.

"Ah, we all know that, Levi. We're all grown men. The funnin' is just a way for all of us to pass off the danger. Don't take us the wrong way," Mr. Calahan spoke quietly in their defense.

"Oh, I'm sorry, fellows, I wasn't looking at it like that," Levi apologized.

"No, no, ya don't need to apologize. You were right. We shouldn't be puttin' it so lightly. We probably gave ourselves some false hope or maybe some false bravery. But whatever we do, we're gonna stop that Tanner bunch from rustling cattle," Mr. Calahan replied.

The group was united once again, more serious and stalwart. Levi was proud of the way his ancestors were handling the situation.

"Well, it sounded like we all agree on what to do," John stated as he pushed off from the tree and glanced over the group. "Now how do we do it, or maybe I should ask when do we do it?"

"It's a little after noon," Mr. Calahan stated as he glanced at the sky.

John Cagle pulled a pocket watch from his overalls and adjusted the distance from his eyes. "It's one-twenty," he confirmed.

"I figure it'd be three-thirty or four o'clock before we could all meet with all our cowhands. Then by the time we got to town and convinced Amos, it'd be almost dark," Mr. Calahan calculated. "I reckon gettin' an early start in the mornin' would make more sense. Huh? What da y'all think?" He scanned the group.

"I'm agreein' with ya, Tom. It'll give the boys a chance to round up our hands this evenin', and we'll meet up with ya come daylight," John stated.

"Levi, does that give ya enough time to round up Pop's crew?" Mr. Calahan questioned.

"Sure. We'll be ready."

"Then it's settled," Mr. Calahan proclaimed.

"Where'd ya want to meet?" Levi questioned.

"We'll meet up at Pop's front gate at daylight," Mr. Calahan added.

Everyone nodded to sanction the plan as a different suggestion came from Pete. "Hey, Pa, ya know we could call in Colonel Mackenzie over at Fort Concho. Ya know what they did to those Comanche warriors at Palo Duro Canyon in seventy-four."

"Yeah, Pa. Pete's got somethin' there. Mackenzie did his doin's in the panhandle," Samuel agreed with a grin.

"What'd he do, Pete?" Levi asked before thinking.

"Ya ain't never heard of Mackenzie's attack at Prairie Dog Town Fork on the Red River?" Paul questioned, very surprised.

Before Levi could answer, Pete commenced to tell the story so as not to embarrass his newfound friend. "Well, come September two years ago, this colonel over at the fort took six hundred troopers and went looking for a Comanchero named Tafoya. He's done a lot of tradin' with those redskins. After they caught him, it only took a little bit of persuadin'." Pete smiled, and his brothers chuckled. "And he told 'em everything. This Indian Quanah was in Palo Duro Canyon. The cavalry got there in the middle of the night. Some friends of ours over at the fort said that canyon was full of tepees. They said those campfires were strung out for miles down the riverbank. Well, Mackenzie struck right then. What really got 'em was Mackenzie had their horses shot, over a thousand of 'em. Then he burned their tepees and all their food and hundreds of repeatin' rifles, burned all of it. They said a few hundred got away but not for long." Everyone knew the story, but they all listened as Pete acquainted Levi with the history lesson. "They still have a hundred or so of the squaws and kids in a compound over at Fort Concho. Quanah was one of those who got away, but he didn't last a year. He couldn't run very far. He couldn't hunt, and he couldn't fight. He surrendered a year ago this month."

"Wow, that's a hell of a story. It makes ya kinda feel sorry for the Indians," Levi commented.

"Ah, nah, it doesn't, son," John piped in, "that renegade Comanche Quanah had massacred 190 settlers that summer. He went into New Mexico and then up to Colorado and Kansas and even found a few settlers in the Indian Territory north of the Red River.

"North of the Red Riv—oh, in Oklahoma," Levi responded before thinking there was no Oklahoma yet.

"What? Yeah, probably there too," Mr. Cagle added, not really knowing what Levi meant. "So don't think they didn't deserve what they got."

"I see what ya mean, Mr. Cagle. Ya gotta have the whole story," Levi said. Cagle nodded at Levi's reply.

"Well, John, we'll leave ya be. We're gonna get back to the ranch. I reckon we got a lot to do," Mr. Calahan stated as the three men walked back to the horses and mounted.

"We'll see ya in the mornin'!" Pete yelled. The three riders waved and rode off.

Levi glanced over his shoulder as they topped the crest, taking one more look at the scenic view of the Cagle homestead. Pete was still standing in the large clearing in front of the house and waved once again as the riders rode out of sight.

"That was some kinda story the Cagles told," Levi commented.

"Ya mean about Quanah Parker, that Comanche chief?" Tom questioned.

"Quanah Parker!" Levi stated, surprised. *I bet I've heard that name a hundred times in old movies and always thought he was just a fictional character,* he thought as Tom began to talk.

"Yep, don't ask me how he got that name, but John didn't tell ya the best part."

"No?"

"Well, I really don't know what got 'em started on that wide-ranging killing spree, but I can tell ya what really got 'em pissed. There was a group of professional buffalo hunters camped at Adobe Walls, that's up in the panhandle," Tom explained. "Well, Quanah Parker and seven or eight hundred warriors attacked that bunch of hunters. Now mind ya, these professional marksmen were using those fifty-caliber rifles. You know, those long, long barrels." Tom stretched out his arms to emphasize the length. "Well, even having those carbines, the Indians couldn't get close to those hunters." Levi laughed, and Mr. Calahan joined in. Tom snickered as he kept on with the story. "They fought 'em off for days, and finally, that bunch of redskins just rounded up their dead and went on."

They all chuckled as the trio continued to ride, and Levi listened intensely to the Texan history lesson firsthand. "Well, that defeat really got 'em riled. They started massacring every settler they could find. That's when President Grant ordered the cavalry to track 'em down," Tom explained.

"Damn, what a story," Levi commented as the Calahan homestead came into view. "I can't believe we're already back." The time had passed quickly.

Elizabeth, watching the road for what seemed like hours, finally spotted the three horsemen. The day had passed very slowly for her. Although she enjoyed the rare treat of women talk, she wasn't used to the waiting. She also hadn't realized how much she was missing Levi until he came into view.

Elizabeth stood and walked from the veranda, stifling an urge to run as Levi stepped from the horse. "How did it go?" she asked. Restraining an urge to hug him, she pretended to listen as she only saw his face.

The three men told only the high points of their plans. It must've been a Calahan trait to keep the womenfolk from worrying too much. They did mention that the Cagles were going to ride with them tomorrow but nothing about the danger involved. They seemed nonchalant as they talked about the trip, but Elizabeth knew the consequences of a showdown with the Tanner gang and figured the Calahan women could surmise the same.

"I guess it's close to three," Levi said as he took Elizabeth's hand and started toward the buggy. "I think we'd better mosey on back to the house." They climbed aboard the buggy as Elizabeth expressed how much she had enjoyed the day to her two neighbors. They all waved good-bye as Levi turned the buggy around.

"We'll see ya in the morning!" Tom shouted as they pulled away.

"Yeah, in front of the Morgan's gate, right?" Levi yelled. Tom nodded to confirm. They headed north up the main road. The couple had ridden for only a quarter of a mile or so when Elizabeth spotted an obscure wagon trail leading off to the east.

"Turn right! Turn right!" she shouted.

"Whoa." Levi pulled back on the reins. He looked over at Elizabeth. "Are ya sure the road's that way? That trail doesn't look like it's been used this year," he questioned.

"It's not to the main road. It leads to the line shack," she said. Levi looked confused. "Aren't ya gonna show me your wild horse with four wheels?"

Levi smiled. "Well," he paused for a second, "sure, I guess we got all afternoon." He pulled tight on the right reins and eased the horse onto the overgrown trail. The old path was very rough. It was only used occasionally by the chuck wagon when the herds were taken up north to the market. Luckily, it wasn't a very long ride because the washouts and the rocky terrain made the buggy ride almost impossible.

Levi fought the trail for twenty minutes or so. They came to a spot where he felt he left the Bronco. He looked up the trail in both directions and confirmed his beliefs. He recalled a few landmarks: some large boulders mixed with a few scrub trees off to the right and a small clump of bushes up the trail on the left. Everything was right. He was convinced this was the exact location. The only problem was that there was no wild horse with four wheels. Levi jumped down from the buggy in a frantic search, looking for anything that might be linked to him.

He already had mixed emotions about his new life. The girl he loved was here, but his only sister and his whole life were someplace else. He had thought maybe one day he might have to make a choice, but now there was no choice. His only tie to his world was gone.

Levi, feeling depressed, looked up at Elizabeth still sitting in the buggy. "Are ya sure this is the place, Levi?"

"Yeah, I'm sure. There's no doubt about it," he replied as his head lowered.

"You know, I did warn ya about it."

"Warn me about what?"

"I told ya if you didn't tie it up, it may not be here when ya got back."

Levi looked up and then smiled. *This girl may be Gracie Allen in a previous life,* he thought as he returned to the buggy. "Ya did warn me, didn't ya?" "

I know it was a machine. I was just kiddin'. I wanted to take your mind off of it for a moment."

"Well, ya know the really bad thing about this, don't ya?" Levi asked seriously.

"What?"

"You're stuck with me forever," he said as he looked into her eyes.

"Oh, darling, I never want ya away from me ever," Elizabeth replied as she melted into his arms. Their emotions ran high as they kissed but especially for Levi. Just experiencing a tragic setback, his tolerance was at an all-time low. Elizabeth couldn't possibly realize how important her love meant to him at this time.

After a moment of long kisses, Levi pulled back. "Ya do know how to take my mind off my problems," he commented with a smile. "I guess we'd better get back to the ranch."

"Do we have to?" Elizabeth teased.

"Yeah, I think we better get out of here, before something happens," he replied with a devilish grin.

"Levi, you're no fun at all," she replied jokingly.

Levi nudged the horse, and before long, they were back on the main road, nearing the entrance to the Morgan spread. Elizabeth's arms were locked in Levi's as the contented couple reached the gate. She hopped down to unlatch it when she noticed the latch was ajar. "It's already unlocked," she stated as she pushed the gate open. Levi drove the buggy on through, and Elizabeth climbed aboard. "I wonder who's visitin'."

"Maybe Ricardo had to go into town," he guessed.

"But what if Dad took a turn for the worse? He might have had to get the doc back out here," she said worriedly.

Levi picked up speed, feeling Elizabeth's eagerness to reach the house. They spotted the doctor's carriage tied at the hitching rail long before they got there. One of the hay wagons was pulled up to the front steps, and a strange feeling came over them both. All the signs pointed to a serious problem. "Your dad must have taken a turn for the worse if the doc's gonna take him into town," Levi thought out loud as he brought the buggy to a halt.

Rosita came running from the house, crying, straight into Elizabeth's arms. "Rosita, what's happened? What is it? Has something happened to Dad?" Elizabeth yelled as she too began to cry.

Ricardo came up hurriedly, behind Rosita, placing his hands on her shoulders. Then he looked at Elizabeth. His face was badly bruised, and blood ran from his eye. His clothes were half torn from his body.

"Your *padre, mi amigo*, is gone," Ricardo said as his head lowered.

"Ooh, noo! It can't be!" Elizabeth cried as she released Rosita and started for the front porch. Levi was by her side as she ran hurriedly up the steps. He placed his hand on her shoulder so she could feel him near as she entered the door. Not only Doc Jones but also Sheriff Gore was waiting inside. "Doc, what's happened? Did something go wrong with Dad's leg?" she questioned as Doc Jones clutched her hands.

"No, it wasn't his leg, Elizabeth. It was his heart that gave out." Elizabeth looked puzzled as the doctor continued. "Ricardo said the Tanners came by, looking for Levi around noon. They roughed up Ricardo, and when he wouldn't tell 'em where Levi was, they started in on Pop. His heart couldn't take it."

Levi was still standing behind Elizabeth as her head fell forward to rest on her old friend's chest. Doc Jones put one arm around her shoulder and pulled her to him as he held his black bag in the other.

Levi looked at the sheriff. Amos, sensing the stare, looked back at Levi. Levi nodded toward the front door, and the sheriff moved in that direction with Levi right behind. As the sheriff reached the yard, he turned to face Levi. "I know what you're thinking, son, but even if ya went along with me and my two deputies, we couldn't stand up to that Tanner bunch," Sheriff Gore stated. "The only thing we can do is get the troops over at Fort Concho."

"How long would that take, Sheriff?" Levi asked as he walked to the rear of his buggy.

"Well, I'd say a man could make it over there in a day's ride. A day to get the troops ready and a day back, three days or maybe just two if he could get the troops to move faster," he estimated.

"I don't think the Tanner boys will stick around for two or three days, Sheriff. Let me show ya something. Maybe I can give ya a better solution or, let's say, a faster solution." He unwrapped the branding iron and explained the whole story to the sheriff, including his last conversation with the Calahans and Cagles.

"I think that Matt probably feels safe for a day or so, but he's probably thinking the same as you do. He's gonna have to be gone from here in two days because of the army. So I think if we hit 'em tomorrow early, we could surprise the whole bunch," Levi laid out his plan.

"It might just work, son. Anyway, it's our best shot to catch Matt before he can leave the country. He'll take tomorrow to gather up his belongin's and all that money he's stolen, and then they'll be across the border in two days," the sheriff figured.

"You're right. That's probably what he's thinking, all right," Levi agreed. Ricardo pulled the wagon down by the barn and waited to follow the doc into town.

Elizabeth came out with Doc Jones by her side. Her face and eyes were red as she stepped into the yard beside Levi. His arm went around her shoulders as she drew near.

"Elizabeth, I'll take care of my friend. You don't worry about a thing," Doc Jones said as he climbed into his buggy.

"Elizabeth, I'm sorry about ya dad. I think he'll rest in peace, just knowing ya got this young feller by your side," the sheriff stated. He joined Doc aboard the buggy. The buggy started down the road, and Ricardo pulled in behind with the wagon housing Mr. Morgan's body.

Elizabeth's head laid on Levi's shoulder as the wagon pulled out of sight. The tears began to fall, and Levi pulled her tight as she tried to muffle the moaning. "Let it out, just let it all out," he said as the tears fell from his cheeks also.

Levi walked up the steps with her and steered her to the swing, where he sat her down and snuggled up to her. They sat for quite some time without a word.

The darkness settling in was brought to Levi's attention as

Rosita lit the lamps in the parlor. "Let's go inside, pretty. There seems to be a chill in the air." He nudged her up and turned her toward the door. Elizabeth quietly followed his directions. The crying had long stopped, and she walked very serenely into the house.

"I'll bet Rosita's got something good to eat," Levi said, trying to take Elizabeth's mind off her sorrows.

"No, I don't want anything to eat."

"Maybe you should lie down," he suggested. She turned toward her room without another sound as Levi followed.

Rosita folded the spread as Levi pulled back a single sheet. The inside air was warm and motionless. Levi kissed her cheek and left the room.

He sat at the dining table as Rosita came from Elizabeth's room. "Señor, will you eat now?" she asked.

"No, *gracias,* Rosita. I couldn't eat a bite either. Why don't ya take that food home with you? I'm gonna wait up for Ricardo. I need to talk to him for just a few minutes before he turns in, okay?"

"Okay, *Señor,*" she replied with a saddened smile.

As Rosita left, Levi opened a door on the sideboard. He lifted a bottle of whiskey and poured a small glass about half full and retreated to the porch. He sat down on the swing in his favorite spot and stretched his legs across the seat. He looked up at the bright moon and took a large sip from the glass. He then laid his head against the chain that held the swing.

"Señor, Señor, Señor Lee." Levi was abruptly awakened by a tugging on his shoulder and the calling of his name. "I'm sorry to wake you, but Rosita, she tells me you want me before I go to bed." Levi's eyes blinked as he heard Ricardo speak.

"Oh, yeah, Ricardo. I … must have fallen a-a-sleep." Still in a drowsy state, Levi pulled himself together enough to explain the plans for the next morning. "And be sure to have all the men up at least a half an hour before sunrise. And please check on me too,

Ricardo. I may not be awake myself," he added with a slight grin.

Ricardo smiled. "Of course, I will, *Señor*."

Levi stood and walked toward the door. He turned back to Ricardo. "We're gonna take 'em for Mr. Morgan, *mañana*," he said as he smiled and opened the creaking old screen door. Ricardo smiled and nodded.

CHAPTER 8

A DAY OF RECKONING

THE PEACEFUL NIGHTS and easy rest didn't hold true for this night. It was filled with relentless aggravation. Many trips were made between Levi's feather mattress and his window view of the moon, which seemed to be suspended in time. He was anticipating what the daylight had in store. Levi's restless body and mind never seemed to slow down. Drowsiness prevailed, but sleep was impossible.

He stepped from the bed to check the window one more time. It was then he heard the sound of kitchen utensils rattling ever so faintly. Relieved that the night was drawing to a close, he lit the old cut-glass lamp and slipped on his jeans. Pouring a small amount of water from his pitcher into the ceramic hand bowl, he rinsed his face as hurriedly as possible. Only a few minutes had passed, and Levi was slipping on his boots.

As he grabbed the knob, he took another look around the room. Draped over the back of a chair was his holster. A cringe went through his body as his eyes focused on the object. He had slipped the gun on every morning, all week, without any real intent to use it. This day would be different. He knew the weapon would be called upon to serve its purpose today. He walked over to the old high-back chair and lifted the holster and swung the belt around his hips. The buckle was hooked, and the leather tie was strapped to his leg. The procedure was smooth and with confidence. He blew out his lamp and headed for the kitchen.

The wood-framed mantel clock displayed a quarter till five as Levi passed through the parlor.

Elizabeth was standing in front of the wood-burning stove as he entered the warm kitchen. She turned to find Levi looking into her eyes. Her long white cotton robe stood open to reveal a white cotton nightgown trimmed with lace around the neck. A small lace hem trimmed the bottom of the garment about knee length.

Although her attire was simple, her hair hung loose down her back, and her beauty shone ever so brightly in Levi's eyes. He felt her pain and sorrow as he pulled her near. Her arms clutched his body, and the tears flowed down her cheeks. No words were said, but the meaning was clear. Their love for each other was obvious, but Levi felt helpless to rid her of her grief. He didn't realize the comfort it gave her just to have him by her side.

A tapping on the back screen door broke their trance. Rosita spoke. "Miss Elizabeth, pardon, maybe me fix you breakfast?"

Elizabeth backed away from Levi's chest as she looked through the screen. "Come in, Rosita, come on in. I've made a pot of coffee, and we'll make ya some breakfast, Levi. Sit here." Elizabeth gestured as she spoke in monotone.

"No, *gracias*, just coffee. I don't think I could eat a bite. Rosita, maybe you can fix a little something for Elizabeth. She didn't eat anything last night," he said for Elizabeth to hear.

"No, no, I don't want anything right now. Maybe a little later, Rosita. Why don't ya just fix somethin' for Ricardo? I don't guess either of us wants anything just yet," Elizabeth suggested.

"Oh, he said he wasn't hungry either. He's in the barn, saddling the horses," she replied.

"Oh, Ricardo's in the barn. Let me have a swallow of that coffee. I'd better get moving," Levi said. Elizabeth grabbed a cup and started to pour.

"Rosita, I don't guess ya have any takers this mornin', but I'm sure we'll all be ready for a big supper tonight," Levi said with confidence, thinking it might instill a little encouragement in the two dismal females. They both smiled ever so slightly, knowing Levi's intent but also knowing the danger facing their loved ones.

Levi took a second large gulp. "Well, I guess I'd better get out of here," he said. Rosita walked out the screen door as Levi's eyes trained on Elizabeth. "We'll be back in a few hours. Don't worry about a thing, pretty," he said as his hand grasped her arm.

"Oh, darling, be careful. I couldn't bear to lose you," she replied. Her arms went around his waist, and Levi held her tight for a second and then kissed her with deep affection.

He stepped back. "I'll be back. You're not gettin' rid of me," he said with a smile. He walked toward the door. Elizabeth followed him out and walked by his side to the barn. Ricardo and all the other cowboys were armed and in the saddle. Levi swung up on to Crimson's back and leaned down for one last kiss as the riders began to move. "Rosita, take care of my *señorita*." Levi smiled. The young woman smiled back as he turned to catch his compadres. Crimson pulled to the lead as the seven riders galloped in unison. The thought that they all were possibly going to face their maker made the hair rise on their necks. Daylight was still weak as the group reached the entrance gate. The Cagles were sitting ten strong in the saddle as the Morgan riders joined the posse. When their horses quietened, the roaring sound of trampling hooves could be heard from the east.

"Well, it sounds like everybody's gonna make it on time," Mr. Cagle remarked as they all listened to the thunder of the oncoming riders.

Levi rode up to the family members as Pete pulled forward to meet him. "Good mornin'," he said.

"Good morning, Levi," Pete replied as Mr. Cagle and Pete's two brothers added their howdies. "I thought about this shoot-out all night, Levi. Ya once told me you wished I'd been there. I guess I'm as ready as I'll ever be."

"No, Pete," Levi said as Crimson pulled even closer between Pete's and Mr. Cagle's horses. "After I tell ya what happened yesterday, you'll be more ready."

A concerned look came over their faces as Pete questioned, "What do ya mean?"

"Yeah, what's happened?" John chimed in.

"While we were at y'all's place yesterday, the Tanners paid a visit to the Morgans' home. Mr. Morgan's dead," Levi stated as his head dropped a little.

A stunned look on the faces of the Cagle family expressed deep lament and dismay. But the silence was short-lived as the Calahan forces blazed in and infiltrated the band. Tom Calahan's horse came to a halt as he reached the center of the cluster.

John Cagle sat erect, both hands on his saddle horn as he spoke. "Tom, Levi's just telling us Matt Tanner killed Pop Morgan yesterday."

"Oh my God! Is that right, Levi?" Tom questioned in a helpless tone as the daylight began to appear on their faces.

"Well, he didn't shoot 'im or anything like that. He worked over Ricardo," Levi started to explain as he pointed to Ricardo's face. "But when Ricardo wouldn't tell 'im where I was, he caught Mr. Morgan and started working on him," his eyes lowered, "until he died. The doc said his heart gave out."

"That sorry bastard. What are we waitin' for? Let's go get 'em!" Tom Jr. shouted as a roar came from the hostile pack.

"Wait, hold it!" Mr. Calahan yelled as a few horses were breaking away. "Matt Tanner's gonna get what he's got coming, but we're gonna do it right. We've worked a long time to get the law as far as we have. Let's get the Tanners, but let's get 'em legal. Okay?"

A little grumbling came from the group, but everyone knew Tom Calahan was right. "All right, let's go!" he yelled as the big white stallion led the charge.

The pounding of hooves could probably be heard from a mile away. The twelve riders from the Calahan spread made a total of twenty-nine men, united in one cause—Matt Tanner.

The pace was set at a fast gallop as the cowboys rode their horses into a lather. The sun was high. The air was hot and still by the time the banded group reached town. The roar intensified as they passed small buildings down the main street of Dorado Ciudad. The shopkeepers stepped from their stores. The passersby stopped. The people came from the hotel and the stables and even the sweeper stepped from the saloon as the massive group stopped in front of the sheriff's office. A touch of fog filled the streets, but the townspeople recognized the leaders of the group and knew no harm was to come to Dorado. Everyone looked on as Sheriff Gore stepped from his office. Amos Gore seemed to be a little more erect this morning. The slouchy, sloppy manner he possessed had subsided for this very important task. All the old-timers could now recall the sheriff of twenty years before and why he had been left to fill this job for so long.

"Good mornin', Tom, John, Levi," the sheriff said as he nodded his greeting and walked to the edge of the boardwalk. The three men nodded as a silence fell over the group of horsemen. "Men, I know all of ya had some special feelings for Pop Morgan," the sheriff said as his eyes passed over the riders, "but this ain't gonna be no lynching party." His voice was stern as he preached to the large body of men in his slow Texan drawl. "I've been thinkin' about this all night. There'll probably be a bunch of men shot today. Matt Tanner ain't worth another man gettin' shot, but he's gotta be stopped and brought to trial. I wantcha all to understand what I'm sayin'. We don't want our town to regret our actions down the road." Amos paused and looked for questions. "Well, I guess everybody agrees with my thinkin'. Everybody, raise your right hand. Do ya all solemnly swear to uphold the laws of the fine state of Texas to the best of your ability?"

A loud roar blared back at the sheriff, and a small grin of satisfaction came to his face. "Men, I deputize all of ya with my authority as sheriff of this county."

The sheriff started toward his horse as John said, "Amos." The sheriff stopped and looked up at his old friend. "Ain't ya gonna carry a gun?" Laughter overtook the newly formed posse. The sheriff felt and then looked down for his holster. He walked back inside the jail and returned shortly, wearing his hat and buckling his gun belt as the chuckling continued.

In a matter of seconds, silence prevailed. The sound of a stampede came rumbling through the small wooden buildings. A mushroom cloud of dust was formed at the north end of town and was moving toward the center. The dust bowl halted short of the posse, about one block. As the particles settled, the posse could make out a large group of riders positioned around the front of the Concho National Bank.

Levi analyzed the situation immediately. "I think Matt Tanner's making one last withdrawal from the bank before he hightails it."

The sheriff looked over at Tom, and in a low tone, directions were given. "Tom, cut through these building with your bunch, and block off the other end of town." Tom nodded and led off between the buildings. The Calahan cowboys filed off around the sheriff's office, and Tom Jr. followed up the rear. The sheriff looked at the remaining posse. "We'll give Tom's bunch a couple of minutes. Then we'll just mosey on up the street."

"Don'tcha think we should rush 'em, Sheriff?" Paul Cagle asked.

"No, it might make 'em jumpy, and they'd start firin'. Maybe they'll see us and what's behind 'em, and they may just stop. It might just save some innocent lives."

"I think the sheriff's right," Pete remarked.

"Yeah, it looks like fifteen to twenty horses at the bank," John commented.

"That's right, Paw. I bet when the Tanners see what they're up against, ooohh, ol' Matt's not gonna know what to do. Ha ha ha!" Samuel stated.

"Shhhh," John replied. The sheriff motioned the posse to start the tense ride up the street.

A couple of shots rang out as four men rushed from inside the bank. The outlaws were still calm, but their horses were churning as they were spooked by the gunfire. Dust had filled the air as the four gunmen reached their horses. The posse was only a half a block away when they saw the elderly banker stepping through the doorway. He cocked his pistol and lifted it with both hands to fire. Matt Tanner's horse twirled as he mounted the animal, but with great speed and accuracy, he drew and fired before setting the saddle. Right before their eyes, a split second had passed, and a man lay dead on the boardwalk in front of the bank.

Levi felt sick to his stomach and helpless because he couldn't prevent the killing. The entire posse picked up speed. The outlaws turned to the roar of the oncoming horses.

"Matt, it's the sheriff and that son of a bitch who shot Clyde!" Billy Tanner yelled. Matt turned to face Levi and the sheriff. He was surprised by the size of the posse behind the two men. It was almost equal in quantity to his own band of outlaws. Matt instantly realized, however, that the posse was only ranch hands. He readied himself for a charge at the posse, but his men didn't have this little insight shared by the Tanner brothers. The posse gave the illusion of a strong body of gunfighters. Several members of the gang contemplated desertion and started to swap directions. The Calahan troops were in full view, blocking the other end of town. "Hey, Tanner! They got us hemmed in. There's just as many behind us!" Matt heard the cries from several voices. "What we gonna do?" another voice cried out.

"We're gonna fight! These jackleg ranchers ain't gonna hurt anybody," Matt conveyed. The posse, only a couple of hundred feet away, front and rear, stopped to let the Tanners call the next move. "Matt, you better throw your guns to the ground and give yourself up!" the sheriff demanded.

"I ain't turnin' myself in to a bunch of brainless cattle pushers! You ain't got a chance in hell against my boys, Sheriff!" Matt yelled.

"Matt, why don'tcha just step down from that horse and fight it out with me? I'm the guy ya really want anyway!" Levi shouted for the gang to hear. Matt stared at the posse. He glanced over his shoulder as if to keep the rear posse in check. He turned back around and stared at Levi. Moments that felt like hours to some of the outlaw gang ticked away as Matt figured his odds.

"I ain't waitin'! Don't shoot, Sheriff. I give up," one gang member whimpered as he plunged forward, spurring his horse.

Matt's pistol gave no quarter. A shot rang out before the outlaw could move ten feet from the gang. Silence prevailed as everyone watched and then heard the thump of the lifeless body as it hit the ground.

"Tanner, I'm waitin'! Are ya just plain yellow?" Levi yelled as a tingle went up his spine. Levi knew the ranch hands wouldn't stand a chance against the hired killers. The sheriff and the entire posse were truly impressed as Levi made the challenge.

Everyone understood Levi's gesture and sat in silence. They could almost see the hair rise on Matt's neck. Matt figured most of his gang would probably throw their guns to the ground if he charged the posse. Plus, there would be a certain satisfaction in killing this bastard in front of the whole town. It would give his band of lowlifes some much needed backbone. Never doubting his ability, Matt decided his only way out was to accept Levi's challenge. He thought, *As soon as I kill this bastard, I'll exterminate that weasel of a sheriff. Then my gang can handle this bunch of cow punchers.*

Matt never took his eyes off Levi as his right boot came over the saddle horn, and he landed on the ground. His dismount was chilling. He exuded confidence with every move as he cleared the saddle. Levi doubted his own sanity as his challenge echoed in his head. Only a week before, he was a peace-loving twentieth-century rancher, and now he faced death at the hand of a gunslinger in the 1800s. Both sides waited helplessly for their fate as Levi stepped down from Crimson's back. He took several steps forward as the cold, calculating Matt Tanner stared through him. Levi's mind relived his first encounter with the dead ancestor of Matt's. The face still gave him chills as he faced this killer. He took several more steps forward. Matt finally moved. His arm hung loose by his side as he stepped toward his victim. Matt had an advantage: like a coiled viper, he had no compassion about the strike. Levi started to move again as Matt continued forward. Only seventy feet apart, Matt stopped and came to a firm stand.

"I've already killed one nosy son of a bitch named Levi, and you're gonna die just as fast." Matt broke the news only to disrupt Levi's train of thought and possibly create a second of hesitation in his draw. Levi's heart was racing. He could see the whites of Matt's eyes enlarge only a split second before Matt's hand went for his gun. With the automation of a high-tech machine, Levi's hand secured his weapon, drew, and fired. The blood splattered through Matt's shirt as his gun cleared the holster and discharged into the ground. The stern look on Matt's face was replaced with surprise as he fell backward into the dirt.

In the moment of silence, a bloodcurdling scream blared out from Billy Tanner. "You sorry son of a bitch! You killed my brother!" As Levi looked up, Billy's pistol was already aimed at him, and he heard the sound of gunfire. But the bullet exploded into Billy's chest.

Levi twirled to see the smoke still floating from a rifle held by his ancestor, Tom Calahan. Tom Sr. brought the rifle down and stared at Billy's body. Levi figured Mr. Calahan just released a little of his own anger and received a little satisfaction from the Tanner clan. He acknowledged his gratitude with a nod to Tom as Tom Jr. looked on proudly.

Looking through the posse, Levi spotted the Morgans' buggy. Elizabeth was sitting in the background, waiting for the finish. He turned back to check the outlaws and saw their guns being tossed to the ground. The posse closed in as the gang surrendered.

The Calahans and Cagles all dismounted to congratulate Levi and each other. Smiles had returned to everyone's faces, and the men had clustered around Levi. He recalled that Elizabeth was close by. Scanning over the tops of the surrounding heads, Levi saw her stepping from the buggy. He immediately worked his way through the crowd to reach her as Pete looked on. The townspeople filled the street as well. There wasn't any grieving for the loss of the Tanner siblings anywhere. It seemed to have lifted a heavy burden from the whole community.

Elizabeth spotted Levi and moved toward him. The happiness she felt with his victory over the Tanners had taken a little of the pain from her mourning. Their eyes met ten feet before the two could work their way to each other. Levi grabbed her around the waist and gave her a twirl high in the air. They were both laughing as the immediate crowd of townspeople who watched laughed with them.

Pete walked over as Levi returned Elizabeth to the ground. "Oh, Pete, isn't it great?" she commented as she jumped from Levi's arms and hugged Pete.

"Sure 'nough," Pete said as he hugged her back. Pete looked at Levi as he embraced Elizabeth. He knew she was only hugging him as a friend and out of happiness. Levi smiled about the hug; he was glad just to see Elizabeth happy. Pete hugged her out of happiness and because of the love he felt for her as well.

Elizabeth, chipper for the moment, grabbed both men by the waist. "Let's go congratulate your dad and Mr. Calahan, okay?" she shouted.

The two friends looked at each other. "Let's go," Pete said.

Levi yelled, "Vámonos!"

Hand in hand, the three worked their way back across the crowded street to where the Calahans and the rest of the Cagle clan were talking to the sheriff. Everyone was in a festive mood.

"Hey, Levi. We're all just talkin' about ya," the sheriff said.

"Yeah, and I don't care what they say. I think you're all right," Tom Jr. stated jokingly as everyone laughed.

"We're all real proud of ya, son," Mr. Calahan stated. Levi just smiled, but he really appreciated the praise coming from his great-

great-great-great-grandfather.

"Hey, we can't forget Tom. He did some fair shootin' too." Mr. Cagle spoke up.

"Yeah, that's right. You sure did, Tom. Y'all both did a good job," Pete confirmed, and the group all nodded.

"Well, nobody appreciates that shot as much as I do. Thanks a lot, Tom," Levi said. He looked at Tom and stuck out his hand to shake on it.

"I want to thank you too, Tom Calahan," Elizabeth said as she put out her hand also. Tom looked at Elizabeth, smiled gently, and kissed her on the forehead.

"Are ya the man who shot Matt Tanner?" a high-pitched voice asked from Levi's back.

Levi turned before answering as Pete and Elizabeth looked on. A short, small-framed man stood meekly, waiting for Levi's response. Levi just looked at the man, trying to figure out what he wanted. "I'm gonna take a picture of the two outlaws," the man said as he pointed to the bodies. Levi's glance followed the direction of the man's finger, only to do a double take at the bodies. They were laid out on two wide boards about six feet long, held up on one end by the hitching rail in front of the blacksmith's shop.

"That's sick," Levi commented.

"No, they're dead," the little man replied. "I didn't mean them. I know they're dead. I meant you. Why do ya want a picture of two dead men?" Levi questioned.

"It's for the newspaper, Levi," Pete explained in the man's defense.

"Yes," the man confirmed, "and I'd like to take y'all's picture with 'em."

"Whose picture?" Levi asked.

"Yours and Tom's and Sheriff Gore's. I think it'll make good copy," the man explained.

"I don't know about the sheriff and Tom, but I don't want myself in that picture," Levi stated.

"Not me either," Mr. Calahan agreed. "Amos, I think ya should get in that picture." Everyone smiled.

"Oh, no, not me. I'm not gettin' in that picture," Sheriff Gore replied.

"Hey, Amos. A little free publicity right before elections can't hurt a thing," Mr. Cagle prompted as the group chuckled. Everyone could tell he had mixed emotions about it, so they all chimed in at once. "Go on, Amos, do it. Go get in the picture," they all agreed.

The sheriff reluctantly decided it might be the best thing for him. Tucking in his shirt and pulling his jeans over his belly, he walked over to the hitching rail to stand between the two bodies. He still had a very serious look about him as the little disheveled man fumbled around with the focus and fired off the gunpowder in the handheld flash. Everyone clapped and yelled as Amos took a bow. The crowd cheered as he walked back to his friends in the middle of the street.

"What's that man's name with the camera, Elizabeth?" Levi asked.

"Rufus."

"Rufus!" Levi shouted as the man turned to look for his caller. "Would ya mind taking a picture of all of us live people together for me?" Levi smiled.

"Oh, no. Y'all gather in here real close. I'll be glad to do it," the little man said with a smile.

The group was surprised at Levi's request, but no one seemed to mind at all. The Cagles and the Calahans moved in unison to the photographer's directions. Levi had caressed Elizabeth's hand and walked with the group. "Hey, Sheriff Gore, we want ya in this picture too. Come on." The sheriff smiled. Feeling accepted again by the ranchers, he moseyed on over to Levi's side.

Levi could hardly believe the group. They became very rigid as Rufus leaned over the camera. "Hey, this is a friendly picture. Y'all don't look so serious. That camera doesn't bite," Levi jested.

On that note, the whole bunch smiled, just as the blast from the flash went off. He knew it would be a good picture. The group had loosened up at just the right second. All the onlookers clapped as the group laughed and began to dissipate.

The townspeople too began to disperse, clearing the street and returning to their routine. Everyone would remember this day for a long time.

"Elizabeth, would ya like to stop by the funeral parlor for a little while?" Levi asked quietly as everyone started to go their own way.

"Yes, I would. Can we go over there now?"

"Sure, we can. I'm sure everything's ready," Levi answered.

"Elizabeth," Mr. Calahan called softly as he stepped forward, "I wantcha to know how sorry we all feel about Pop. You know how special he was to all of us. Anythin' any of us can do, you just holler. We'll help in any way we can," he said, holding his hat in both hands.

Elizabeth caressed his hands as the tears fell from her cheeks. "I know how much you cared for Dad, and I really appreciate what you're saying. Thank you," she whispered as she turned and started toward the funeral parlor. The tears flowed even more freely. Levi nodded at the group of saddened faces and then caught up with her, putting his arm around her shoulder.

Pete looked on, wishing he could share these troubled times with his secret love.

Stepping between the hitching rails and up the steps to the boardwalk, they reached the front door to the makeshift funeral parlor. The local barber was the only prospect for grooming or makeready for the deceased. The funeral director, or mortician, was none other than the businessman and local barber Arthur

Gore, the sheriff's elder brother. The front of the small barbershop had been divided, and the narrow entrance to the funeral parlor opened up into a quaint room in the rear.

Levi had not attended a funeral or been in a funeral home since his grandfather had died. It brought back a lot of sad memories as he walked back to the body. He had grown very close to Mr. Morgan. But maybe the greater pain was the helpless feeling he had as Elizabeth broke down in front of the casket. Levi caressed her shoulders as she leaned over the casket and clutched her father's hands. Levi hadn't cried at his grandfather's funeral but had often wondered since if it might have made it easier to accept. The small display room was just that, just for displaying the casket and body. The room was small and had no chairs for one to sit and mourn in the presence of their deceased loved ones. Levi led Elizabeth—her eyes filled with tears—and guided her out the front door.

Mr. Calahan and Mr. Cagle were stepping on to the boardwalk as they came outside. The sheriff yelled at Levi as the two friends stopped to talk to Elizabeth. "I'll be right back," Levi said as he stepped swiftly from the boardwalk.

"What's up, Amos?" Levi questioned as he walked up to the sheriff.

"In all the excitement, I'd plum forgotten about the reward."

"Reward! What reward?" Levi asked.

"The state of Texas has a $2,500 reward out for any information leading to the capture and conviction of any murderers in the state. Since Matt Tanner confessed to killing the Calahan boy, and he's already been executed for it, I'm gonna authorize the bank to make payment to you right now," Amos replied with a smile.

"Really, aahh, I couldn't take that money," Levi said as his eyes shifted to the ground with embarrassment. "It would be like blood money. I couldn't take it."

"Levi, ya deserve the money. The whole town would feel better if you took it," Amos pleaded.

Still shaking his head, Levi turned to walk away as Amos frowned in disappointment.

"Hey, Amos." Amos turned back as he heard Levi's voice. "Could ya put it in the Morgans' account at the bank?"

"Sure, I could," he answered with a grin. Amos proudly reached out to shake Levi's hand and then turned and walked away.

"Hey, Amos!" Levi shouted and then asked with a grin, "Ya think maybe ya could deposit twenty-four hundred and give me a hundred of it?"

Amos smiled. "I'll bring it to ya at the hotel." Levi smiled and started back to Elizabeth.

"Levi, you talk to this woman. We told 'er we're gonna treat y'all to a big meal over at the hotel, and she's got some kinda excuse about gettin' back to the ranch. Says she has to get a dress ready for tomorrow," Mr. Cagle stated.

"Yeah, son. You tell 'er y'all got plenty of time for that, okay?" Mr. Calahan added.

"Elizabeth, they're right. We've got plenty of time. What do ya think about just staying here at the hotel tonight?" Levi asked with a smirky grin. Not knowing about the reward, Elizabeth just stared at Levi as he spoke and continued in a cocky way, "I figured after a good meal with these two fine gentlemen, we could mosey on down there to Hattie's Dress Shop and just buy ya a new dress for tomorrow." She just continued to stare at him; Levi grinned as if he had just eaten the canary.

"Levi, can I have a word with you?" she asked as she grabbed him by the elbow and pulled him over to one side. "Have you forgotten your money won't spend here? And what's with this little grin you've got all over your face?"

"Don't worry so much. We've got plenty of money." Elizabeth looked on with confusion. "The sheriff just gave us a reward for Matt Tanner."

"Really? Aahh, there's no reward out for those rustlers," she stated in disbelief.

"No, not for the rustling but for the murder of Levi Calahan. Oooooh," Levi paused, "that sent cold chills up my back."

"Is that the truth?"

"Yes, it really did send cold chills up my back."

"No ... I mean, about the reward."

"Verdad."

"Why didn't ya tell me?"

"The sheriff just told me," he said with the grin still intact. "I haven't had a chance."

Elizabeth rolled her eyes back. "Okay, let's go to lunch," she agreed.

"Okay, compadres. I have convinced this lovely young lady that she is starving."

"All right!" the two men shouted as Elizabeth shook her head. The foursome headed for the hotel restaurant.

Tom Jr. spotted them as they entered the hotel. "Hey, Pete, I just saw our dads and Levi and Elizabeth headed into the hotel. Come on, let's join 'em."

Pete, a little disheartened, dropped his head momentarily and then came up smiling. "Sure, let's go." The two friends broke into a vigorous trot.

The table was enlarged by adding another. This made room not only for Pete and Tom but for the two remaining Cagle siblings too. It gave the group of neighbors a chance to eat away the tension, which had been so strong just an hour before.

Another hour or so had slipped away, and everyone had enjoyed a good meal. Mr. Calahan stood with a shot glass in his hand and said, "I'd like to make a toast to our newfound friend. May he remain among us forever."

"Here, here," everyone said. Levi smiled and lowered his head, embarrassed, as Elizabeth looked on with pride.

It cut deep into Pete's heart as he sat and watched Elizabeth's eyes follow Levi's every move.

Soon the feast was over, and the group broke up. Levi stopped to check in at the front desk. The other men told Elizabeth they would see them at the funeral Friday morning but just to holler if she needed anything. Levi walked out on the boardwalk as Tom Sr. and John were waving good-bye.

"Tom told me to tell you he was bringin' an extra suit for ya in the morning."

"That's a couple of fine men," Levi said as he waved, and then he placed his hands on Elizabeth's shoulders. She smiled and nodded as she watched the two amigos ride down the street.

"Well, are ya ready for that new dress?" Levi asked as he saw the sheriff coming toward them.

"I don't know. It's gonna take a big one after all that food."

"Hey, Amos, how's everything?" Levi started the conversation.

"Oh, everythin's fine, son. How ya doin', Elizabeth?" the sheriff replied.

"Oh, I'm fine, Amos. Thank ya."

"Good. I got that money put in the Morgans' account, and here's …" Amos stopped talking as Levi gritted his teeth, and Elizabeth looked surprised.

"You put the reward money in our account? Why'd ya do that?" she asked.

"Well," Levi said as he scrambled for an answer. "I didn't have an account of my own. I had to put it somewhere."

"And here's that cash ya wanted," Amos said.

"Thanks, Amos. I sure appreciate it." Levi grinned and avoided the heated stare from Elizabeth.

Levi jumped off the boardwalk with the first words coming from Elizabeth, just to avoid any questions. "Let's go get that outfit for ya." He knew that was one line that would keep any woman quiet. He grabbed her hand and started down the street. Elizabeth hesitated a little, but the farther they walked, the more receptive she became.

Naturally, her selection was limited to black and not very ornate. This brought the number down to only three or four dresses. But Elizabeth's beauty made the simplest of dresses stand out as perfection. High button heels and a large-brimmed black hat and veil completed the outfit for just under sixteen dollars. Levi had only seen her in a white cotton dress one time; she usually wore her tomboyish clothes, never this feminine attire. His mind couldn't believe the beauty his eyes beheld, and he marveled at this ravishing sight. She stood in front of the long body mirror as Levi looked on. "What do ya think? Is it okay?" she asked as she looked over her shoulder. Levi, just taking in the view, hesitated for a second.

"Okay? That word couldn't possibly describe you in that dress. You are beautiful. Even beautiful shortchanges you. I just can't think of any words to describe you in that dress. If you looked any better, I don't think my heart could take it," Levi said. Hattie swooned, and Elizabeth smiled as she reached for his hand.

"Then I guess that means we'll take it," she stated as Hattie smiled, and Elizabeth returned to the dressing room.

Levi paid the bill, and Elizabeth returned with the outfit and helped Hattie package it. He carried one box with the dress in it as she carried the other two. The couple had started for the hotel when Levi spotted the drugstore on the corner. A little more shopping for some essentials was in order. The afternoon spending spree was well-spent therapy for Elizabeth's downhearted spirits. Having Levi by her side meant even more. The sun had started to set, and the air had cooled by the time the couple reached the hotel. "We have two rooms on the second floor. Why don't ya go up and take a bath and rest a while. We can wait a couple of hours before we eat," Levi suggested.

"That sounds good to me," she agreed. He accompanied her to her room and dropped off the packages.

Levi then started back down the staircase. The saloon was to the right as Levi reached the bottom of the stairs, just across the lobby from the dining room. Unbeknownst to Levi, Pete had stayed in town for the afternoon and had gotten slightly inebriated. Two troublemakers at the bar had heard about the earlier gunfight between the lightning draw of Matt Tanner and the new stranger in town. The two men were harassing Pete about his friend and the Morgan girl, almost to the point of another gunfight. Levi entered the bar just in time.

"Come on, Cagle, stand up and show us how your friend took Matt Tanner. We've gotta see this for ourselves!" one of the men shouted as the other laughed and prepared to draw.

"Fellows, if ya want to see that draw, you'll need to look this way," Levi said as the startled duo swirled and reached for their guns. Levi's pistol had cleared leather and was pointed in the faces of the mouthy scums. Neither gunman's pistol had moved from its holster.

The two men removed their hands from the pistol grips in a slow fashion as Amos came in behind Levi. "I'll let these two sleep it off in the jail. Can ya get a room for Pete?" Amos asked. "He's in no shape to ride home."

"Sure, Amos. We can't let him drink and drive ... I said he'll survive. I'll take care of 'im," Levi stated as he grabbed Pete and started up the stairs.

The two wranglers stared as Levi left the room. "You're two lucky men. It's a wonder ya ain't dead," the sheriff commented. The two men knew the sheriff was speaking the truth, and not a word was said as he carted them away.

Levi climbed the stairs with Pete over his shoulder as the desk clerk's eyes followed. Dropping Pete off in his room, he headed back downstairs. "Let me have one more room please."

"This one's on the house," the clerk said as Levi reached for his money. They both smiled as Levi nodded to the man and walked back to the saloon.

"I think I need a whiskey."

The bartender promptly moved down the bar and poured Levi a shot glass to the rim. "Here, son, I think ya need it too," the old gray-haired bartender said with a smile.

"What started that ruckus with Pete a while ago? I wouldn't have thought Pete could have an enemy in the world," Levi questioned the bartender.

"Aahh, those two are just troublemakers. They knew he was gettin' a little lightheaded. He'd drunk damn near half that bottle." The bartender focused on the table where the half-filled whiskey bottle sat as he spoke. "It's better if I don't say any more."

"What, you're stopping in the middle? What's going on?" Levi's tone got a little more serious. "If that had anything to do with me, I want to know about it."

The bartender, not really knowing Levi's character, didn't hesitate to finish the story. "Well, as I was saying, they knew the Cagle boy was drunk. So they started picking on 'im, about that Morgan girl."

Levi interrupted, "What about the Morgan girl? What did it have to do with Elizabeth Morgan?"

"Well," the bartender stammered, "they knew how Cagle felt about the girl." Levi was stunned by the bartender's reply.

"Okay, okay, that's enough. Forget it," he answered as he stared at the bar.

"Listen, I didn't want to say anything," the bartender explained.

"It's okay, don't worry about it," Levi stated as several instances crossed his mind and confirmed the bartender's accusations. Only three or four old men sat in the bar as Levi looked up and caught them staring at him. He turned and walked out of the bar as the bartender shook his head.

Knowing he didn't want to lose a good friend or the one he loved, Levi started up the stairs, feeling a need to talk to both. He knew there was no way to talk to Pete. He was passed out cold. He then headed for Elizabeth's room as she stepped into the hall.

"Hey, were you gonna let me sleep forever? I'm starved."

Levi forgot the problem for a second as he looked at Elizabeth. "You are? Well, let's eat." He smiled as she tucked her arm in his and started down the stairs.

They started across the lobby. "Hey, aahh, Mister, aahh, Mr. Levi, you forgot your key to your extra room!" the clerk shouted as the couple were almost to the dining room.

Levi looked back to see the clerk dangling the key in the air. "Oh, yeah. I'll pick it up on my way out, thanks."

"What are ya gonna do with two rooms?" Elizabeth asked.

"Well," Levi fumbled for words, "Pete decided to spend the night in town."

"So ya gave him a room?" she questioned. "Why didn't he get his own room?"

"Well … ahh, he wasn't feeling too good."

"Oh, did ya get the doc?" she asked, concerned.

"No, I think it was something he ate. He's just a little sick to his stomach," Levi squirmed out an answer.

"Hey, you two. Won't y'all join us for supper?" a voice interrupted. Levi sighed with relief and appreciated the interruption. They both looked up to see the sheriff waving his arms.

Oh no, it's the sheriff, Levi thought. No tellin' what he'll say about Pete.

Elizabeth started toward the sheriff as Levi whispered, "Hey, wouldn't ya rather eat alone?"

"What could ya say?" she whispered back as she covered her

mouth. "We'll have to go over there anyway." Levi thought maybe the sheriff would be discreet.

"I guess old Pete's sleeping it off" were the first words to roll from the sheriff's mouth. "Y'all sit down. Levi, ya ain't ever met my wife. Levi, this is Flo. Honey, this is the fella I was tellin' ya about."

"Oh, hi, nice to meetcha," the short and very chubby wife replied.

"Hi, Mrs. Gore. It's nice to meetcha too," Levi answered. He dreaded his next look at Elizabeth.

"Well, Elizabeth, it's nice to see ya too. I was sure sorry to hear about your father," Mrs. Gore stated.

"Thank you. I appreciate ya thoughts," Elizabeth answered as she stared at the side of Levi's face.

Being one of the town's leading gossipers, Mrs. Gore continued to rattle through the meal, and Elizabeth soon forgot she was supposed to be mad at Levi for lying to her about Pete. She was, however, still wondering why he would lie about Pete's condition. *Pete wasn't known for his drinking*, Elizabeth thought, *but he wasn't known as a teetotaler either*. She just couldn't wait to get Levi alone.

Levi took the hint. "Well, we hate to leave good company, but we've got a long day tomorrow," Levi remarked.

"Aahh, we understand. Y'all go ahead. The dinner's on us," Amos said as his wife took another bite and smiled at the young couple.

"Thanks a lot, Amos. Nice seein' ya, Mrs. Gore." Elizabeth smiled and nodded. As soon as they reached the lobby, Elizabeth asked the question, "Levi, why did you say Pete was sick? I don't care if he gets drunk."

"Wait just a second." He stopped by the desk to pick up the extra key. "Let's go up to your room and talk," he said quietly as he took her arm and started up the stairs. The desk clerk rolled his eyes and shook his head as he thought, *I've heard that line a few times.*

Elizabeth could hear the seriousness in Levi's voice but had no idea what was going on in his mind. He took the key from her and unlocked the door. "I can't wait anymore. How do you feel about Pete?" he asked as he shut the door.

Elizabeth was confused as she looked at him. "I like Pete. He's just like a brother to me. He's been my best friend, I guess, all my life," she replied.

"Do ya love 'im?"

"Of course, I do. Not in the way I love you. Is that what you're asking?" she questioned.

"Yes, I guess that's what I'm asking."

"What brought this on? Did Pete say something different?"

"No, Pete didn't say anything. He wouldn't. There was a little talk in the bar about maybe you were his girl," Levi said as his eyes glanced at the floor.

"Levi, darling, Pete's a very dear friend I've known all my life. But I love you with all my heart. There's no one else," she stated as he clutched her hand and pulled her into his arms.

"Oh, I love you so much. I couldn't stand the thought you may love someone else," he replied. Their passionate kisses ran freely, and their emotions ran wild.

Elizabeth pushed back and shook her head. "I think we'd better call it a night," she panted. "I can't quite handle this right now." Levi stepped back too.

"I'm just glad I'm the one you want. I'll let you go to bed. It's gonna be a long day tomorrow." Levi smiled, and she smiled back. He leaned for a light kiss and then opened the door. He looked at Elizabeth and winked and pulled the door closed. The much anticipated day had come to an end.

CHAPTER 9

TEARS AND PASSIONS

A LIGHT RAPPING at the door served as Levi's alarm as his eyelids slowly opened, and he stared at the strange high ceiling. Again, the soft rap struck the door as his totally relaxed mind and body began to function. "Levi, are ya awake?" A soft feminine voice carried through the door.

"Elizabeth! Sure, I'm up!" he shouted as he rolled to his feet. "I'm almost dressed. I'll meet ya in the dining room, okay?" He scurried for his clothes as he answered.

"Well, okay. I'll wait downstairs," she replied.

Levi washed his face in the fancy porcelain bowl as fast as possible, wondering about the time and if maybe he had overslept.

The funeral was at ten o'clock. But without a timepiece, it was impossible to keep up with the hours. He slipped on his boots and was out the door in minutes. As he made the bend in the staircase and started down the second half, he saw Elizabeth sitting elegantly on the round tufted sofa in the middle of the lobby.

She stood as Levi approached. "You are beautiful," he stated as he took her hand. "You didn't have to wait for me. Ya should have gone in and got a cup of coffee anyway."

"Well, I know. But it's not really proper for a lady to be in a dining room or anywhere they serve whiskey without an escort."

"Boy, I know a lot of women who wouldn't stand for that very long." Levi smiled as he spoke, and Elizabeth's eyes rolled back as she shook her head and smiled at him.

"Right this way, Miss Morgan." The hostess—a young French woman, not particularly pretty but pleasantly dressed and well mannered—showed the couple to a table. Levi thought back on his many trips to the old ghost town and had never really thought about real people living there. The old town had some class, he pondered as they sat down for breakfast.

"You seem to be miles away. What are ya thinking about?"

"Oh, how I remember this town and how it is right now." Levi smiled. "It really is a different place. Boy, is it a different place!"

Elizabeth smiled. "Well, are ya disappointed?" she asked with a teasing grin.

"Well, ah … let me think about it for a minute." Elizabeth looked on with a smile. "No," he answered with the same grin as their eyes never left each other.

"Coffee?" the waitress asked as she broke their trance.

"Sure," Levi replied, "both cups please." Glancing over Elizabeth's shoulder, he spotted Pete coming through the door. Untidy would not begin to describe Pete's condition—a leftover five o'clock shadow, disheveled hair, a slept-in shirt, and a face that showed deep pain. Levi figured it was safe to assume Pete had a hangover. "Pete, over here! Ma'am, maybe ya ought to fill another cup," Levi commented as the waitress looked up at Pete.

"I think he's gonna need more than coffee," the waitress replied with her own brand of humor.

"Don't holler. Don't even speak," Pete replied with both eyes almost closed and one hand pressing his head as the other pressed down on the table to cushion the act of sitting. "Boy, do I feel bad."

"Pete, if you feel one-tenth as bad as you look, I don't think you'll make it," Levi replied with a nonsympathetic smile.

Elizabeth, on the other hand, was very concerned and truly sympathetic to Pete's well-being. "Pete, I've never seen you like this. I don't think you've ever been drunk in your life. How did ya get like this?"

Levi, knowing Pete's obsession with Elizabeth and also Pete's frame of mind at the moment, decided to answer this unanswerable question. "Hey, we were out there under fire yesterday, a lot of pressure. Give 'im a break. He felt like gettin' drunk, so he got drunk." Pete looked up at Levi as he heard him come to his defense. "But he probably won't feel like doing it again for a while." Levi grinned. Pete looked up at Levi again and raised his eyes to show a touch of animosity for Levi's help.

The waitress returned and took the order as Pete's head faced the table. "And how about you, Pete?" the young waitress added. A long silence came from Pete, and his eyes continued in a fixed position.

"Pete, you need to eat something. You'd feel a lot better," Elizabeth sympathized.

"Y'all leave 'im alone. Pete, what ya really need is the hair of the dog." Levi smirked as he enlightened Pete. Pete's head lifted slowly as his glassy red eyes pierced Levi's face. "What I mean is," Levi grinned, "you really need to drink a beer." Pete's head slowly reclined back to the table, staring into space as Levi continued to explain. "It's really the best thing for a hangover. Bring him a beer," Levi continued as Elizabeth and the waitress stared at him. "I'm telling the truth. He'll feel better after he drinks a beer." The two women reeked with skepticism, but the waitress momentarily returned with beer in hand. "Drink it down, Pete. You'll feel better, I promise."

Pete's head slowly raised as he grasped the mug with both hands and chugalugged the beer. Breakfast was served, so Elizabeth and Levi ate as they observed Pete's recovery. By the time the two had finished, Pete was in an upright position. "Pete, how are ya feelin'?" Elizabeth showed concern as Levi continued his good mood.

"Well, I think I'll live," Pete remarked. He had forgotten it was the day of Mr. Morgan's funeral. He started to apologize to Elizabeth but decided he would probably do better just keeping his mouth shut. Levi cringed at the remark, but he too thought better of opening his mouth.

"Hey, Pete!" a voice shouted. Levi turned to see the youngest of the Cagle brothers walking their way.

"Hi, Sam. Don't speak too loud. Your brother's head may fall off," Levi remarked.

"Ya think you're funny, but when Paw gets through with him, he's gonna wish his head was off," Sam stated.

"What's wrong, Sam?" Elizabeth asked.

"Ahhh, Paw had us out looking for 'im last night till one of the hands told 'im Pete stayed in town. Boy, was he mad."

"Hey, Sam. Go find your Paw, and tell 'im Pete had told me to tell 'im he was gonna stay in town, and I just …" Levi stopped his tale as he looked into Pete's enlarging pupils. They were staring over Levi's shoulder. Sam also had a frown across his face as Levi looked at him. Of all people, standing behind Levi and listening to his plot was none other than John Cagle. His face was stern and looked mean as anyone twenty years your senior can look. "Oh hi, Mr. Cagle. How's everything?" Levi stated as he stood for politeness sake, an old habit.

"What was that ya wanted to tell me?" John asked, knowing the answer.

"Oh, ahhh, I had asked Pete to stay in town yesterday. He told me he'd need to let you know, and I told 'im I'd tell ya." Elizabeth proudly listened as Levi executed his plea of defense for his good friend of less than a week. She knew full well Mr. Cagle was not swallowing the story at all. "I just forgot."

John Cagle, always known to hold a firm rein on his clan, was also known as a reasonable man; he realized the day of his old friend's funeral was a good time to back off. "Well, it sure made me worry for a while last night, but I don't guess I can get too mad at Pete since it wasn't his fault."

Levi, knowing Mr. Cagle was biting his tongue, laid it on a little thicker. "I know you had to be worrying last night, and I do apologize."

"Oh, it's okay. Let's forget it." John smiled, and the tension eased.

Everyone was standing around the table as Tom Jr. approached. "Good morning, fellows, and morning to you too, Elizabeth."

"Howdy, good morning" was heard from the group as Tom joined in. "I've got that suit for ya, Levi," he whispered as he drew Levi to the side.

"Oh, that's great. Thanks a lot, Tom. I sure am lucky we're the same size."

"Yeah. Dad even mentioned how much we're alike. He said it looked like we ought to be kin." Levi smiled, and Elizabeth grinned from a few feet away.

"Sam, did you bring in Pete's clothes?" Paul asked as he stood behind Mr. Cagle.

"Oh, I sure did, Pete. You'd better get dressed," Sam replied.

"Hey, Tom, where's your paw?" John asked in a pleasant mood.

"Oh, he's ridin' in on the buggy with Maw and Karen. They'll be in shortly."

"I guess we'd all better get dressed," Levi stated as the group began to break up. The two friends started up the stairs as the rest of the bunch walked to the front of the hotel.

Elizabeth turned to the Cagles as they reached the boardwalk. "Would ya mind tellin' Levi I've gone on over to the funeral parlor?"

"Would ya like for me to go along with ya, girl?"

A small smile came to her face. "No, that's okay, Mr. Cagle. I think I need to spend some time alone with Dad." Mr. Cagle just nodded as she turned and stepped down into the street. A tear trickled down his cheek as he watched her walk away. His memories of her dated from the time she was a new foal, and he had known her dad even longer. He recalled helping Ben Morgan dig the grave for his bride of only four years. But nothing seemed to be as tough as his old friend's child, now a young lady, being left alone in this old world without any real kinfolk.

"Here come the Calahans, Paw," Sam remarked as John wiped the tears with his sleeve hurriedly and looked down the dusty street for the Calahan buggy.

John regained his composure as Tom and the missus and Karen came to a halt in front of the hotel. "Good morning, ladies, and you too, Tom," John stated with a large grin as a tear puddled in his right eye.

"Good mornin', John," came from the elder Calahan.

"Good morning, Mr. Cagle," was heard from Karen simultaneously.

"Where's that big boy of yours, Karen?" John asked, just for conversation.

"Oh, we left him with Consuelo. He'd be worn-out if he'd made that long ride," Karen explained.

"Not to say how we'd feel," Tom added with a chuckle; John and the ladies laughed.

"We were sure shocked to hear about Pop last night when Tom got in," Mrs. Calahan stated.

"Yeah, it was a hard thing to accept, Mary," John replied.

"How's Elizabeth doin', Mr. Cagle?" Karen asked.

"I think she's doin' fairly well considerin'," John replied.

"I'd give that credit to that young Levi fellow. Wouldn't you, John?" Tom remarked.

"Yeah. She sure needed someone, all right."

"Where is she, John? Maybe we should go to her for a little while," Mrs. Calahan stated as she looked back at Karen in the backseat of the buggy.

Karen nodded as John looked up the street by the barber sign. "She's up there at the funeral parlor, Mary. I think it would be the thing to do. I sure didn't want to see her go up there by herself to start with, and I did ask her if she wanted me along. Maybe it'd be more fittin' with a woman's touch anyhow."

The women climbed down from the buggy as Tom tied off the team. "John, where's your better half?" Mary asked as Karen smiled, and Tom kinda chuckled out loud.

"She'll be in shortly. She's coming in the buggy with my daughters-in-law. Them women take too much time dressing for me. They'd rather for me to leave anyhow." John grinned. "Of course, that old buggy won't hold very many anyway," Mr. Cagle explained.

The Calahan women smiled and started up the street to the funeral parlor. Tom stepped on to the boardwalk, and the two remaining old friends walked into the hotel.

As the two men entered the lobby, they spotted Levi coming down the stairs, with Pete a few steps behind.

Levi's suit was a light gray color in wool. Maybe not the ideal color for a funeral and surely not the ideal fabric for this hot summer day, but it did fit fairly well. The long, lanky-bodied Calahan seemed to have a lot of the same family traits as his ancestors. "Hello, Tom," Levi started off the conversation with a zesty smile as he reached the bottom of the stairs and reached out to shake Tom's hand.

Tom shook Levi's hand as he grasped his arm with the other to show a warm reception for this almost stranger, who for some inner feeling felt very close.

Pete followed up with a "howdy" and a nod as the four men clustered in the center of the lobby. The other two Cagle boys came in from the dining room as Tom Jr. walked in the entrance. "Mr. Cagle, your buggy's coming up the road."

"Huh? Oh, thanks, Tom. Maybe we'd better get on over to the funeral parlor, fellows," John suggested. "It looks like the womenfolk have made it."

"I guess Elizabeth's already over there, huh?" Levi questioned the group.

"Yeah, she is. But Maw and Karen went over to be with 'er,"

Tom Jr. explained.

"Oh, good," Levi commented as the group stepped from the boardwalk and headed toward the funeral parlor.

Paul tied off the Cagle buggy in front of the barbershop, and the womenfolk climbed down.

A large group of the townspeople was standing around the entrance to the funeral parlor in their Sunday-go-to-meetin' clothes; Pop Morgan's closest friends started into the doorway. Worried about Elizabeth, Levi led the pack as they filed into the small reception room. The room was filled with the city friends also. Levi's height gave him the advantage, and he spotted Elizabeth standing behind the casket. A large set of double doors were opened at the rear of the room, but the air was calm, and the crowded room made it almost unbearable. The Calahan women were by Elizabeth's side, and Levi was assured she was among her friends. It seemed like the whole town had turned out for Mr. Morgan's funeral. He stopped a few feet short but close enough for Elizabeth to know he was near. The people continued to offer their condolences, and shortly, the Cagles had also worked their way to Elizabeth's side. Levi stepped closer as she looked back and held out her hand toward him.

The room got quiet as Pop Morgan's best friend, Tom Calahan, stepped up beside the plain wooden casket, which still scented the room of freshly cut timber. He placed his hand on Mr. Morgan's hands.

"Friends," Tom paused as the room quieted even more, "I know I'm not the perfect person for a eulogy. Heaven knows I could stand a lot of correcting myself." A small grin came to his face as he stared out into the crowd. "But since we don't have us a man of God yet in our growing community, I'd like to say my piece about this man." Tom's hand moved from his friend's hand to the rim of the casket as he turned slightly to face the main body of friends. "I've known Benjamin Morgan for the greater part of my life, and it has been the greater part because of Ben.

Last night, sitting at home, I recalled a lot of old memories of 'im."
A slight grin came to Tom. "And one in particular comes to mind.
It was the first time Ben came into town after we'd hired our first
schoolteacher. He didn't get into town very often back then, but
after that trip, he was here every week." Tom grinned a little larger
as a little laughter came from the crowd, and even Elizabeth was
paying close attention to Mr. Calahan's every word. "He'd fallen
hook, line, and sinker in love. Well, of course, ya all know what
happened. When her contract expired, and it was time for her
to go back east, she became Mrs. Morgan." Tom laughed as the
crowd laughed with him, and even Elizabeth smiled. "I wasn't for
sure at first if she was gonna make a good teacher. She showed up
on the stage one morning after we'd hired her off her résumé. She
was so shy and so quiet. I didn't know whether she'd ever be heard
over all the boys in school, includin' Tom here," Mr. Calahan said
as he looked over at Tom Jr. and smiled. "I asked her if she thought
she had the strength and the imagination to make the kids learn.
She told me about her mother dying a few months before and
about how she almost didn't go on with her life." Elizabeth looked
up and listened intensely as Tom Calahan spoke. "She told me
about how she pulled herself together and was determined to start
her life again in new surroundings. Then she handed me a poem
she had written. I found it last night as I was looking through an
old box of memories, and I want to read it to y'all and especially to
her daughter." Elizabeth still looked up at him as most eyes were
on her. Tom looked down at an old yellowed piece of paper he was
unfolding. "'Life Goes On,'" he started.

The dawn awakens as new life begins,

the evening falls, for some, life ends.

Life goes on for the remaining fold,

to lose a loved one weakens the soul.

The beginning of life is like the breaking of dawn,

the youth will grow, and life goes on.

The survivors of death are pained and alone,

as friends perish, but life must go on.

It's always hard to accept death's moans,

but the heartaches fade, as life goes on.

"She wrote this for her own peace of mind, Elizabeth," Mr. Calahan said as he turned to hand the folded paper to her. "But somehow, I think she had you in mind when she did it." A tear rolled down his cheek. Elizabeth looked up with tears in her eyes and thanked Tom as she accepted the poem. Levis could hear his heart beating wildly as he saw the tears fall around the room. The poem was clutched in her hand and her hand to her bosom. Her head went down as Levi's arm pulled her tight, and the tears on her cheek spotted his shirt.

The crowd began to disperse as Elizabeth, being guided by Levi and accompanied by Tom Calahan, started toward the front. The Calahan clan and the Cagles trailed close as the threesome made their way onto the boardwalk.

Mr. Gore lifted the casket lid from the floor where it leaned against the wall and placed it on the casket. He motioned for Ricardo, who was standing by the wagon, as one hired hand climbed to the driver's seat and backed the team of horses to the double-door opening. The funeral director, Ricardo, and a few of the Morgans' ranch hands loaded the casket. Rosita observed from a nearby shade tree as her husband slid the casket in and put the tailgate in place. That was Rosita's clue to board the wagon, and without a spoken word, Ricardo helped her on to the seat of the high-sided hay hauler. The Morgan cowboys mounted and filed two abreast behind the wagon as it slowly made its way out the back alley and onto the main road to the Morgan spread.

Some of the townspeople were still giving their condolences to Elizabeth as Levi stood close with the Calahans and the Cagles. Hearing the sound of a few riders approaching, the men looked up to see the sheriff riding in with a couple of deputies. Doc Jones was close behind, driving his black buggy with the surrey top. The sheriff nodded to acknowledge the group and started toward them as he dismounted. Surmising the sheriff was in a quandary, the group of men moved toward him and away from the women.

"I'm sorry I couldn't make the funeral," the sheriff began as he approached Levi. "But that old housekeeper from the Tanner Ranch woke me up at four o'clock this morning."

"What's the problem, Amos? Has Mr. Tanner found out about his boys?" Levi asked as the group of friends listened in concern.

"No, he never heard about his sons yesterday. The old woman said he started coughing up some blood around midnight and died shortly thereafter." The whole group lowered their heads. Their emotions were already running high.

"Well, it was probably for the best, Matthew being like he's been for the last few years," John said as the rest agreed.

"Well, he was down to probably seventy pounds and hadn't known anybody for quite some time, accordin' to the old woman. I couldn't see bringin' 'im into town. I just had my boys to bury 'im up on that knoll by his wife, under that big oak. It's a pretty spot," the sheriff said as everyone agreed. "They'd already buried Clyde up there, so I think I'm gonna get my brother to take Matt and Billy out there too. No use separatin' 'em or using up the town cemetery with 'em," Amos added as he squinted his eyes and wiped his brow.

"It's the proper thing to do," Tom commented as the sweat ran down his face, and he slipped off his suit coat. The noonday sun was working like an oven. Levi followed by taking off his jacket and slinging it over his shoulder. "Sheriff, did ya ride up to the old mine shaft, where it cuts through to the Morgan Ranch?" Levi questioned.

"No, I didn't get a chance to run up there. We were kinda busy right there at the ranch house. But I did check out a couple of hundred head they had penned by the barn. They all had that funny-looking brand. I figure most of their cattle's gonna have the Morgan brand. I ain't got to talk to the circuit judge yet, mind ya, but I think he'll go along with my thinking. Confiscate all Tanner property for the county," the sheriff smiled, "and turn over all the cattle to the Morgan Ranch."

"Hey, hey, yeah!" the group shouted in laughter.

"Hey, all right!" Levi shouted.

"Hey, Amos, I don't want to pour beer on your apple pie, but don't ya think Matt's wife's gonna contest that call?" Mr. Calahan projected.

"Matt Tanner's got a wife?" Levi questioned.

"Nah, they weren't ever married," the sheriff explained.

"Amos, they had two kids," John added.

"Listen, that girl moved back home over two years ago. She ain't lost anything here. Besides, most of those cattle are clearly marked with the Morgan brand. She probably knew about the whole operation. If she raises a fuss, I'll get 'er for withholdin' evidence or somethin'."

The womenfolk and the townspeople all turned to see what the commotion was and found it hard to believe this fine upstanding group of men would be so disrespectful under these conditions.

Elizabeth figured it had to be something very important for this bunch of friends to shout and carry on in that manner. She slowly turned from the group and walked toward the noisy bunch as Levi spotted her from the corner of his eye. He turned and started toward her. "Elizabeth, the sheriff just told us Mr. Tanner passed away last night."

"Oh, Levi, that's what y'all are laughing about?" she asked.

"What? Huh? No, pretty." Levi smiled. "He also said you're gonna get all the cattle that're on Tanner land."

Elizabeth's eyes lit up, and then a big smile came over her face. "We can keep the ranch," she stated as the tears started to flow. She jumped into Levi's arms, and they both laughed out loud.

The sheriff, followed by the group, sprightly walked over to Elizabeth. The inquisitive townsfolk moseyed in a little closer also. "Elizabeth, now I'm not saying this for a fact as I told the boys. I ain't talked to the judge yet, but I'm thinking it'll be all right with 'im." Everyone cheered again for her good fortune as she stood clutching Levi's hand. Those proverbial tears of joy fell down her cheeks.

"When does that circuit judge come through, Amos?" Levi asked.

"Well, let's see. It's the first Tuesday of each month. So it's still about three weeks off. But all those cattle that're double branded, we could start moving those back to ya tomorrow. That is, if ya want 'em," the sheriff said with a smile. Everyone laughed, including Elizabeth.

Levi, still clutching Elizabeth's hand, said, "That's great. We'll get Ricardo and the rest of the boys rounded up and ride in to your office in the mornin'." Then he looked over at Elizabeth and asked, "What ya think?"

Her smile faded some. "Maybe we should wait a few more days, Levi," she replied. The group quietened; everyone was caught up in the excitement and had forgotten for a moment the reason they had all gathered, even Elizabeth. Reality was back, but the overtone had lightened. The bleak side of the days to come evaporated, and Elizabeth's prospects were bright.

"We'll just play it by ear the next few days, Amos. Ah, I'll get with ya later. Okay?" Levi asked. The group began to disband.

"Oh, sure. That'll be fine. Just come by the office when ya get ready," Amos replied. Levi shook his hand and turned and walked away.

"Listen, you two. When ya decide to round up those cattle, let us know. We'll loan ya a few extra hands," Tom said as the whole family looked on with support.

"Yeah, you can take a few of our boys too," John added as the family members all smiled.

"We'll have those cattle rounded up in no time and back on the Morgan spread," Pete added as Elizabeth looked up at him and smiled.

Everyone started to their buggies as Elizabeth took Levi by the arm. "Are ya ready to go home?" she said with a smile.

"Let's go. I think a little breeze will go a long way," he said as he laid the jacket in the back.

"Vámonos," she replied as they both smiled.

It looked like a parade as the carriages strutted down the main street of Dorado Ciudad in single file. Many of the male family members were on horseback, and it made the cavalcade stretch out for a couple of hundred feet. Most of the townspeople waved as the caravan passed. Levi nodded to the storekeeper and his wife as they reopened the store. Soon the ranchers were out of sight, and the town resumed the normal hustle and bustle.

The old buggies traveled slowly but still churned the dust, and the carriages drifted a little farther apart. The young couple could still hear the chattering from the others, but the noise faded, and the ride was pleasant as they rode along in silence. Elizabeth put her arm through Levi's and slid in a little closer as he handled the reins. He leaned over and kissed her on the forehead as she laid her head on his shoulder. Crimson watched from the rear as he followed along, tied to the buggy.

Levi finally broke the silence after a long period of deep thought. "Pretty."

"Huh?" she answered in a contented tone.

"Tom said something back there about Matt havin' a couple of kids and a wife."

"Yeah, that's right, he does, or I guess he did. I heard she was working in a cantina in Big Spring when he met her, about ten years ago."

"Ten years ago?"

"Yeah, I'm sure it was. Of course, I was only eleven at the time, but it seems it wasn't long after the war, and Matt was workin' for his uncle at a feedstore. Well, anyway, when Mr. Tanner found out Matt had a kid by this girl and he was only eighteen, he made Matt come back home."

"What happened to the girl?"

"Well, that caused such a big scandal in Borden County that Mr. Tanner had to let her and the boy move in with them. Then just a year later, she had another boy."

"So Matt had two sons?"

"Yep, two of 'em. They never did get along too well. Then about two or three years ago, she up and moved back to Big Spring and took those two young'uns with her."

"So somewhere around Big Spring, Texas, there's a nine- or ten-year-old Matt Tanner loose, huh?" Levi stated as he smiled and shook his head.

"That's right," Elizabeth grinned. "Hey, we're almost home."

The younger of the Cagle boys reached their gate and swung it open. The carriage made the turn without a delay. The whole family waved as they peeled off down their private road. Pete rode up alongside the rear buggy in a trot as Levi and Elizabeth looked up at their friend. "Y'all let me know if I can do anything. When you get ready to round up those cattle, just send one of your riders over, and we'll give ya a hand."

"Thanks a lot, Pete. I'll call ya," Levi caught himself and smiled, "I'll talk to ya later." Pete nodded and smiled back, not really understanding Levi's inside joke. He looked over at Elizabeth, nodded, then spurred his animal, and hurriedly rode onto the Cagle property. An odd sensation came over Levi as he watched Pete ride away. He realized if anything happened to him, Elizabeth would be well looked after. He picked up a little speed, still thinking of the funny feeling that just went through him, and then slowed down as he turned in at the Morgan gate.

The Calahan carriage stopped as Levi leaped from their buggy to open the gate. "Levi, we're going to head on to the ranch. When ya get ready to move those cattle, just holler!" Tom shouted as the rest of the Calahan family waved to Elizabeth.

"Elizabeth, we'll come over to see ya in a day or so. If ya need us to do anything, you just let us know," Mrs. Calahan yelled as Karen agreed with a nod. Their carriage was moving on down the road as Elizabeth smiled and waved, and soon they faded out of sight. Levi pulled the buggy through the gate and hopped back down to shut it.

"Ya sure got some good friends there," Levi stated as he stepped back on to the buggy.

Elizabeth smiled. "We've got some good friends there. They're your kinfolk."

Levi smiled. "We've got some good friends there and there." He laughed as he looked toward the Cagle entrance. Then he let the brake off and popped the reins to start the old buggy on its final leg of the trip.

The sun was beaming from overhead without a cloud in the sky. It was midafternoon, and the temperature was reaching ninety, but one might think it was a cold, wintery day. Elizabeth's arm was locked in Levi's, and she was snuggled close as the buggy wound down the dirt road through the trees.

No one seemed to be at home when the buggy reached the hitching rail, and the young couple stepped down from the long dusty ride. "The place looks deserted. I don't think anyone's back," Levi remarked.

"Yes, they're here. They're all back at Peaceful View," Elizabeth stated.

"Where?"

"Peaceful View. It's a place Dad picked out when Mother died. It overlooks a small valley a few hundred yards behind the house." A couple of tears fell down her cheek. "He used to go up there a lot and talk to her when he needed to work things out." The tears flowed a little stronger as she reminisced aloud.

"Would ya like to walk up there?" Levi asked. He felt her pain, and a few tears filled his eyes and trickled down his cheeks.

Elizabeth looked tenderly at Levi. She watched his eyes water, and it made hers run even faster. Levi pulled her close and hugged her as she softly cried against his chest. "Let it go, pretty. It'll do ya good," he commented as his hand patted her back.

A few seconds passed, and Elizabeth regained her composure. She lifted her head and looked up at Levi. "Can we walk on up there now?" she asked in a muffled tone.

"Sure." He took her hand, and they started around the side of the house. She led the way down the bank of a small ravine only forty or fifty feet from the back door. There, nestled in a clump of mesquite trees, was a shallow clear water stream. Elizabeth stepped from stone to stone, like she had done so many times before. Reaching the far side, they started up a shallow incline, where the trail narrowed, and the woods got thicker. Soon the ground leveled, and they reached a secluded clearing overlooking a small but beautiful valley. Ricardo knelt beside a fresh mound of dirt as he piled some white limestone rocks around the base of a cedar post. A crudely hand-carved plaque was attached, matching the one next to it. The other Morgan cowhands were assembled around close by. Some were leaning on their shovels as others gathered stones, but all were dripping with sweat. The air stood as still as the large boulder where Carmita sat, attempting to avoid the heat.

The amigos stepped back as Elizabeth advanced. She stood looking down on the grave. Levi stepped up behind her and placed his hands on her shoulders. "He's not really down there, pretty. He's up above, looking down on you right now."

"I know. Mother's standing beside 'im," Elizabeth whispered low. "But now that you're here with me, she needs him more than I do. I know they're both happy now." She turned and laid her head on Levi's chest as he reassured her with a gentle hug.

The caballeros gathered their tools in silence and started down the shady trail. Carmita walked over and laid her head on Elizabeth's back and hugged her tightly. Then Ricardo took Carmita by the hand, and they started down the slope behind the cowboys. Still holding Elizabeth in his arms, Levi turned and started down the hill behind the other couple. He thought it might be better if Elizabeth didn't dwell on this heartache too long.

Slowly, the group made their way down the hill and across the stream. Soon they were back at the Morgan ranch house. The silence was broken when Carmita spoke. "Elizabeth, you want me to fix you something to eat?"

"No, I'm not hungry right now, Carmita. Thank you." Carmita was saddened. She frowned and looked down and then started to turn to follow Ricardo.

"Yes, Carmita. She is hungry, and she does want ya to fix dinner, if ya don't mind," Levi answered. Carmita turned and smiled. Elizabeth only listened as she looked up at him, knowing that he was doing what he thought she really needed. If nothing else, she knew she needed him.

Carmita scurried up the steps and through the kitchen door as Levi led Elizabeth in the same direction. Many bowls of food filled the table as they entered through the back screen door. Carmita stood dazzled as the food caught their eye. "I think maybe the good angel has come," she stated.

"Yes, I think so," Levi replied as he watched Elizabeth's face brighten.

"Oh, isn't this nice?" she remarked.

"You really think it was the good angel?" Carmita questioned.

"In the form of good neighbors, Carmita, I do mean good neighbors. This is really a spread, huh, pretty?"

Elizabeth smiled. "It really is thoughtful of them to go to all this trouble." Her voice had perked up as she walked to the table and sat down.

"Pretty, don't ya think Carmita should ask the caballeros and their families to share all this food with us?" Levi suggested.

"Sure, that's a good idea. Would ya like to ask the men to come over?"

"*Si, Señorita*. I think it would be very nice," Carmita replied, very excited. Elizabeth smiled as Carmita hurried out the back door. Levi walked up behind her and placed his hands on her shoulders as she placed her hand on his hand.

Soon the kitchen was full as the scruffy but well-mannered caballeros filled the room with sombreros in hand. A couple of the Mexican cowboys had wives, and many children ran in and out the screen door. Elizabeth had grown up around them all. The best medicine she could have received, a really festive get-together, was underway. The fiesta was to honor their friend, Mr. Morgan, and no one took it as disrespect. Slowly, the kids settled as their plates were filled. They formed a small circle outside on the ground. The close-quartered kitchen was downright hot, so the cowboys and the women migrated to the outdoors also. Watching everyone enjoy themselves made Elizabeth forget some of her own grief, and soon she began to eat. Levi watched closely, and the tension subsided in his new world.

Time passed fast when things were good, and soon the sun was setting over the hills toward Dorado Ciudad. The cowboys began to pay their respects and to thank Elizabeth for her kindness as the women gathered the dishes and stacked them neatly in the kitchen. Then the group began to dissipate. "Hasta mañana" and "buenos noches" could be heard loudly over the compound as darkness fell on the Morgan Ranch.

"Carmita, don't worry with those dishes tonight. We'll take care of that tomorrow."

Carmita turned from the large pan sitting on the drainboard, drying her hands on a dishcloth. "Are ya sure?" she asked.

"Sure, I'm sure. It's been a long day. Go home." Elizabeth smiled. "I'll see you in the morning."

Carmita smiled. "Hasta mañana," she said.

"Carmita," Carmita turned back to Elizabeth, "thank you," she added as Carmita smiled and walked back to Elizabeth, hugging her tightly, and then turned and scampered out the screen door.

The air was calm, and the heat still lingered heavily in the wood-framed house. The young couple passed through the parlor and onto the porch, where Levi found his favorite spot on the front porch swing. Elizabeth sat close to his side and snuggled as if it were a winter night; neither seemed to care about the heat. Levi held her tightly. He draped his arm over her shoulder as the swing moved ever so gently. Soon the movement stopped as she turned to face him. He leaned forward, and their lips met. Her hand went over his shoulder to reach the base of his neck, and she pulled him even closer. The passion was spurred even deeper. His hand flowed from her tiny waist, up her body, and on to her breast. The feeling was a new experience, and it sent a warm craving over her entire body. His sensitive fingers continued to massage and be felt intensely through the dress. Passionate moans flowed from Elizabeth as Levi dragged his lips from hers. He lightly kissed her cheek and then trailed light kisses down her neck and across her shoulder. The night was pitch-black. Dark clouds had rolled in and covered the moon. The movement of the old wood swing was the only noise heard over the background sound of the crickets. Levi's hand dropped from her breast and slowly traveled to her waist. When he reached her hip, he pulled her so close they felt almost as one. Their kisses ran even deeper till she felt the sensation in her toes. His hand lowered to her thigh as he felt the muscles tighten in her back. Elizabeth pulled back as her hand slipped from his neck to his arm. "We need to stop," she said breathlessly. Their faces were only inches apart, but in the darkness, nothing could be seen.

"Darling," she called softly, not hearing a response from Levi.

"I'm here."

"I know you're here. I don't want to make you mad. Are you mad?"

A long silence. "No, I'm not mad."

"You sound mad."

"I'm not mad.

Maybe a little disappointed, but I'm not mad. I know you're right. Let's just call it a night."

"Levi."

"Yeah."

"You promise you're not mad."

"Pretty, I can't be mad at you. I love you way too much." Levi stood, holding Elizabeth's hand, and pulled her to her feet. "I promise I'm not mad." He leaned over in the still darkness and kissed her gently on the lips. "We'd better turn in. We've got a lot to do tomorrow." He turned and led the way across the porch and into the house. He stopped to put out a single lamp as they passed through the parlor.

"Levi," Elizabeth quietly whispered as the light faded into darkness. "I love you too, and I want you more than anything in the world. But you know, everything's a little mixed up today. It's not the right tim—"

Elizabeth was cut short as Levi's finger rubbed across her lips in the darkened room. "I love you, and I know you love me. I know the reasons. You don't need to explain to me." The understanding in his whisper made her stretch up and kiss him.

The light in Elizabeth's room was dim as they reached the hall, and Levi waited by the door as she brightened the lamp. He turned and started into his room across the hall. "Levi, I love you. Good night."

He slowly turned and smiled. "Good night, and I love you too." He walked into his room and closed the door. Slipping off his shirt, he poured some water from the pitcher into the large ceramic bowl and rinsed off his face and arms. He sat down on the edge of the bed and lazily removed his boots and then his jeans. He looked over at the door as he stood and thought about Elizabeth lying in the room across the hall. Thinking about a lifetime together, he decided against rushing things. He pulled back the spread and proceeded to turn out the lamp. The light under the door caught his eye as his head hit the pillow. Still thinking about his desires and mixed feeling for Elizabeth, he had a difficult time relaxing. The heat of the summer air didn't seem to help the situation, but his common sense finally took control. It was all in vain. Levi's bedroom door swung open. Elizabeth stood in the doorway. The light from her bedroom lamp glowed through the thin-laced cotton gown that pulled off her shoulder. Her naked silhouette stood revealed through the sheer material, and her freshly brushed blond hair hung softly down her back. The stimulation that was aroused in Levi could not be measured. Elizabeth walked closer, and her image grew more distinct. She stood by the edge of the bed, and Levi watched as the gown came off her shoulder and fell to the floor. He rose up on one arm and, without speaking a word, slowly pulled back the spread, and Elizabeth slipped between the sheets.

CHAPTER 10

LOVE CONQUERS

LEVI LUNGED FROM deep sleep to an upright position as a loud burst of thunder seemed to slam into the house. The pounding of rain hitting the roof and the panes of the windows were painfully sobering as the short nap came to an end. The loud, booming noise had also roused Elizabeth. "What's wrong?" she asked.

Levi was in deep concentration, glancing out the window and then back at Elizabeth. "My Bronco is back, Elizabeth!"

"What?"

"My Bronco. You know, my truck." Elizabeth looked puzzled as she stirred from her deep, drowsy state.

"Oh, the Bronco. Is it outside?" she asked.

"No, I don't think so. I just have a funny feeling that it's back in the same spot on the Calahan Ranch," Levi replied

Elizabeth began to awaken as she sat up in bed. "Oh, on the Calahan property."

"Yeah, that place I showed ya," he responded as he slipped on his jeans. It was pitch-black outside, but Levi was assisted by the lamp that still burned in Elizabeth's room.

"What are you doing?" she questioned.

"I'm getting dressed. I've got to go get that Bronco," Levi explained excitedly.

"What makes you so sure it's there?" she asked. She leaned over on one arm, watching Levi hastily slip on his boots.

"I don't know, but something's telling me it's there. I've got to find out. Will you go with me?"

"You want to go now?" she questioned.

"Yes, it's got to be now. I need to get that truck, and it won't be there long. I just know," he hastily replied.

"Okay, let's go." She climbed out of the bed, still nude, and bashfully picked her gown off the floor and hurried to her room.

Levi grabbed his shirt and walked to the door as he watched Elizabeth dress. "Will you go back with me if it's there?" he asked. She buttoned her blouse as she sat down on the edge of the bed and proceeded to slip on her boots.

"I have a funny feeling inside," she started as she looked up. "I'll never fit in your world."

"Hey, pretty. I fit in your world. You'll fit into mine. I won't go without ya."

"If you really want me to."

"If I want you to! I'm telling you, I wouldn't go without ya." Levi grabbed her by the arm and pulled her close. "I love you, and I'll only go if you'll go."

"I wouldn't let ya go without me. Sure, I'll go with you." She smiled shyly, and Levi leaned down and kissed her with deep emotion.

He smiled. "Vámonos!" Elizabeth smiled.

"Grab your raincoat, and I'll saddle up the horses," Levi said as he ran through the parlor, noting the mantel clock showed a few minutes after midnight.

"Okay!" she yelled as his steps faded into the kitchen.

The intense downpour covered Levi as he made his way to the barn. Opening the double doors, he could hear the neighing coming from the stalls. The constant sound of thunder pounded, and the lightning bleached the sky. Crimson stood tall and didn't seem to mind the unnerving weather. He seemed to know what was happening and was eager to travel. Elizabeth was bundled from head to toe in a leather slicker suit as she came running into the barn. She handed one to Levi as she reached his side. "Here, I know Dad would want you to have this. We used to use these on the cattle drives."

"Oh, this is great." He slipped the pants on over his jeans. "Boy, these things are heavy."

"They're oiled-down cowhide. They're waterproof," she proudly stated as he slipped on the jacket with a hood. "But I'm no boy." She smiled.

"You're telling me." He grinned and kissed her quickly. "Are ya ready?"

Elizabeth slowly swung upon her horse with the heavy rainsuit. "I'm ready."

"Let's go!" he shouted as he mounted Crimson, and they galloped from the dry surroundings into the thundering cloudburst. Reaching the front gate with great speed, Levi swung it back, and their journey gained momentum on the open road.

Levi felt time was of the essence as the team of horses galloped stride for stride. The old dirt road was covered as the water came down in sheets, and the sureness of the four-footed animals became almost unmanageable as the slippery mud covered their hooves. But still, the twosome never broke stride, and soon they reached the entrance to the Calahan Ranch. Levi slowed down just long enough to unlatch the gate, and the horses returned to a full gallop. The brush-covered trail was rocky and unfamiliar, but the constant bolts of lightning kept the sky bright as they made their way to their rendezvous. They rode up on a long stretch of clearing that Levi recognized as the place. He looked up the washed-out road and then back down the gully as the water flowed like a small river. A lightning bolt illuminated the sky as it struck a huge oak tree just ahead, and the flames ascended into the darkness. A black shining object sat half on the road and half in the gully. They both surged forward up the knoll and dismounted only forty feet from the shiny object. Levi ran forward as Elizabeth, reluctant to venture too close, hung back to watch Levi. She grabbed the reins and held the horses in check as he reached the vehicle. He anxiously tried the door. "It's open!" he shouted over the loud noise of the pounding rain. "This is it, pretty. It's all ours." He grinned.

He could tell it frightened her as he stepped into the black machine. Levi hoped she could see that it was only a machine. He smiled again. "If it'll run, I'll get it onto the road!" he yelled as he slammed the door. Elizabeth stood in the downpour, holding the reins of her horse and that of Crimson's, as she saw a smoky gray ring engulf the shiny black object.

In only a split second, Levi and the black machine disappeared before her eyes.

"Nooooooo!" she screamed, and she fell to the ground. The smoky, swirling funnel vanished before her. "Nooo, no, no," she cried, rising to her knees as the drenching rain continued to fall. "Don't take 'im. Oh, Levi, come back." She continued to cry as the lightning began to subside.

The sweat dripped from Levi's nose. He was draped over the steering wheel, unconscious. The sun's rays beamed with intensifying heat through the glass as his drowsiness wore thin. He felt he had been drugged. His hand slid onto the dash, which felt like a hot plate. He jerked it back as he came to a rude awakening. Pushing his body from the wheel, he gained stability and reached for the door handle. The ninety-degree air felt cool as it rushed inside. His mind was still foggy as he slid out of the seat and stood beside the Bronco.

Holding on to the door, he began to collect his thoughts. "Elizabeth, Elizabeth. No, my God, no!" he yelled in a saddened moan.

He leaned against the cab as his fist pounded the top of the vehicle. "Oh, Elizabeth, no," he continued. He was almost in a faint as he realized the heaviness of his garments. Looking down, he saw the leather slicker Elizabeth had handed him only hours before. He shed the jacket immediately, and life was restored when the air started to penetrate his skin. But the pain in his heart could not be corrected so easily. He stood almost in a trance as he reached down and unbuttoned the leather slacks. Staring at the ground, he leaned against the black machine and slipped them down. His clothes were drenched with perspiration, but the light breeze began to dry them. It also felt exhilarating to his body. His mind started to function as he pictured Crimson standing at Elizabeth's side. He quickly walked to the rear of the trailer, where he hoped to find a miracle. *Maybe Elizabeth's back here with Crimson.*

But the trailer was empty ... So was his heart ... So was his life.

He stood disheartened as he slowly regained his composure. He unbuckled his gun belt and walked back to the cab. Levi leaned down and picked up the slicker suit and folded it gently as he achingly reminisced about Elizabeth. Shaking his head, he crawled into the cab and laid the heavy leather outfit on the passenger seat with his holster.

He started to turn the key and wondered if it would start. *Maybe it won't start, he thought. If it won't, maybe I'm still in the past. Maybe Elizabeth's just gone after help.* His eyes brightened as the key turned. But without hesitation, the engine roared to life. Levi's dreaming had ended with a single switch of a key. The Bronco backed to higher ground in seconds, and he turned the vehicle for home.

Two hours had passed as he daydreamed in silence, riding over the rocky terrain. The ground was dry, but this time, it doesn't confuse him. He now understood the game. He just doesn't understand the rules. The Bronco started down a small incline and then over a flowing creek as Levi decided to stop. Stepping out of the cab, he stepped toward the water as he took a whiff of his shirt. He shook his head and unsnapped the grimy garment. Soon the boots, the socks, and the jeans were lying by the creek; and he sat naked in a small pool. It felt refreshing as he lay back in the cold, spring-fed water with the sun beaming from overhead. *Well, the Bronco was full of clean clothes,* he thought as he relaxed in the sun. A few minutes passed, and soon he hobbled across the rocks to the rear of his vehicle. Before long, he was back on the road in a clean wardrobe but had acquired a hell of an appetite. A few beers were in warm water in a small ice chest behind the front seat. Without hesitation, he popped the top, and the warm beer was devoured in seconds. This act of self-preservation was a good sign. *He who helps himself or something like that,* Levi joked to himself as he narrowed the distance to the ranch house. *At least I will get to see Dyanne. Oh, she'll be a good sight to see. I hope Elizabeth made it back home. I hope she's okay. What am I thinking? That was 120 years ago. Oh, Elizabeth, why did I leave?* The torment continued as he made his way down the rough road. Soon Levi spotted the red clay rooftop of the old hacienda, and the helpless heartache temporarily receded. Anxious to be home, he really got excited as he passed over the cattle guard at the last cross fence. Manuel and a couple of the hands were working in the barn and came trotting out as they heard Levi's rig entering the grounds.

Manuel stood in the path with a big smile as Levi pulled up to him. "Oh, Señor Lee, did you have a good trip? We never hear from you, so we say you have a good time, no?"

"Yeah, it was a good trip, amigo," Levi answered as he stepped from the Bronco. "But it's good to be back too." He pulled down the tailgate, and Manuel watched.

"Did you go all the way back to the waterfall, Mis-ter Lee?"

"I went back a lot farther than that," Levi stated as a little smile came to his face, and a puzzled look came to Manuel's. The other cowboys smiled pleasantly and nodded as Levi nodded back.

"Oh, Mis-ter Lee, we have somethin' to show you," Manuel said as he looked back at the other men. "Juan, trae la sorpresa," Manuel said as Juan smiled and ran off into the barn. Only a few seconds passed as Levi watched the doorway. The caballero came running out, leading a newborn colt as Levi and Manuel looked on. The deep red colt hopped around as Juan led him out the door. Levi was all smiles as he watched the colt. "He look just the same as your horse, no, Mis-ter Lee?"

"He sure does, Manuel, he sure does. We've got a new Crimson," Levi said as he reminisced about his horse, and that brought on more thoughts about Elizabeth. Levi stood in a daze for a second.

"Mis-ter Lee, Mis-ter Lee, you okay?"

"Oh, yeah, Manuel, I'm okay," Levi assured Manuel as he pulled himself together. "Well, now we know why Buttercup didn't want Crimson to leave last week, don't we?"

"Yes, she have the little one only the next day, after you leave," Manuel said.

"She must've known something was gonna go wrong," Levi commented.

"Somethin' go wrong, Mis-ter Lee?"

"Oh, no." He paused. "Did everything go okay here?"

"Oh, si, Mis-ter Lee. Eveer'thin' was fine. No prrooblem. Didn't you catch anything?"

Levi stopped and thought, *That was what I was going to do.* "Yeah, I did, Manuel, but I never got to go fishing," Levi replied as he pulled out his suitcase.

Manuel was really puzzled by Levi's reply. "Maybe my English no too good. You say you no fish? Then you say you caught somethin'?" he questioned.

"That's right," Levi stated as he started toward the house, carrying his luggage.

Manuel followed along, not paying any attention to the fact that Levi was unloading the Bronco himself. "Mis-ter Lee, what happened? Why you no fish?"

"I just got too busy," Levi said with a smile. "I just didn't have time to fish, and before you come tell me Crimson's not in the trailer, I already know it."

"What?" Manuel still looked confused as he followed Levi all the way to the kitchen door.

"Amigo, don't worry so much. One day soon, we'll sit down, and I'll tell you all about my trip back to Dorado Ciudad." Levi smiled. "Now would ya open the door for me?" he asked with both arms loaded.

"Oh, pardon, Mis-ter Lee." Manuel hurriedly reached down for the knob and swung the door open. "Don't worry about your things. Me, I will unload your trucka."

"Okay, Manuel. That'll be great," Levi answered as Manuel closed the door behind him.

Levi heard Manuel shouting at the other men outside to unload the Bronco as he made his way across the kitchen. Rosita was coming through the dining room door as Levi started out the opposite side. "Mis-ter Lee, you're home," the little woman stated with a welcoming smile.

"Yeah, it's good to be home," he replied, knowing that wasn't the real truth. "How's everything going?"

"Oh, ever'thin's fine. The *señoritas* plan a big party tonight, Mis-ter Lee."

"*Señoritas?* A big party?"

"Oh, si. Miss Dyanne and Miss Beth have a big, big party here tonight."

"Oh, yeah, that's right. Today's Saturday. Maybe that's what I need. A party," he commented with a grin.

"*Si,* you need a party. Ever'baady needs a party," Rosita answered in her jolly way, not knowing Levi's reasoning.

"Where's Dyanne?"

"Oh, Miss Dyanne's in your study, Mis-ter Lee."

"Thanks, Rosita. I'll pick up these bags in a little while," Levi remarked as he looked down at his luggage and swung open the door.

Rosita nodded as Levi walked from the room. She walked to the rear door and hollered out in Spanish to Manuel for him to carry Mister Lee's luggage to his room.

Levi walked across the grand-sized family room as he wished he was back in the small wood-framed house with Elizabeth. He made his way to his study entrance, where he found Dyanne slouched on the couch with her feet propped on the coffee table. "Hey, girl, what ya doing?" he asked as he leaned down to kiss her on the forehead.

"You made it back on time. I'm proud of you, big brother," Dyanne joked as she looked up but then continued to look through a large box of old pictures. "Levi," she said with a very serious look on her face, "I thought you told me you hadn't seen Beth for seven or eight years."

Levi thought. "That's about right, I guess. Why?" he questioned.

Dyanne grinned. "I know that's not true. I don't know why you think ya should keep it from me, but I've got proof," she stated as she held up a small photograph. "You'll have to tell me why you glued this old twenty-dollar bill," she started as she looked closer at the bill, "to the back of it. Levi, this bill has a brand-new date, but it looks so old."

Levi started toward her. "I don't know what you're talking about, Dyanne. Why would I keep anything from you?" he asked with a smile as he took the picture and stepped back into the light.

"Elizabeth," he said as he looked at the old photo made in the dirt street at Dorado Ciudad. He flipped it over to find the twenty-dollar bill he gave Pete. A short communiqué in a feminine hand read, "Maybe we'll see you again someday. Love, Pete and Elizabeth." Levi's mind relaxed as he understood the message. His worry for her was at rest but not forgotten.

"What's all this about a picture of Levi and me?" a feminine voice interrupted.

Levi knew he recognized the voice and turned to the doorway behind him. "Elizabeth!" he shouted as he stood stunned and unable to move.

"Levi, she likes to be called Beth. You're not making a good first impression," Dyanne remarked jokingly. Levi, still mesmerized, stared at the beautiful blonde standing in the doorway.

"Dyanne," she replied as she looked straight at Levi, "he can call me anything he wants to." Beth could feel Levi's thoughts because, for some unknown reason, she had had a crush on him all of her life. *Maybe the age difference was not so bad anymore,* she thought.

Dyanne smiled. "Well, I guess you told me, but I still want to know when y'all had that picture made." She couldn't believe how entranced they were with each other.

Beth was curious about the photograph Levi held. She slowly walked over, and their eyes stayed fixed on each other. She took the picture from his hand, still looking into his eyes. Knowing they had never been in a picture together, Beth was not expecting what she saw. She was overwhelmed, almost to a faint, as she glanced at the photo. She looked back at Levi and then again to the picture.

"I recognize those old-timey clothes y'all are wearing," Dyanne rattled on. "But who are all those people with ya? Y'all sure have had me fooled."

Levi waited for Beth's reaction as he listened to his sister ramble.

Finally, Beth explained as she studied the picture closely, "Oh, I ran into Levi at the carnival last year. We didn't know any of those people, but everybody wanted to get their picture made in those crazy old outfits."

Levi was happy with her reply, and he knew she understood somehow as he took her hand and started toward the front door. "Elizabeth, would you like to sit on the front porch swing with me?"

"Would I?"

"Hey, did I ever tell you the joke about this guy with a wooden eye?" he started as they walked out the door.

"Hey, you two! We don't have a front porch swing!" Dyanne yelled.

Not the end but a new beginning.